TAKE NO NAMES

TAKE NO NAMES

A NOVEL

DANIEL NIEH

ecco

An Imprint of HarperCollins*Publishers*

TAKE NO NAMES. Copyright © 2022 by Daniel Nieh. All rights reserved. Printed in the United States of America. No part of this book may be used or reproduced in any manner whatsoever without written permission except in the case of brief quotations embodied in critical articles and reviews. For information, address HarperCollins Publishers, 195 Broadway, New York, NY 10007.

HarperCollins books may be purchased for educational, business, or sales promotional use. For information, please email the Special Markets De-partment at SPsales@harpercollins.com.

Ecco® and HarperCollins® are trademarks of HarperCollins Publishers.

FIRST EDITION

Designed by Paula Russell Szafranski
Fronitspiece © trentemoller/Shutterstock.com

Library of Congress Cataloging-in-Publication Data has been applied for.

ISBN 978-0-06-288667-5

22 23 24 25 26   LSC   10 9 8 7 6 5 4 3 2 1

For my sisters:

Susie, Ari, and Camellia

NOTE ON LANGUAGE

In this text, Mandarin that the narrator hears is rendered in pinyin transliteration: "Zhège yàngzi!"

Chinese characters that the narrator sees are rendered as written: 就像这些

All translations of Chinese and Spanish appear in italics, like the narrator's internal monologue. Quotation marks indicate what Victor hears; italics represent the experience of language in his mind.

TAKE NO NAMES

1

A habit established without discussion: Mark Knox and I sit in silence for several seconds before we exit the van. For me, a moment to steel my nerves. Fear takes up its proper position inside my rib cage, and my senses awaken to the night: the spit of the rain in the yellow headlights, the steady pit-pat as it drums on the roof, the sour odor of the van's mildewed upholstery.

As for my employer, I don't know what goes through his head. Maybe Mark is like me, saying a prayer for a good haul and muttering his gratitude for some work to do on a Friday night. Or maybe he's just waiting for Ty, the guy we bribe for parking, to emerge from his single-wide.

The door of the trailer cracks open, and Ty sticks his head out.

"I'm Matt," Mark whispers. "You're Dave."

I make my eyes big like, *Duh.* I screwed up the fake names once, and now he never fails to remind me. We hop out of the van, sling our backpacks over our shoulders. Mark ascends the three steps to the door of Ty's trailer. I hang back.

"My man Matt." Ty proffers his fist.

Mark leans against the side of the trailer, taps Ty's fist with his own, and palms him a ten-dollar bill.

Ty tucks the ten into the breast pocket of his blazer. Still in uniform—he must've had to work late. The three of us tip our heads back in unison as a passenger jet roars overhead, rending the air with twin six-ton engines. The world feels changed once it's gone, the unseen throngs of crickets and chorus frogs chastened into silence. Ty glances at his watch. "Delta red-eye to Newark, that's a Dreamliner. Y'all want rolls?"

Mark grins as he produces five more dollars from his rain pants. Ty works as a concierge at the Visa Crown Elite Lounge, where Obsidian cardholders are served the same defrosted croissants every day until they're gone. But at the Cinnabon in Terminal Three, where his girlfriend cashiers, day-olds go home with the staff.

Ty pockets the five, disappears for a moment, and then reappears holding a plastic bag.

"There's extra icing in there." He hands the bag to Mark.

"My man," Mark says.

"You good, Dave?"

"Hi, Ty," I say.

"Lotta new tents out there." Mark jerks his head back toward the entrance.

Ty's lips press into a tight line, and he shakes his head ruefully. "Land of the free. Well, good luck, my dudes. Bag mucho amphibians."

He salutes us with two fingers and pulls his door shut.

Mark puts the cinnamon rolls in the van, and then we set out through the rain, navigating the puddles in the potholed pathway between the netless tennis court and the empty pool. Making our way toward the reservoir behind the mobile home park.

"Six rolls for five bucks," Mark says, scanning the cloud layer for upwind gaps. "That's like fifteen calories a cent."

"Diabetes can add up," I say.

Mark chuckles and says, "We need happy Ty."

We skirt the muddy banks of the reservoir, trace the chain-link fence to where it vanishes into a thicket of blackberry bushes. Then the work gloves and headlamps come out of our backpacks. Peering into the darkness that surrounds us, I seek signs of others out roaming the night, but we're alone.

So I click on my headlamp in red-light mode and pull aside the thorny vines that hide our tunnel through the thicket.

Mark crawls in first. I follow behind. The bushes have grown since we last cut them back, and for the final several feet of the tunnel, on the other side of the hole in the chain-link fence, we're wriggling forward on our elbows and bellies.

"Think maybe we should trim again?" I clamber to my feet on the other side.

"We've only got a couple trips left," Mark reminds me.

We're standing in the corner of a large field, its soggy expanse arrayed with a grid of shipping containers listing in the mud.

Hull Secure Facilities. Or as we call it, the Lost and Found.

Mark shucks his backpack to the ground in front of the nearest shipping container. Kneeling next to him, I knit my fingers together and boost him onto the top. After I've passed up both backpacks, I grasp his hands and launch myself upward, and he heaves me onto the container beside him.

The first thing I do is check for our two-by-fours: right here where we left them. Then I follow Mark's gaze to the cottage on the hill at the far end of the Lost and Found.

A light glows in one window.

"Jerry's up late," I say, glancing at my watch, a black rubber Casio I found among Dad's things after his murder.

Ten minutes to midnight.

Mark narrows his eyes at the cottage. The window flickers. Dimmer. Brighter. Yellow. Blue.

"Watching TV," Mark concludes. "Rain might clear up by four. I say we move."

June on the forty-seventh parallel north: the sun lingering in the sky until nine, rising again at five. Seattle averages eight nights of rain in June. July only gets six. The window for our visits to the Lost and Found is closing.

I pick up one of the two-by-fours and lay it across the gap to the next container over, and Mark places the second board parallel to the first. We cross this makeshift bridge one at a time, moving our feet in short, wide steps like inept roller skaters. Then we move the boards and cross the next gap, working our way toward the only four containers that we haven't searched yet: the ones closest to Jerry Hull's cottage.

A single footstep on the paths among the containers could result in a felony burglary charge or a spray of buckshot in the back. It would trip the network of seismic sensors buried beneath the ground, and that would trigger an alarm on Jerry's phone that would send him scuttling to his gun cabinet.

But the vibrations caused by our steps on top of the containers, dampened by the seismic static of the rainfall, aren't strong enough to trip the sensors. And there are dead spots in the network, including the far corner by the blackberry thicket.

All this from Mark. He knows all about the ground sensors. He installed them.

It takes us about half an hour to reach the first untouched container, the one labeled Bin Four on Mark's hand-drawn map back at the office. Now we're within a hundred feet of Jerry's. The light has migrated from the front of the cottage to the rear.

"That his bedroom?" I ask.

Mark shakes his head. "Bathroom. Brushing his teeth, I suppose."

"Impressive hygiene for a parasite."

"Well. He doesn't floss."

I smirk at Mark. "You searched his cabinets?"

"I don't know about 'searched.'" His tone is defensive. "I wasn't fiending for Vicodin. You don't peek behind the mirror when you use someone's john?"

The question gives me pause. Do I? Would I? Nobody's invited me into their house since I arrived in Seattle sixteen months ago. And before that, well. I was a different person before that. I had a home and a future back then. I had a name.

Mark's gaze shifts from my face to the darkness behind me. He puts his hands on his hips, sticks out his chin, and says, "Huhhh."

I turn around and see what he's staring at: a rectangular pool in the mud, twenty feet long and eight feet wide, where Bin One used to be.

I say, "Oh."

We peer at the absence of Bin One for a long moment. Conjectures float through my head with all the dependability of helium balloons. Meanwhile, the rain thickens.

"Maybe we should get the hell out of here," I say.

"We'll make tonight our last." Mark glances back at the cottage. All dark now. He opens his backpack, pulls out his climbing harness and the rope.

"You sure about that, boss?" I say.

Mark nods. "A few more hours, Lao. One last hurrah at our dear Lost and Found."

I pull out my own harness and tighten the straps around my waist. We tie the ends of the short rope to our carabiners with figure-eight knots. Then I sit down on the roof of the container and brace my heels against the steel lip of its front edge.

Mark drops off the front of the container, hangs for a moment with his hands on the lip, then sets the soles of his boots against the container door. As his weight falls into his harness, the rope between us stretches taut.

I hear a beep from his watch. Mark's gotten pretty handy with his pick and tension wrench. He opened the padlock on Bin Twelve in ninety-two seconds. He hasn't come close to that record since, but he hasn't given up.

I follow along on Dad's Casio. A hundred and fifteen seconds later, I hear him pop the shackle on the lock and slide open the bolt.

He climbs back to the top of the container with a grin on his face. I get to my feet, unclip the carabiner from my harness, and make a show of stretching my legs.

"A few more cinnamon rolls and we're gonna need a thicker rope," I say.

"Hit the squat rack," Mark scoffs. "I'm trimmer than a sprinter."

The chummy banter feels forced, undermined by the conspicuous absence of Bin One and the increasingly stormy skies. The wind is really ripping now, the rain blooming into a downpour. And when we're shifting the two-by-fours to the next gap, rushing a little so that we can get out of the weather, I trip over the rope, lose my footing, and drop the board all the way to the ground.

We freeze, lock eyes, and then turn as one to look at the cottage. Long seconds pass in which the only sounds are the splatter of the rain on the steel containers, the whistle of the wind through the gaps.

I check my watch. One minute. Then two. No lights snap on. No door flies open. No sign of Jerry.

I look down at the errant timber, one end still resting on the lid of Bin Three, the other sunk into the mud beneath us.

"Is this a dead zone?"

Mark shrugs, still watching the cottage. "I guess so." He turns to frown at me. "Think you can keep your shit together, Lao?"

"Line management is *your* job, *Matt*."

He looks down at my feet, where the rope lies in a heap.

"All right, all right. Just watch where you're going, you big baby," he says. "Can you cross a single plank?"

I don't answer, just step out onto the remaining two-by-four.

I fix my eyes on the far bin and move quickly. Then I turn around and extend both middle fingers toward Mark.

He gives me a golf clap. I reach down and retrieve the second board for his use. We repeat our routine on Bin Three, and Mark picks the padlock in ninety-eight seconds. Then we look at the skies. Plenty of rain left.

"Three hours?" he says.

"Oughta do it." I set a timer on Dad's Casio.

"You need some puréed pumpkin to tide you over?" he asks.

"I'd kinda like to purée your face right now."

He flashes his snaggletoothed grin, then crosses back to Bin Four. He dangles himself over the front edge, pulls the door open with one hand, and drops into the shipping container with the grace of a jungle cat.

I watch the dark cottage for another minute, a scowl on my face, resentment nesting in my intestines.

Think you can keep your shit together, Lao?

Typical Mark. Mister Teflon. Not a mistake-owner. Leaves a rope coiled around my ankles in a rainstorm and snaps at me when it trips me up. I'm still fuming in his general direction as I slip into Bin Three, shut the door behind me, and switch my headlamp to white light.

But when I look around the humid interior of the shipping container, anticipation floods my veins, warming me from scalp to fingertips. Gratitude returns to me, gratitude to my boss and only friend, the man who introduced me to the one thing I ever feel like doing anymore: searching through stories sealed in plastic, each one a life to glimpse into, a lottery ticket to scratch. Purses, wallets, backpacks, suitcases.

The confiscated belongings of people ejected from the country.

2

We first visited the Lost and Found on a drizzly night in April. We searched Bins Twenty-One and Twenty. Our cumulative haul was a pearl necklace, an e-reader, two film cameras, and 386 dollars in small bills.

We'd burgled federal property for a little more than what we could've made bouncing the door at a Cap Hill nightclub. On the giddy drive back to the office, I tried to figure out why it felt so good. In the weeks that followed, I developed a few theories.

Theory One: the dance with danger. Mark and I were weaned on adrenaline. Cable sports, console gaming, online poker, laser tag. Here was a game with real stakes: sneaking around in the dark, evading shitbag Jerry and his shotgun collection. After a night at the Lost and Found, air hockey felt like quilting.

Theory Two: the lure of fortune. Each plastic bag was a face-down hand of cards, radiant with possibility. "There's a big score in here somewhere, I know it," Mark said on that first night, rubbing his palms together. "A score that will change everything."

We'd hit several times, no royal flushes but plenty of straights: the Rolex in Bin Sixteen, the sock full of engagement rings in Eleven, the vintage dreadnought guitar in Eight that Mark fondled for a week before consenting to sell.

I inferred Theories One and Two from Mark, that hop in his step each time we came here, that daredevil desire to linger until dawn. Theory Three came later. As I lost myself in the excavation of other people's tragedies, an unfamiliar feeling washed over me. I had trouble naming it at first. Too warm for pity. Too far removed for compassion. Eventually I made up a word for it: "intonymity." The combination of intimacy and anonymity. Like watching a sad movie. You see someone up close: their eyes, their teeth, their tears.

But they never see you.

I shed my rain gear to the floor of Bin Three, swap out my work gloves for disposable latex, and make a pile of bags from the nearest shelf. The first one I open contains a trifold wallet, all nylon and Velcro. Eight bucks in ones. A few neatly creased receipts, an expired condom, and a punch card for a movie theater: BUY SEVEN LARGE POPCORNS, GET THE EIGHTH FREE! One punch short of redemption.

And an Idaho driver's license. Chambi Musa Jabril: 5'9", 155 pounds, eyes brown, hair black, date of birth May 28, 1994. The photo shows a man with bushy eyebrows and pointy ears. Address: 6213 Overlook Street, Boise. Once upon a time.

"Chambi Musa Jabril. So close to free popcorn," I mutter, tucking the cash into one of the dry bags in my backpack. "Happy belated, Chambi. I hope you got cake."

Next up, a tiny denim backpack. Butterfly barrette, three sticks of fossilized chewing gum, and a high school ID card. Aracely Garcia. Rosacea, shy smile, eyebrows very plucked. The inner zip pocket contains a worn wooden rosary, a Korean smartphone in a bedazzled case, and a family photo from one of those green screen booths at tourist attractions. Aracely stands with her parents and her brother, superimposed on a stock image of the Space Needle, all four of them smiling that same shy smile.

I stare at the photo, studying their faces. Did this family fall to pieces, like mine, when they were shaken awake from their American dream? Or are they still together somewhere south of the Rio Grande, taking new photos and assembling a new life?

I put the photo, the rosary, and the phone into a different bag—the one Mark doesn't know about. This is the bag I'll send to Leon Few, the director of a nonprofit in Nogales that helps deportees get back on their feet. I close my eyes for a moment, imagine the surprised smile that would light up Aracely Garcia's face if she ever gets these items back.

The third bag of the night is a carry-on suitcase. The Border Patrol label says SEATAC. I dig through folded clothes. Suit pants, dark stockings, sheath dress in scarlet red. High heels, strappy sandals, and a pair of black training shoes made by Li-Ning, China's biggest sportswear brand, its logo laughably similar to the Nike swoosh.

Quality stuff. Not worth enough to bag, but promising.

Near the bottom of the suitcase, I find a small notebook clamped shut with a plastic hair clip. The clip catches my attention. It feels a millimeter too bulky, a gram overweight. I examine it in front of my headlamp, spy within its recesses a micro-USB port.

What's this, a cleverly disguised flash drive? My pulse quickens as the intonymity surges through my veins. This suitcase belonged to someone with a secret.

I open the small notebook. Sticking out of it like a bookmark, there's a boarding pass for one Song Fei. November of last year, Seattle to Washington, DC—a flight she never boarded. The pages of the notebook are filled with handwritten Chinese characters. Addresses, names, places, dates. 旧金山—*Old Gold Mountain*, that's San Francisco. 亚特兰大—yàtèlándà, phonetic for Atlanta.

Another page has an address in Spanish. And a price, sixty-five thousand US dollars per 克拉—kèlā—whatever that is. The

price is followed by a seemingly random list of elements: 铝—lǚ—
aluminum; 钙—gài—*calcium*. Others I don't recognize.

On the last page, six vertical lines of ten characters each: a
poem in classical verse.

"Who are you, Song Fei?" I wonder aloud. "An undocumented
chemist? A roving bard?"

I push my damp, unkempt hair out of my eyes and unzip her
toiletry kit. Upscale cosmetics. Clippers, tweezers, emery board.
And a felt box—my pulse quickens—containing two rings! Both
gold, both set with gemstones: one emerald, one sapphire.

I've gotten good at assessing jewelry ever since Mark and I
streamed a master class in gemology. He wanted to make sure
we weren't being ripped off by pawnbrokers. I'd expected the six-
hour course to be dull, but in the end, we were both mesmerized
by the instructor, "Doctor" Ontario Heffelfinger, who had a loupe
chained to his bow tie, tiny rubies embedded in his incisors, and
a mustache like Salvador Dalí. Uncut stones, synthetic stones,
conflict stones from Sierra Leone or Myanmar—now we know
all about them.

And Song Fei's rings are definitely nice jewelry. The small emerald is eye-clean, and the setting is an intricate gold weave. The
large sapphire has some inclusions, but they're well masked by the
Asscher cut.

My mouth turns up at the corners as I tilt them around in the
light of my headlamp. Mark will be stoked.

I'm packing Song Fei's things back into her suitcase when I
notice a rectangular shape in the exterior pocket. I zip it open, dis-
cover a block of wood about the size of a hardcover book.

A puzzle box. A thrill flutters through my chest. Dad used to
bring home a pair of puzzle boxes every time he came back from
Beijing. One for me, one for Jules. Whoever opened theirs first got
a ten-dollar bill.

Jules lost interest in her early teens, around the time that Mom died of stomach cancer. "I'm sick of him making us compete with each other," she said.

So after that, I got to solve two.

I hold the box in front of my face, rotating it in the light of my headlamp, feeling for moving parts—*aha*. This one is basic. One of the ends, pressed just so with my thumb, slides a few millimeters on an interlocking track. That allows one of the long sides to slide perpendicularly, unblocking—*it must be*—a hidden spring in the center of the box. I squeeze the wide sides toward each other, and the other end pops off like a bottle cap.

Squinting into the open end, I see a layer of red fabric, run my finger along it—velvet. I flip the box over, tap tap tap, and a gusseted bag slides into my hand.

Inside, a second puzzle box, this one about the size of a deck of cards. The polished dark wood is inlaid with a dizzying pattern of ebony and nacre. I give it a shake next to my ear, hear little pins move within. This box is much more ornate than the first.

"What are you hiding, Song Fei?" I ask the red dress in the suitcase. "Launch codes? Kennedy nudes?"

I could put the puzzle box in my dry bag, work on it later in the comfort of the office. But I don't want to share it with Mark. I'll turn over whatever's inside, sure. I would never hold out loot.

But the experience, that's for me. That's Theory Three.

I don't know if Mark feels it. It's not the kind of thing we talk about, and we always work separate bins. That's what builds the intonymity: being alone with someone else's story. The clues, the hints, the heartbreaks, and not a thing I can do about it. Who, me? I'm nobody. A scavenger, a collector of mementos, an archaeologist of woe. Even if Leon Few can find Aracely Garcia and give her back her phone, she won't know it was me who reclaimed it for her. There will be no gratitude. There will be no debt.

On the cold steel floors of the Lost and Found bins, I meet dozens of people who will never meet me back. We can lower our defenses because they're already gone. I don't have to lie to them about who I am. I don't have to treat everything like a big joke, like I do with Mark.

Another habit established without discussion: Mark Knox and I keep it light. We've spent almost every day together for six months, but he's never told me why he was discharged from the military. Why broken glass makes him vomit. Why he never visits his son. He hasn't told me, and I haven't asked. Because I'd rather not answer any questions myself.

Mark pays me in cash. I think he suspects that I'm a wanted man, but he has no idea why. He doesn't know about Beijing, about Sun Jianshui and the men I watched him kill. He doesn't even know my real name.

He doesn't know the first thing about Victor Li.

3

I arrived in Seattle sixteen months ago. It was February. I was a fugitive. I'd just wrapped up a weeklong intercontinental crime spree with the man who killed my father.

It wasn't what you'd call a period of peak mental health.

At the time that Sun Jianshui slit Dad's throat with a folding knife, I was a senior at San Dimas State University. I thought the world was a pretty solid place about the size of Los Angeles County. I thought Dad ran a chain of Chinese restaurants. Part taskmaster, part cornball, all love.

Sun Jianshui changed all that. He came looking for me after killing Dad, and he told me a secret: before our family moved from Beijing to LA when I was a toddler, Dad had been the designated head-breaker in a Chinese crime syndicate. He'd pulled Sun off the streets as a kid and trained him to hurt people. Sun was Dad's ticket to a better life. Once Sun was old enough to take over as the syndicate's enforcer, Dad abandoned him, moved our family to Los Angeles, and set up his restaurants to launder money for his gang.

Now Sun was an expert in violence with the emotional breadth of a rattlesnake. He'd come to the States to ask Dad for his liberty, and in a moment of blind rage, he'd killed the only person he'd ever loved. But he left out that teensy-weensy little detail when he came to find me. He asked me to go with him to Beijing and expose the syndicate's criminal schemes. Then he used me to bait his traps.

I was a world-class sucker, a leading nominee for the Nobel Prize in Naivete. The moment I figured out Sun's game, I was standing in the kitchen of a safe house in Pasadena with a stolen gun in my hands, watching him cut another throat. When I confronted him, he confessed to everything, promised not to kill me later, and jumped out a window. I let him go. After twenty years of servitude to Dad, Sun Jianshui was finally free.

Me, not so much. I was spotted by a cop at that house in Pasadena. When Sun vanished, I became the prime suspect in the murder he committed that night.

So I fled from LA to Seattle, started living underground in Chinatown, got a cash job washing dishes at a noodle joint called Chow Fun Fun. Back in those days before I met Mark Knox, I worked six twelve-hour shifts per week. As I hunkered over that cramped sink, scrubbing sesame oil out of clunky plastic bowls, I often wondered what had become of the mild-mannered assassin who'd shattered my world.

"Hŭ sĭ bu biàn xíng, láng sĭ bu biàn xìng," Dad would say— *Wolves and tigers will die before changing their ways.* I imagined Sun Jianshui lying low in Canada. Forging signatures, drilling safes, scaling drainpipes. Or back in Beijing, handing out beatdowns for some new kingpin.

Or hell, maybe he stayed in LA. Maybe he was teaching kung fu to children in Claremont. After all, the police weren't looking for him. They were looking for me.

"Their warrant is for the stolen gun," Jules told me on the phone. "Not the murder. They said you'd serve a year at most."

It was a drizzly night last May. I'd been in Seattle for three months, and my case hadn't cooled. Plainclothes detectives were dropping by my sister's apartment, plying her for crumbs. I told her that we shouldn't speak, but she insisted on calling me anyway. Always late at night. Always using an encrypted VoIP app to circumvent the pen/trap order that the police had likely placed on her phone.

"They're lying to you!" I hissed, pacing the alleyway behind Chow Fun Fun. "Do you really think they're knocking on your door because they need that larceny collar? They know I stole the gun. They know I fled the scene. If I turn myself in, they're going to pin me with manslaughter. That's three to six years, Jules!"

"Yeah, well." I seemed to hear her tip her head from side to side. "That lawyer said that you'd definitely be acquitted. One? You have no priors. Two? The gun you stole was not the murder weapon. And three? You didn't do it! They can't convict you on circumstantial evidence."

I rolled my eyes. "She's saying that because you're a potential client. What does she charge, three fifty an hour? Whether or not I rot in prison?"

"I have the money, Victor. I already told you that."

I choked back a snort of disgust, kicked a sodden cardboard box across the alley. Jules had Dad's money. Money soaked in blood. Blood spilled by Sun Jianshui.

There was no way I would touch that money.

"I have to go, Jules."

"Just promise me you'll think it over, okay?"

"Fine," I lied, and I hung up the phone.

I closed my eyes, took a deep breath, and reminded myself that Jules didn't know what she was talking about. My old life was gone forever, and hoping otherwise, even for a minute, would be dangerous and stupid.

Then I rejoined my coworkers, who were sitting on milk crates by the restaurant's back door. Even though I didn't smoke, I cherished the cigarette sessions in the alleyway after closing because they constituted the entirety of my social life. The other employees sipped 120-proof báijiǔ from Dixie cups and waxed wistful about their hometowns. Hardly anyone preferred living in America. No—they planned to return to Fujian or Anhui, reunite with their aging parents and patient sweethearts. Buy a concrete house with a solar water heater, a compact Geely with front-wheel drive.

It might be possible in a decade or two if they saved every penny they didn't spend on their counterfeit cigarettes, which they smoked down to the filter. The cashier's mom, in Foshan, was getting a dog. The cook's daughter, in Anxi, was turning six. I took some comfort knowing that I wasn't the only exile living in the past, the possible, the purgatory of unrealized dreams.

Chinatown knew me by an alias: Dennis Lao. I was renting half a bunk in a tenement flop for undocumented mainlanders. Twenty-eight men shared the fourteen bunks in our apartment, snoring around the clock in shifts, but I didn't mind that. I felt comfortable among these recent arrivals to America's margins. My roommates were shadow people. You never spoke to them, you rarely even saw them, but they cooked your food, starched your shirts, and vacuumed your office. They pulled eighty-hour weeks for half minimum wage, and they thanked you for the opportunity. It beat the shit out of assembling iPads in Dongguan for thirty bucks a day.

As for me, I'd grown up with a white mom, a free-spirited sister, a golden retriever, and a PlayStation 3. Dad had sheltered me from the dirt he'd done to build my world. Now I was soft and he was dead. Once I knew my cushy childhood was a sham, only raw deals felt real.

I tried hard to blend into Chinatown. I spent long nights in an all-hours internet café, working on my vocabulary, learning to read handwritten characters. At first, my roommates and coworkers seemed to like having me around. They called me hùnxuè'ér—

the mixed-blood kid. After I helped our chef contest some parking tickets, word got around that I could write English like a native speaker. People came to find me when they needed to edit a menu or answer a letter from the government.

Unfortunately, business at the restaurants was crappy, and the letters I translated were mostly bad news. Code violations. Eviction notices. Deportation orders. Being a Chinese immigrant had always involved certain amounts of maltreatment, but it got a whole lot worse last year. Our fellow Americans were letting us know that they'd always see us as aliens, even if we'd been here for generations.

It all began when the president labeled China an "Enemy of Freedom" for propping up the genocidal Burmese junta. The Chinese premier responded by accusing the president of "imperialistic hypocrisy." Before long, relations between the two superpowers deteriorated from treaties to tariffs, tariffs to sanctions, sanctions to boycotts. Journalists and diplomats were expelled; consulates were shuttered. The vicious Chinese were the villains of every news cycle. And the new Cold War was trickling down to Chinatown.

—*Yes, Auntie, the spray paint says, 'Monkeys get stomped.'*

—*I believe you have sufficient credit history, Uncle, but that's not what the letter says.*

—*He called you what? Oh. It's a slang word for 'person of Asian descent.'*

I filled out forms, filed appeals, and pressed zero to speak to representatives, but most people still got screwed. Eventually they stopped asking for my help. The Cantonese and Fujianese stopped switching from their regional languages into Mandarin so I could participate in conversations.

I was no more at home in Chinatown than qīngtíng diǎnshuǐ— the dragonfly that skims the water's surface.

I told myself that I didn't care. I had to keep a low profile anyway. I retreated to my internet café, stayed up all night sipping energy drinks, delved ever deeper into my language studies—

having decided that total fluency in Chinese would be the best way for me to disappear completely. In particular, I spent a lot of time on the Language forum of Huayiwang.com, an online community for people of Chinese ancestry. I learned about zhengkai calligraphy, about traditional and simplified characters, about oracle bones and the *Book of Changes*. And when I'd read every post in the Language forum, I clicked on History and Politics.

The Politics posts overflowed with heated arguments in the comments sections, although everyone seemed to agree that American politicians were stoking public fear of China in order to shift attention away from their own repugnant corruption and quagmire wars of choice. The History posts were the real revelations. The Chinese Exclusion Act. The mass lynching of Chinese workers on Calle de los Negros. I spent a whole weekend studying the murder of Vincent Chin in Detroit in 1982. Two autoworkers decided to blame him for the decline of their industry, so they beat him to death with a baseball bat in the parking lot of a McDonald's. These white men were sentenced by a white judge to three years of probation and a three-thousand-dollar fine.

I'd grown up in the San Gabriel Valley, the largest community of Chinese-Americans in the country. How come none of this stuff was in my textbooks? I roved onward to more message boards, stared wide-eyed at more disgusting truths that contradicted the myths I'd been raised on. COINTELPRO and MKUltra. Salvador Allende and Operation Cyclone. Monsanto, Tuskegee, redlining. There was no melting pot. It was not A Small World After All. Everyone was pointing fingers, hoarding privileges, staking out fiefdoms. And where the hell was *my* niche? Hùnxuè'ér—*the mixed-blood kid*. I had gone from legal to illegal: I was immigrating in reverse. No tribe, no home, no name.

I started training at the gnarliest MMA gym I could find, a place in Delridge popular with gangbangers and vets. Dead-eyed guys with cauliflower ears taught me the practical stuff: Brazilian jiujitsu and Krav Maga. How to jab eyes, break fingers, and escape the choke holds favored by the cops.

In Delridge, I discovered how much of a cupcake I truly was. Dudes twice my age were submitting me in half a round. I heaved air on the mats after tapping out, the bare bulb in the pendant lamp dazzling my eyes like a guiding star. Heart pumping like a coal train, taste of blood in my mouth.

That was where I found myself again. I felt most alive when someone had just kicked my ass.

"You're sick," Jules said. "You've been traumatized. You're turning your self-loathing into a violent game."

"You're not hearing me, Jules," I said. "It's not a game, it's survival. It's real life. Nothing has ever felt more real."

"Victor, there is so much more to real life than grown men beating the feces out of each other."

I stopped walking at a red light. It was after midnight on a windy Wednesday in November, and the chill cut right through my cheap cotton sweats. I had just finished an hour of wind sprints along Elliott Bay. Jules was taking a break from binge-watching documentaries. Like Dad, we were both night owls.

Jules had been knocked off her orbit by Dad's murder, too. She'd dropped out of design school and enrolled in a new grad program, this one in documentary filmmaking. After two more years of expensive education, she'd be ready to start healing the world by recording its problems.

It began to rain again. That was Seattle for you. I covered my head with the hood of my sweatshirt, even though I was already soaked.

"I'm just doing the things that make me feel better," I said. "You should be happy for me."

Jules sighed. She sighed just how Mom would sigh. I could remember the exact way Mom sighed, even though she'd died when I was twelve.

"I am happy for you," Jules said. "I would like to be slightly more happy for you. Can we talk about Thanksgiving?"

"What about Thanksgiving?"

"Um, it's a family holiday?" She told me that she was inviting some people over for brunch, including my college roommates. "How about a video chat? They'd really love to see you."

A Thanksgiving chat with my sister and my friends—oh, joy. They could tell me all the things they're grateful for. Their new apartments, their cool jobs. Maybe they had girlfriends now. And I could tell them that I'm well, too. Thanks for asking. I'm absolutely frickin' stellar.

I dug the fingernails of my free hand deep into my palm and squeezed my eyes shut so hard I could feel my pulse in my skull.

"Victor? Are you still there?"

"Yeah. Sure. Sounds great," I said. "What time?"

When the day came, I made sure to keep my phone off throughout the morning, which I spent deep-cleaning the restaurant with my boss. Old Leung was a bewhiskered curmudgeon from Kowloon. He'd arrived in Seattle twenty-five years ago, spooning a stranger in the false bottom of a refrigerated Canadian beef truck. The only thing Old Leung knew about Thanksgiving was that hardly anyone wanted lo mein on Thanksgiving.

In the afternoon, I ran to Delridge, but the gym was closed. Bummer. I guess even the guys who taught crotch kicks wanted to eat yams with their families and commemorate the genocide that paved the way for this fine nation.

I sat on the curb, powered on my phone, and swiped away a series of angry messages from Jules. I started mapping out a circuitous run home involving as many hills as possible. Thursday was my night off, and the impending hours of holiday solitude sucked at my stomach like a black hole.

Then another guy trotted up to the gym entrance.

"Balls!" he exclaimed.

I glanced up and quickly glanced back down. I'd seen this guy around the gym, working out almost as hard as I did. Average height, slender but broad-shouldered, muscles on muscles on muscles. Severe burns had turned the skin on his forearms several different colors.

He sat down on the curb next to me and said what's up.

"You work out here, right?" he asked me.

"Yeah," I said. "So do you."

"I know," he said. He had purple semicircles beneath his pale green eyes, brown hair all spiky with gel, and an inch-long scar on his right cheek shaped like a slice of pizza. He looked like a buff insomniac with a broken nose.

He stuck out his hand and said, "I'm Mark."

4

Dennis Lao," I said, and we shook hands. Mark's palms were calloused, and he had a grip like a firefighter. He studied me with those pale green eyes until I felt uncomfortable.

"So, no turkey for you?" I asked, just to break the silence, even though it felt like the awkwardest possible subject.

"Yeah, no." Mark frowned, and then his face lit up. "Hey, wanna race to the sculpture park?"

"The Olympic Sculpture Park? Like north of Pike Place?"

"That's the one."

Confusion knit my brow. It was at least six miles to Pike Place. I had nothing better to do. I already knew I was in, but I wanted to know why he was.

"What's the finish?"

Mark scratched his chin and squinted. "Let's say Calder's Eagle."

"Okay, but—" I began, and then he hopped up and took off.

I passed him on Harbor Island and never looked back. I'd been stretching for a few minutes when he limped up to Calder's Eagle.

"Oh, God," he wheezed, hands on his knees. "I hate your guts."

Weeks later, I would learn that Mark had lost a chunk of his left calf to an IED in Mosul. For now, unsure of how to respond, I said nothing.

When he'd caught his breath, he said, "I bet I can eat more chicken wings than you."

"C'mon, man," I said.

He looked at me disdainfully. "I put you at about twenty-four wings, tops, and five lite beers."

"Go fuck yourself," I said.

"But we have to walk there. In fact, you have to carry me."

"I don't have my wallet."

"I'll buy. You won."

"But I don't have ID."

Mark scoffed. "You think I don't know the bartenders?"

We didn't end up having an eating contest, which Mark admitted was a disgusting idea. But we did compete for the rest of Thanksgiving at Big Needle Brewing. The footrace ended up being my only win. Mark swept pool, darts, and skee-ball. I kept video poker close, but Name That Tune was a landslide.

Mark didn't crow or gloat. After each victory, he gave me a fist bump and then headed to the bar for another round. Without consulting me, he ordered two of whatever was next on the tap list. Mark was skilled at drinking beer. He took a sip, looked at the ceiling, and then nailed the tasting notes just like he'd nailed the corner pocket with the eight ball.

He sipped the saison and said, "Buttery barnyard."

He sipped the porter and said, "Leather glove and German chocolate cake."

By the time we got to the barrel-aged cherry stout, the brewery had filled up with bloated Seattleites who seemed relieved to be free of their families. I was soaked in my first drunk of the year, lolling around in the warm, beery noise.

Mark took a sip of the stout, screwed up his face, and said, "Abandoned bird's nest."

I took a sip and said, "Sewer smoothie."

Mark guffawed. Then he poured out the stouts at the hydration station and bought another round of pilsners.

We didn't get to know each other. We didn't discuss what we did for work or where we came from. We talked about the Seahawks, who were losing badly on the bar TVs, and the gym. We debated which wing sauce was best (Nashville Hot). When karaoke started at ten, Mark suggested that we rate each performance for song choice, inebriation, melodic accuracy, and spunk.

By midnight, we'd assimilated into a broader group of shout-talking, dance-standing survivors. At one, Mark put in a song and tipped the KJ to bump him up the list. The song was "Walking in Memphis." Mark brought the gusto. By the second chorus, he was soaked in sweat and possibly tears—it was hard to tell with all the sweat. I gave him a nine in inebriation, an eight in melodic accuracy, and a twelve in spunk. Half the bar sang along, and the other half left.

I left, too, just after last call. Mark was using his whole body to describe the merits of potato cannons to a trio of irked hipsters. I wanted to thank him for the beers and the wings, but the bathroom stalls were full, and I simply had to puke. I staggered outside and paid my penance on the sidewalk. Reentry was out of the question. I walked two miles back to Chinatown, humming.

After that, Mark and I played bar games and drank beer on most Thursday nights. He knew which bars had League Pass, which bars had shuffleboard, which bars had deals on nachos. I insisted on picking up every other tab. We didn't always get as loaded as we had on Thanksgiving, but it was still a strain on my dishwashing income.

"What did you say you do for work?" he asked one night in January as I counted out fives and ones.

I hadn't said. "I breed heirloom artichokes."

He nodded. "Me, too."

I told him that I washed dishes at Chow Fun Fun. He looked taken aback. He asked if I'd gone to college.

"Didn't finish."

"And you speak Chinese."

"Uh-huh."

"Other languages?"

"I was a Spanish minor."

Mark pursed his lips and nodded. "And you make, what?"

"Fuck you," I said.

It was the first personal conversation we'd ever had. I felt like he was violating an unspoken pact. I didn't realize it was a job interview.

"I'm looking to expand my business. I can pay you"—and right then, Mark doubled my hourly.

"I can't really—"

"In cash," he interrupted.

I paused.

"To do what?" I asked.

"Logistical Solutions. Number One in the Seattle Area for Making Things Run Smoothly." He framed the words in the air between us, making L-shapes with his hands.

"'Things'?"

He jerked his head toward the door and said, "I'll show you."

We pulled up the hoods of our jackets and walked through the rain to the Industrial District. The vacant city streets were cool, quiet, and full of possibility. Mark walked a few paces ahead of me, his shoulders hunched against the wind. Despite his slight limp, I perceived latent energy in his stride.

It occurred to me that a year had passed since Dad's death. *Maybe this is the beginning of the rest of my life*, I thought. *Or maybe he'll murder me, and that will also more or less be fine.*

After half an hour, we arrived at a storage facility. Mark had a key to the concertina wire gate, which was padlocked, it being two in the morning. He had a good relationship with maintenance, he said.

We walked through the dark facility, asphalt lanes sloped to grated drains. Mark told me he'd been a communications engineer in the army. He knew everything there was to know about drones, cameras, microphones, Comsats, magnetic fields, and electronic pulses. He'd done three tours in Iraq before ISIS blew off his gastrocnemius.

We stopped in front of a roll-up door, which Mark unlocked and threw open. The unit had climate control and electricity. There was a big desk, a pleather couch, and chrome wire shelves stacked high with gadgets.

Mark had mounted a TV on the wall and covered the concrete floor with faded rugs. He had a mini-fridge and a toaster oven. The big desk was an old door set atop two stacks of cinder blocks. On its surface there was a pearl-handled balisong knife and a padlock in its deconstructed parts.

He'd hung a couple of monthly calendars on the wall by his desk: last year's *Sports Illustrated* Swimsuit Calendar and this year's Great Castles of Europe. On brand for Seattle, he had a turntable and a crate of vinyl. He put on a Steely Dan record, set the needle to a snide song about an alcoholic saxophone player. Then he produced two bottles of beer from the mini-fridge and popped off the caps with his teeth.

I remained standing in the doorway, trying to make sense of

what I was seeing. The roll-up door smelled of metal and dust. The drizzle had stopped, and the wind had kicked up. The moon peeked through a gap in the puffy charcoal cumuli, shining bright there in that part of the city with low ambient light. Its crescent sliver was waxing.

Mark handed me a beer. He turned up a palm as if to say, *Well?*

Expressions of gratitude were outside of our mutual language, but I held up my bottle.

"Logistical Solutions," I said.

"Logistical Solutions," he solemnly repeated, and we took a sip. Pale ale. Mark's favorite.

"Lemon and hay," he said.

"So what do we actually do?"

5

What we did turned out to be a little bit of everything. Mark's expertise was valuable and diverse. But most of his gigs were one-off, so he was constantly scrambling for work. His bread and butter was surveillance detection. We swept corporate offices for bugs, then wiped the computers of malware and bots.

These jobs couldn't be done during business hours, so we'd meet with the IT and security guys at eight or nine at night. Before we left, Mark would casually ask: Hey, are y'all happy with your CCTV cameras? Your conference phones? Your stun guns? He'd sell them a few gadgets from the stash in the back of his rickety van, or he'd leave them with a couple of catalogs and a pitch for a customized workshop. Preventing Corporate Espionage. Third-Gen Office Security. Advanced Market Research—which really meant How to Spy on Your Customers.

There was a lot of potential demand. People just needed to be shown what they were afraid of. We advertised on B2B sites, on Craigslist, on the dark web. Are your networks secure? 你的网络安全吗? Sabes cómo proteger tus secretos industriales?

I could use my Chinese and Spanish to help Mark reach new customers, and a second pair of hands was useful during installs. He also tasked me with making his invoices. Mark could sketch a diagram with the sure hand of an architect, but when he had to write, he gripped his pen like an ice pick. On a keyboard, he hunted and pecked at a dismal rate, and he tended to pore over emails as if they were written in hieroglyphics.

Within two weeks, I surmised he was dyslexic. After three, I suspected he was broke. We had regular work only because Mark charged bargain-basement rates. It didn't make any sense for Logistical Solutions to have a second employee, even though he underpaid me. There was no schedule, no time sheet. There was just an envelope, containing a random quantity of twenties and labeled LAO CHEESE in purple Sharpie, that materialized in my backpack every Friday.

I didn't complain. It was still more than I'd earned washing dishes. And I was relieved to be spending less time in Chinatown, which had recently become subject to patrols by bullies with paintball guns, rolling down King Street in trucks adorned with American flags. I bought a secondhand bicycle, which made me a faster-moving target and gave me an excuse to wear a helmet. I rode to the gym in Delridge each morning, then spent the rest of the day with Mark: working jobs, spitballing new schemes, or just kind of hanging out. Logistical Solutions became my life. Except for two or three nights a month.

"I vote we take tomorrow off, whatcha say?" Mark said one evening in mid-February. We were standing in the lane outside of the storage unit. He'd just pulled the big door shut. He asked me the question while he was facing away from me, securing the lock.

I glanced at Dad's Casio, confirmed that it was Wednesday. Mark wanted Thursday off. Why Thursday? Had I done something wrong?

"Fine with me," I said, trying to maintain a neutral tone.

The next day, I ran two six-mile laps around Lake Union. Then I showered at the tenement, where I was lucky enough to have hot water for the first couple minutes. I put on black jeans and a hoodie. It was six p.m. The sun had set, rain was sheeting out of the sky, and I couldn't get back into my bunk until ten. So I rode my bicycle through the downpour to Mark's favorite dive in SoDo. I sat at the bar, eating chicken fingers, avoiding eye contact, and watching the Lakers get whomped.

On Friday Mark was back in the storage unit, acting as if nothing had happened. But a couple weeks later, on a Tuesday, he asked me the same thing. And a week after that, on a Monday. Always at the end of the night. Always standing outside of the roll-up door in the dark.

"I vote we take tomorrow off, whatcha say?"

I spent each day off running in magnitudes of rain that seemed gratuitous. I noticed that Mark yawned a lot on the days we returned to work. And after the third day off, when he rolled his sleeves up before extracting a monstrous Reuben from the toaster oven, I saw a lattice of threadlike scratches on the mottled skin of his forearms.

I didn't say anything. I didn't want to pry. Mark still hadn't said a word to me about his personal life or his past. He never told me that he had a son, either. I found that out when he was under his van, trying to identify a leak. I was using his phone to google the smell of transmission fluid when a message popped up from a contact, with a Montana area code, labeled "Tina": tyler needs more from u than 280/month he needs a dad.

I froze for a moment, and the sweat glands under my arms leapt into action like a pit crew. Then the words of Tina's message vanished, shrinking into a tiny blue envelope on his phone's status bar. I regained my composure and did the search. I appreciated Mark's healthy reverence for secrets. He stayed grounded in the present. He didn't delve, and he didn't dwell.

As for me, my mind was still defaulting to that night in Pasadena: the stolen gun in my hand, the pool of blood oozing across the kitchen floor. Sun Jianshui stole into my dreams and painted them scarlet. I was drawn to Mark's levity like a pigeon to popcorn. And for a while there, Things Ran Smoothly indeed.

Mark kept the mini-fridge stocked with beers craft and lite. He'd finagled a League Pass log-in from one of his bartender chums. We'd play rock records during basketball games, hit mute on the commentary, and do our own play-by-play. We re-created the Great Castles of Europe with beer cans. Then we held whimsical competitions to decide who got to destroy them with a slingshot.

Even after six beers, I could balance on one foot with my eyes closed while I whistled the national anthem. Mark could juggle five tangerines while being pelted with more tangerines. We peed in a milk jug, stumbled out to the lane to empty it in the sewer grate. There were nights when I forgot myself for a whole hour.

But when you spend that much time with anyone, you catch their down moments, too. Mark's downs came at the end of the month. He didn't like to look at balance sheets. He spun in circles in his office chair, throwing paper clips at the swimsuit model on the wall calendar, while the Veterans Benefits Administration kept him on hold. By April, he'd dropped the pretense of leaving at the end of the night. He'd record three basketball games and watch them in sequence. Slumped on the couch, resting a beer on his chest, he compulsively twirled his balisong knife, open and shut, open and shut.

He hardly seemed to notice when I got up to leave. If the record had finished, I flipped it over before letting myself out and biking back to Chinatown through the relentless evening rain.

It was a night like that in April when Mark stopped me as I was leaving.

"Hey, Lao," he said.

I was wheeling my bicycle toward the door. I'd thought he'd fallen asleep.

"Hey what?"

"I vote we take tomorrow off," he said, his eyes still fixed on the TV. "Whatcha say?"

"Fine with me."

I took a couple more steps toward the door. Then I turned to look at him again. He was still slumped on the couch. The game was in commercials.

"You know you can trust me, right?" I said.

Now he looked at me with his head cocked at an angle. "What the hell are you talking about?"

"You know what I'm talking about."

Mark sat up on the couch and crossed his legs beneath him. "You'd better spell it out for me. All these hoppy IPAs have done a number on my noodle."

I dropped the kickstand on my bike and walked back to the couch. "Even with the SCIF job, we barely broke even in March."

"You been reading my books?"

"I don't need to. Plus, your books are incomprehensible."

"Touché," Mark grunted. "So?"

"So I also know I'm your biggest expense. And that you didn't hire me just to entertain you."

"You are quite entertaining," he said.

"But you're not that rich."

"So you assume."

"You live in a storage unit."

Mark turned a palm up between us, as if to say, *Please proceed.*

"Of the five nights we've taken off since I started working here, each one was the rainiest night of the week. The last three, you've come back with scratches all over your forearms. Either you've got a cat that you're not telling me about, or you've been wrestling some thorn bushes. Plus, you spend about an hour a day playing with

Master padlocks. Our customers use smart surveillance and bio-metric verification. We don't work with padlocks."

"Don't we?"

"Do we?"

"Well," he said.

"Well?" I said.

Mark flashed his snaggletoothed grin. "I was starting to think you'd never ask."

6

We drove to SeaTac the next night. Mark parked the van in front of Ty's mobile home and led me through the tunnel he'd cut in the blackberry thicket. We sat there eating cinnamon rolls in the drizzle, our feet hanging off the front of Bin Twenty-One, as he explained his scheme.

"The hardest part was getting access to the trailer park," he said. "I stood in front of that gate for hours, flagging down every car going in. But thanks to the homeless encampment out there, everyone stares straight ahead and side-eyes me like they're wearing an invisible neck brace. Finally Ty rolls up in his beater Geo, holding out a mini box of Apple Jacks."

"And you told him you were here to harvest chorus frogs?"

"He doesn't give a shit. He just wants his ten clams."

I peeled off a strip of bun and dipped it into my little cup of icing.

"Tell me more about these ground sensors."

"It's a stupid, expensive system. They protect the ground instead of the bins. I recommended Bluetooth padlocks, but Jerry said they don't cost enough," Mark said. "You wouldn't believe what a leech this guy is. He says, 'Set me up those fancy-ass ground sensors, invoice me double, and kick me back half.' Homeland Security is paying the bills."

"And you did it?"

"If I hadn't, he would've found someone else, right? So I say to myself, 'You'll do it, Mark, but you'll make him pay.' And here we are. First, we go through the bins and take everything we can sell. Then we tip off the feds that Hull Secure Facilities is anything but. Smoosh." He ground his palms together. "Jerry loses his sweetheart contract. Maybe he gets off his ass, stops staring at the History Channel, starts working an honest job towing jetways around SeaTac. He'll probably lose fifty pounds!"

"We'd be taking things that people are trying to get back." I'd read a hundred tragic sagas of immigration enforcement on Huayiwang. Visa voidance. Family separation. Operation Endgame. "People can claim their belongings after they've been deported."

"Oh, sure," Mark said. "If they spend a month filling out paperwork at the consulate. But if ICE says they can't find the items, there's no appeal process. Jerry's got a whole stack of requests sitting next to the Mudjug on his TV table. He ordered a stamp cut with 'UNABLE TO LOCATE' so that he can respond to them faster."

"Jesus, he told you that?"

"He *showed* it to me. The dude does not get out much. Followed me around barking his life story while I laid the sensors." Mark wrinkled his nose. "Something about me sets these good old boys at ease."

"Because you look and talk like them."

He threw a chunk of his cinnamon roll at me. It bounced off my shoulder and fell to the ground. "I look like Jon Hamm. Jerry looks like Orson Welles's corpse."

"Jon Hamm? Maybe if he did a Unabomber biopic." I stared

down where the chunk of cinnamon roll had vanished. "You're not worried about that?"

"Squirrels will eat it. You in or what?"

I scratched my head.

"Do you want to do this because Jerry's a leech and has it coming?" I asked him. "Or because you found a way to steal a lot of stuff without getting caught?"

Mark shrugged and said, "Potato, potato."

"And you can't do it without me."

"Right."

"Why?"

"I need someone to dangle me." He explained the harnesses, the padlocks, the rope.

I frowned at the mud, weighed becoming a thief with one friend versus going back to being a nobody with none.

"You hired me to do this?"

"I hired you because I wanted to grow my business."

"But I'm fired if I say no."

"I didn't say that."

I was trying to watch Mark's eyes, but in the dark, in the rain, I could barely see his face.

I sit cross-legged on the floor of Bin Three, turning Song Fei's second puzzle box around in my fingers, holding it close to my ears, listening to how the pins inside it move. I try different combinations of orientation and rotation. Clockwise, flat: the *clink* of metal on metal. Counterclockwise, on edge: the *thock* of metal on wood.

One of the ends of the box is a panel that doesn't want to budge. No other moving parts on the exterior. So I have to organize the pins, which I can't see, in some way that will unlock the panel.

Minutes stretch by. The wind kicks up in gusts, drowning out the tiny sounds made by the pins. Sweat beads at my hairline, runs into my eyes. Upside down, counterclockwise, metal on metal, twist the panel, and: still no.

I set the box down and mop my forehead with the front of my T-shirt. Check Dad's Casio: only two hours left, and the shelves of unopened bags call to me. *One last hurrah at our dear Lost and Found. Is this my last taste of intonymity? The* end of my employ at Logistical Solutions?

Over ten visits in eight weeks, Mark and I have extracted almost twelve thousand dollars from the Lost and Found. We split the cash fifty-fifty each night, and Mark pays me for the rest as soon as we've pawned it. These protocols seem to emphasize that our relationship is business. And even as he's made plans to sink his share back into his company—designing more online ads, eyeing the secondhand market for a better van—he's never asked me how I will spend mine.

Think you can keep your shit together, Lao?

I slap myself twice across the face, clear my head of the past and the future. Upright, clockwise, metal on wood. Upside down, clockwise, metal on metal. Gradually, I draw a mental diagram of the inside of the box. Two metal pins moving in channels along the long sides. Tap them to the top and they free up a long pin in a channel along the bottom. Which somehow connects back to the movable panel on the top.

And the tiny amount of wiggle on the panel isn't lateral slide. It's rotation. Rotation means an anchor in the middle. The panel must be attached to a locked axle that runs lengthwise through the center of the box. Which means—*it must be*—the long pin along the bottom is actually *two* pins. And if they could somehow *both* be moved outward—*centrifugal force*—they'd unlock that central axle.

I flip the box upside down, set it on the ground, and give it a spin with my thumbs. Then I pick it up again, turn it right side up, press the edges of the top panel to twist it open—*finally!*—

revealing two tiny compartments about a centimeter deep, and each one completely, totally, and absolutely empty.

I close my eyes. *Brilliant work, Victor. You sprinted extra fast around your hamster wheel and still managed to go nowhere. Pat yourself on your furry little back.*

I snap the box shut, toss it aside, and snatch up a few plastic bags at once. Tear through them to make up for wasted time. I pinch cash out of wallets and purses without bothering to read the IDs, my mind still seething over the puzzle box. Such an elaborate mechanism with no purpose except to instill false hope. All puzzle, no prize. There wasn't even room for a prize. The secret compartments were too small.

I freeze for a moment, then scamper across the floor, trying to figure out where I threw the thing. Upside down. Spin. Right side up. Twist.

The secret compartments *are* too small. I twist it shut again. Twist it open. Twist it shut. Peer into it, trying to see the central axle—*yes*: it's threaded like a screw. I twist the panel shut, open, shut, open, but always the same way this time, always clockwise, and the false bottom of the two narrow niches recedes into the depths of the box, moving past two more niches: the true secret compartments.

And then the panel won't twist any further. I turn the box on its side, tap tap tap. Nothing in the niche on the right. Tap tap tap on its other side. Something plunks out of the niche on the left. I upend the box over my palm, and out drops an oblong red stone.

I pick it up with trembling fingers, hold it to the light, rotate it slowly. Reflections of my headlamp dance across its surfaces. Its center is as translucent as polished glass. An uncut ruby. A huge one, eye-clean, completely unincluded. Unless—*wait.* Something deep within the stone catches the light of my headlamp and glints green.

I snatch up Song Fei's notebook. Skimming pages, skimming

pages, *where was it?* There. 红硅硼铝钙石. *Red* something something *aluminum calcium stone.*

I squeeze my eyes shut, try to remember the exact words of the mustachioed "Doctor" of gemology. Not ruby. Not garnet. Not red beryl. I squint at the characters I don't recognize. 硅 and 硼 both contain 石: the stone radical. Which could indicate the names of minerals. If 硅 is *silicon* and 硼 is *boron*, then—

"Painite"—that's what "Doctor" Ontario Heffelfinger said: "The world's rarest gem. Mined by Chinese extraction firms in the Mogok region of Myanmar, boycotted as a conflict stone in the West since the Rakhine genocide began last year. But even before then—" He chortled merrily and admitted that he'd never seen one bigger than a sunflower seed.

I mutter a phrase that I haven't said since I was twelve, when Mom died and Dad stopped taking us to church.

Sixty-five thousand US dollars per 克拉—kèlā. Per *carat!* And then a street address written in Spanish. Cerrada 5 de Mayo 17.

No city. No country. But a price per carat means a buyer. And a stone the size of a peanut weighs at least three carats. Maybe four.

A score that will change everything.

I push open the door to the shipping container and lean out. The rain is still pouring, the wind still whipping, as a cold front slides off the Olympic Mountains and raises hell in the Puget Sound. I glance up at Jerry's cottage: still dark. In this weather, a hundred feet away, he wouldn't hear me even if I screamed.

"Mark!" I holler at Bin Four. "Mark! Dude! Buddy! MARK!!" No response. I could toss a rock onto his bin to get his attention, but it might skip off, hit the mud, and trip the ground sensors. I can't call him because we never bring our phones out here—we both know too much about cell tower triangulation for that. I decide to close up my bin, gather my stuff, and climb back over to his.

He'll probably be pissed that I'm scrapping the plan. But this isn't a Rolex or a vintage guitar. Song Fei's painite is not the kind of news that I can sit on for two more hours.

I slip back into the bin, roll up the stone in the velvet bag, and shove it into my pants pocket along with the notebook. Then I don my rain jacket and backpack. I switch my headlamp back to red. Push the container door open again.

The red light of my headlamp falls onto the barrel of a shotgun two feet from my chest.

"Not a word," says the face, obstructed by night vision goggles, at the other end of the gun. "Not a single fucking sound."

7

My hands fly upward. My mind plunges into a blank, milky panic.

"Put it in reverse," the man growls, stepping forward, marching me back into Bin Three. He's clad in waterproof pants, a camouflage parka, and combat boots. The shotgun is in his right hand. In his left, a pair of handcuffs.

He reaches over the top of the shotgun and twists a black tube mounted on the barrel. A light snaps on. He flips the night vision goggles up on a hinge attached to his helmet.

Orson Welles's corpse.

Jerry Hull squints into my face. "A fuckin' slant. Figures." He pitches the cuffs at me underhand, and I catch them against my chest. "Wear 'em."

I tighten the cuffs around my wrists, exaggerate the tremble of my hands, try to buy a little time—*For what? What's my play?* Mark might hear me if I scream at the top of my lungs. Or reach up and bang on the top of the container. Jerry's got the weapon, but we outnumber him two to one.

Which he already knows. He must've snuck up to Bin Three after I poked my head out to call to Mark. He's been staking us out in his rain gear, waiting for us to emerge. An image flashes through my mind: the puddle where Bin One used to sit. Jerry knew we were coming, and he could've called the cops an hour ago.

He has other plans.

Jerry must have seen it dawn in my eyes because his lips twist into a sneer as he says, "Absolutely correct, you grubby little worm."

And then he steps forward, swings the gun stock around, and bashes me in the side of the head.

I stagger a few steps, catching myself with my cuffed wrists on a shelf as pain explodes through my skull and orange lights spray across my vision. My headlamp clatters to the ground.

Jerry presses the gun's muzzle into my cheek.

"Listen up now, Table Tennis: you can do exactly as I say, and maybe I'll let SeaTac's finest cart you out of here. Or you can play hero and catch a load of buckshot in the face. Comprenday?"

I look at him and blink.

"You have cost me my livelihood," he snarls. "And I just might have to end you for that. But first we're going to have some fun. Next thing that happens, we go next door and roust your pal. You run? I shoot. You talk? I shoot. You shimmy? I shoot. Now blink again like a good little bitch so I know we're crystal clear."

My head rings with pain. Hot terror floods my brain. I do as he says.

Jerry steps backward, keeping the shotgun trained on my chest. His left hand vanishes into his parka, reemerges gripping a pistol. He lowers his night vision goggles back over his face. Then he twists off the flashlight mounted on the shotgun, leaving me blind.

"C'mon now. Follow my voice," he says with a playful lilt. I walk forward tentatively, my cuffed hands extended in front of me. Step out of the container and into the rain.

"Drop on down to those knees."

I kneel in the mud. My breath catches in my throat as he presses the pistol barrel against the back of my head.

"Hey, Marky Mark! C'mon out, buddy. Jig's up." Jerry's voice comes from directly behind me, scratchy and joyous, and for the first time I catch the whiskey on it.

Jerry must've been keeping himself warm on his stakeout. Which means sloppy. Reckless. And uninhibited.

"I said c'mon out! Nice and slow! Or your girlfriend here gets a slant eye full of lead."

An L of light cuts through the darkness as the door to Bin Four swings open a few inches.

"All right, Jerry, I'll come out," Mark calls. "You caught us. You're calling the shots. There's no need for rude language."

"Rude language, he says." Jerry chuckles. "You're a real hoot, Knox. But tonight, I'll be deciding what's needed or not."

Light spills out of the container and then shrinks to a point as Mark steps out of the door.

"Now slap on those cuffs."

"What cuffs?"

"Three feet to your nine, Private," Jerry says.

"Sergeant," Mark mutters as he peruses the ground. When he spots the handcuffs, he dutifully picks them up and wraps them around his wrists.

"Nice and tight now. Good. Next you lose that light."

Mark drops his headlamp to the ground.

"Now y'all two proceed up that hill."

Half a breath escapes my lungs as the gun moves from my head, and I hear Jerry's boots sucking mud as he backs away from me.

"Go on," he shouts. I stand up and start walking. "There you go. That's right. Ah, thirty degrees starboard, kid. What's your name? Ping-Pong? Bruce? Ichiro?"

"Fuck you!"

"All right, Ichiro it is. Five steps this way, the both of ya. Now back on those knees."

A moment later, a lantern pops on in front of me, blinding white like the sun. As my eyes adjust, I see that we're behind the cottage. The lantern is on the back deck, shielded from the rain by the eaves. Mark's kneeling in the mud a few feet from me.

"Tighten up now. No, you move, Knox, not him. That's it. Now smile! Jessst kidding. Y'all don't have to smile."

Jerry's voice comes from the other side of the lantern. I can faintly discern his triangular shape behind the light. It looks like he's sitting on a camping chair. The shotgun rests on his left knee, pointed right at me.

The bigger gun in his weaker hand. Might matter. Might not.

"Look, Jerry," Mark begins. "Here's the—*nnnh!*"

A pop. Mark doubles over.

"Shit, what is that, an air gun? Are you ser—*nnnnnh!*"

"Woo, I am surgical tonight! Two for two," Jerry crows. "Now practice some silence like your Oriental friend here, if you please, Sergeant. I have some documentation I'd like you to review."

Jerry sets down the air pistol and extracts a folded sheet of paper from the pocket of his parka. He shakes it open with his right hand, keeping his left on the shotgun, and leans forward to read by the light of the lantern.

"I did sniff a hint of the hustler on you, Knox, but I am truly dumbfounded by *this* behavior. I'm hoping you'll enlighten me as to why in the holy hell you thought you had a good idea on your hands. Here we go: 'To Whom It May Concern'—now, this wasn't sent to me, mind you. The feds were kind enough to provide me a copy when they came by to start scooping up their junk. Anywho, where was I? 'To Whom It May Concern: In recent weeks we have received three parcels containing unlabeled deportee possessions addressed to the Border Support Initiative in Nogales, Arizona. Although these parcels came with no accompanying documenta-

tion or return address, we have determined that these items origi-
nate in the Pacific Northwest region. Reuniting people with their
belongings is one of BSI's primary means of supporting deportees
who'—oh, shit, hold on, I feel my indignation flaring up—"

Jerry sets the letter in his lap, picks up the pistol, and *pop, pop*—
Mark's torso spins to one side and a pellet smacks into my chest
like a bee sting.

I hunch into the pain and bite my lip, but a groan still escapes
from my throat.

Jerry pauses, looks up at the sky for a second. "Yup, I do feel
marginally better now. To resume: 'Concerns regarding the in-
tegrity of your'—blah blah blah—'exclusively through the formal
channels'—blah blah blah—'Regards, Leon butt-chew Few, Ex-
ecutive Director, Border Support Initiative.'"

By the time Jerry reads the name at the bottom of the letter, I'm grinding my teeth in outrage. Leon Few at the Border
Support Initiative in Nogales—that was the guy! I researched his
nonprofit before sending him boxes of phones, photos, and keep-
sakes from the Lost and Found. Posing as a conscientious ICE
agent in a bankrupt system, I assured him that this was the only
way these items could catch up to the people who'd lost them.

It never occurred to me that he'd rat me out. And now I'm real-
izing how monumentally stupid I've been. How my selfish desire to
matter to somebody—even somebody I'd never meet—has Mark
and me headed to prison if we survive the night.

And when I look to my left, I see that Mark is staring at me, his
face contorted with disbelief.

I drop my gaze to the ground, my face burning with shame.
And that's when I see it: Mark's right shoe is untied and loose. The
back of it squished down beneath his heel.

And he's not too pissed at me to give his ankle a waggle.

Jerry crumples the letter into a ball and then tosses it behind
him. Then picks up the air pistol again and aims it at Mark.

"Now what's got me all befuddled," Jerry begins.

But I interrupt him.

"It was me, Jerry," I say. "I sent those things to Nogales. Mark didn't—"

Pop. Pop. One in the shoulder like the stab of a stiletto. A pained grunt escapes my lips. But the other pellet misses.

"Did I request your version, Ichiro?"

I twist my wrists against the steel cuffs. "You see this, Jerry?" I hold my hands out. Blood oozes out of my broken skin, trickles off the metal bonds. "Are you ready to kill someone in handcuffs? What're you gonna tell the judge, Jerry?"

"You're on my property. You're robbing my business, you filthy skunk!" *Pop. Pop. Pop.* Two more in the stomach and another miss.

But now my fury drowns out all the pain.

"So if I get up"—I step to my feet, still holding my bloody wrists in front of me, still grinding them against the cuffs—"and turn and walk away, you'll shoot me in the back and claim you caught me in the act? I'm just kinky enough to wear these around for fun?"

"Don't play around with me, boy!" Jerry stands up, too, throws the air gun aside, and starts passing the shotgun from his left hand to his right.

But before he's done, Mark dives to his left, swinging his right foot forward, sending his shoe flying toward Jerry's head.

Jerry turns sideways, takes the shoe in the shoulder, and fires the shotgun into the darkness where Mark disappeared. He's pumping the slide and turning toward me when I hit him in a full horizontal leap, my outstretched hands smashing the gun into his face, my body driving him backward into his camping chair, which collapses beneath us.

I'm up first, kicking him in the gut, once, twice, three times as he curls up fetal. Then I'm on his back, pushing his hands away from his head, wrapping the cuffs around his neck, twisting my wrists together, and I see his eyes bulge and feel his body struggle beneath me. But I don't hear him gasping for air, I don't hear Mark shouting, I hear nothing but my own screams of bright red rage. I don't unlock my wrists from behind Jerry's head until Mark thwacks me in the ribs with the butt of the shotgun, shoves me over, and steps onto my neck with his sopping-wet sock.

Spatter of rain on my face, mad throb of pain in my skull. Mark looming above me, Jerry wheezing beside me. Shadows shrinking and stretching as the light of the upended lantern, rocking on the deck, swings like a frenzied pendulum across the drenched night.

"Has everyone absolutely lost their frickin' minds?" Mark exclaims. "Who *are* you, man? You almost choked him out!"

He steps off my neck and starts hobbling around the deck like a neat-freak pirate. The lantern goes back upright. The air pistol goes into his belt. His shoe goes back on his foot.

I crawl into a seated position. "He knows your identity!" I shout at his back.

"Oh, and if you throttle him to death, I'm in the clear? Are you insane?"

My mind traces forward from Jerry's lifeless body. Sirens, yellow tape, detectives. The tunnel through the bushes. The van parked at Ty's. And somewhere, Jerry's invoice from Logistical Solutions.

Mark is right—there's a trail that leads right to him. If I'd killed Jerry, then he'd end up wanted for murder in addition to burglary and assault.

I press my wet sleeve against my forehead. My heart rate begins to slow from hummingbird to Chihuahua.

"I wasn't thinking," I admit. "I just wanted to kill him."

Mark sits astraddle of Jerry's moaning mass and searches his parka pockets. He finds a phone and a set of tiny keys, holds them up to the lantern light.

Cuff keys. He crawls over to me and uses them to free my wrists. Then he fixes me with an expression I've never before seen on his face. Furrowed brow, wild eyes, lips twisted into a grimace.

"Do you have any idea what it's like to live with that? Having killed someone?"

A scene flashes before my mind's eye: the kitchen of that house in Pasadena, the Cantonese ketamine smuggler with the gash across his throat, the pool of cherry-red blood spreading across the linoleum. Sun Jianshui rifling through the dead man's pockets.

"Kind of." I take the keys from Mark's hand and use them to unlock his cuffs. "Do you?"

He holds my eye for another moment, that deranged look lingering on his face. Then he stands back up, walks over to Jerry, and fires the pellet gun into his gut.

"Not so funsies anymore, is it?" he asks as the ball of Jerry tightens and whimpers. "What's your phone password, Jer-bear?" *Pop.* "Let's go. Six numbers. C'mon." *Pop, pop.* "I won't let this nutjob kill you, but I will shoot one of your goddamn beady eyes out."

"Enough." I get to my feet and snatch the phone out of Mark's hand. Jerry's got his hands over his face, but when I pry his thumb loose, he doesn't fight me. I press it over the phone's fingerprint reader.

"Now you're Captain Compassion?" Mark sneers.

I hand him the unlocked phone.

After a moment, Mark blows out a slow exhale, buzzes his lips.

"The man has twenty-one contacts and only seven of them are names. Want to hear the rest? 'Cable Co.' 'Trash Co.' 'Best pizza.' 'Pizza open latest.' 'Best gyros'—isn't that spelled with a *j*?"

I slump back against the cottage, bury my aching head in my hands, tax my brain to explain how the hell I ended up on this porch with these two men.

"Listen up, Jer. This is a big night for you." Mark squats in front of him, speaks as if to a child. "You'll be hankering to set the blue boys on my trail, so I'm going to lock you in one of those bins for a few hours while I get real scarce. Once I'm gone, I'll call someone to come let you out."

As he talks, he wraps his handcuffs around Jerry's wrists, which are still shielding his face.

"Tomorrow's gonna be a rough one. You've got some lacerations on your neck, but those will heal. What you need to focus on is that heart of yours, which seems to be jam-packed full of lonely and hate. You lost your contract, sure. You got your ass whupped by some deadbeats, I'll accept the label. But you can bounce back, Jerry. Clean slate now. Maybe tonight's the night your new life begins. So who do you want to see, Jerry? Who's gonna help you get right? Not a drinking buddy, mm-kay? Good influence. Give me a name."

Mark thumbs through the phone.

"Len Byrne? Trevor P? 'Bones'? He sounds like your dealer. Chad Nicholls? He's got a 206 number. Chad a good person, Jer?"

"Damn you to hell, Knox," Jerry croaks. "Say whatever bullshit you want. I hired you, and you stole from me, and you deserve to rot in a cell, you bastard."

He spits into Mark's face and rolls a half turn in the other direction.

Mark stands up, wipes his cheek with his sleeve, and heaves a sigh. "'Deserve.' I hate that word."

In the next ten minutes, the ugly evening sinks to even deeper levels of nightmare. Getting an uncooperative Jerry down the hill entails an exhausting amount of pulling, pushing, wrestling, cajoling, and soft-core torture. Finally Mark slams the door of Bin Four shut on Jerry's stream of profane epithets and rams home the bolt.

Then he turns around, strides over to me, and shoves me hard in the chest, knocking me into the mud.

"You sent parcels to Nogales? The Border Support Initiative?" he bellows. "Are you the dumbest person to ever crawl the earth?"

I lie there for a second, catching my breath, wondering if the answer is yes. The night's chill reaches through my wet clothes like an icy hand, but my body is too fatigued to shiver. A trio of awful sensations—the sting of my wrists, the hammer in my head, the bites on my torso from Jerry's air gun pellets—grow insistent as adrenaline drains out of my bloodstream and abject misery takes its place.

The rain has abated now. The pale hints of morning suggest themselves on the eastern horizon. A wet June dawn at five. That's Seattle for you. I prop myself up on my elbows.

"I kept seeing stuff that people relied on," I say. "Things they turned to when they were alone. So I found this organization in Nogales that helps deported people put their lives back together. I'm talking about family photos. Phones filled with messages and contacts. People's identities, Mark! Can you imagine what it would feel like to get that back if you thought it was lost?"

"That's a real nice way to put it, Lao," Mark says. "But allow me to rephrase: You sent some stuff that you stole to some people who would know that you stole it, and then went back to the place you stole it from several times. With me. Without telling me."

"I had to do something to not feel like a total zero all the time. I needed to be more than a raccoon-person." As I say the words, I know how stupid they sound. I let my head fall back to the earth and cover my face with my ice-cold palms, streaked with blood from the cuts on my wrists. "I thought that Leon Few guy would understand."

"Your dumbshit 'need' burned us both to charcoal! You oughta downsize those ideals if you're keen on survival. You know what, Lao? Zero's a small target. And raccoons are smart."

He pulls out Jerry's phone and starts tapping as he talks.

"I'm gonna schedule messages to all seven humans in Jerry's sad-sack life and assume that one of them cares enough to come open this door." He glances at his watch, and then back up at the sky as he does arithmetic in his head. "Let's say six hours to get me packed up and Canadian with some elbow room. You do what pleases you. He doesn't know your name, lucky you. I doubt he could pick you out of a lineup with multiple two-legged humans of East Asian descent."

He pockets the phone and looks back to me, the anger gone from his face, replaced by a mask of weary detachment.

"I don't care for hard feelings," he says. "But you've rolled me royally, and we'd fit quite the description on the lam together. So I think it would be best if you go your way, and—" He trails off, lowers his eyes. "Well. You know the song."

He turns his back and starts walking toward the fence. I push myself up to my feet.

"Mark."

He stops without turning.

"I was wrong," I say. "I'm sorry."

He looks back over his shoulder.

"Doesn't mean a bean anymore, Lao."

"That's not my name."

"I know it isn't."

I glance at Bin Four, take a few steps toward Mark to move out of Jerry's earshot.

"My real name is Victor."

His mouth twitches, the ghost of a smile. "I'll be sure to forget that promptly."

"We agreed to split everything, right? I found something tonight. Something big." I pull the velvet sack out of my pocket, fish out the red gem, and toss it to him underhand, throwing it with some loft, giving him time to track its flight in the dim light of dawn.

He palms it out of the air and holds it above his face. After a moment, he says, "Dear God. Is this—"

"Painite."

"You're sure?"

I hold up Song Fei's notebook. "Says so in here."

"This python came with a manual?"

"Uh-huh."

"How about papers?"

I shake my head.

Mark's face falls. "Painite without papers, shit. That's about as easy to sell as enriched uranium."

After the United States convinced one hundred other countries to boycott the Burmese gem trade, collectors and dealers rushed to get their stones certified as pre-genocide. Now no jeweler will touch a painite without documentation from the International Gemological Institute.

That is, no law-abiding jeweler.

"There's a buyer," I say. "In Mexico. And a price." I tell him how much.

Mark whistles low. "Dónde in Mexico?"

I shrug. "There's only a street address."

He scowls. "Then how the hell do you know it's Mexico and not frickin' Paraguay?"

"The street name is Cinco de Mayo."

Mark presses a knuckle into the bridge of his nose.

"Vancouver's three hours away. Tijuana's twenty. People buy hot rocks in Canada, too, Victor."

When he says my name, the first time in sixteen months that anyone has called me Victor to my face, I have to bury the twin urges to sob and to grin.

"Not rocks like this one, Mark. Not from people like us."

There, I said it. *Us.* I don't have to run, like Mark said. But I want my half of the score.

Or at least I'm happy to let him think that. Better than telling him that I don't want to be left alone.

"Jerry can last twenty hours," I say. "He's got fat reserves."

Now Mark cracks half a smile. "You know, I could tuck this little Valentine into my pocket, call us even, and walk away. Wouldn't bother me a bit."

"You could tag me a couple times with that shotgun, too," I say.

He wrinkles his nose at me, looks down at the painite, and then back at Bin Four. He taps his hairline five times with the heel of his hand.

Then he starts walking back up to the cottage. "Might as well get him a cup of water," he says. "And some chaw."

He flicks the red gem back to me as he passes, and I catch it in my fist.

9

almost tell Mark the bad news before he drops me off in Chinatown. But we're both bruised up, soaking wet, and running on fumes. Better to wait until we're headed south on the interstate, I decide. Sure, he still might take the next exit, leave me at a gas station, and head north for Canada. But Mark tends to avoid covering the same territory twice.

So I exit the van without a word, climb the four flights of stairs to my tenement flop, and limp into the windowless, mildewed bathroom for a lukewarm shower that ranks in the top five bathing experiences of my life.

Mark heads to the storage unit to pack the van with his most treasured possessions. Then he'll go to his credit union and cash out his accounts.

I have no treasured possessions or bank accounts. The tenement isn't the best place to keep cash, so I've invested my modest savings in cryptocurrency. After my shower, I repack my backpack with my Chinese passport and a few changes of clothes. The rest of my belongings go on the kitchen table beneath a handwritten note.

床不用了　如果有人问, 我没来过
My bunk is available. If anyone asks, I was never here.

In the year and a half that I've lived here, someone has vanished like this at least once a month.

At the corner store run by the Anhui aunties who stock a dozen of everything, I procure some first aid supplies and a hundred bucks in pesos. I'm halfway down the block when I realize that I need something else from the store. We stole federal property, so once Jerry tells his story, the case will go to the FBI. The feds will enter Mark's name into their vaunted new National Suspect Database. Next time he pops up on the grid, he'll be flagged as a federal fugitive.

And Mark's phone will be the starting point of the FBI's search. They'll check his records in order to track his associate, the unidentified Asian accomplice, Ping-Pong Doe. There will be more than enough location data to demonstrate that Mark only hung out with one person.

In short, I need to ditch my phone.

The Anhui aunties don't bat an eyelash when I return to the store and buy four pay-as-you-go flip phones. My next stop is Canton Noodle King, where I procure two to-go bowls of congee. After that, as I wait for Mark in the parking lot of the Japanese supermarket, I call Jules.

"NASA," she answers. "How may I direct your call?"

"Reservations."

"Please hold."

"Jules."

"Yah."

I hesitate. What's the least alarming way to say this? Should've figured that out before dialing. Not thinking straight. Been up twenty-four hours, almost got killed.

"Brobi-Wan? You there?"

"Yeah, sorry. I can't use this app for a while. You won't be able to message me or call me. But I'll call you from burner phones, okay? Numbers with 206 area codes. Just try to pick up because I can only use them once each."

A pause.

"What's going on, Victor? Are you in more trouble?"

"I'm fine! In fact, I have good news. I've gotta go, but I'll tell you about it later."

"Good news? Really? Because it sounds like you rode your bicycle through a car wash."

I pinch the bridge of my nose. Lying has never been my strong suit. And the people who know me best always see through me right away.

"I'll explain later, I promise. Any cop visits lately?"

She sighs that sigh that reminds me of Mom. "Not for a couple of weeks," she says.

"Great. Okay, well. Have a good day."

"Wait! Victor, stop stonewalling me!"

I squeeze my eyes shut. "Jules, I can't explain right now, okay? I'm just doing what I need to do."

"What you need to do is face the music, Victor. I'm the only family you've got. When are you going to come home? When are you going to stop blaming Sun for your own stupid decisions and turn yourself in?"

The same questions she asks me every time we talk. The ones I think of when I decide to not call. I grit my teeth. "I dunno, Jules. Maybe five, ten more minutes?"

"Okay, fine. Forget I asked. Forget I even exist."

"I'm never turning myself in, okay? Signing up for three to six years in a racist, privatized prison is not 'facing the music.' And I don't blame Sun. I was an idiot to believe his lies. I know what Dad put him through."

"So if you saw Sun today, what would you do?"

I think it over as an ancient man pushes a nearly empty shopping cart across the parking lot of the Japanese supermarket at a pace that would bore a tortoise. I could picture Sun Jianshui perfectly: his unassuming posture, his attentive eyes, his deadly hands. Sun killed Dad because Dad had taken advantage of him for twenty years. Thinking about it uncorks a torrent of conflicting feelings.

But the strongest of those feelings is that Sun Jianshui cannot be trusted.

"I'd run," I say.

These words hang in the ether as the ancient man reaches the edge of the parking lot, wraps his arms around his lone bag of groceries, and walks off at the same snail pace.

And I seem to hear Jules stare at her shoes. Bite her lower lip. Press her palm against the side of her head.

"I have class," she says.

"All right," I say. "Bye, Jules."

The line goes dead.

I'm feeling awful, thinking about calling her back, wondering what I could say, when I spot Mark's van at a stoplight two blocks away. So I power off my phone and toss it in the trash can at the bus stop on the corner.

Then I glance at my watch. Almost ten in the morning now. Which means we need to make it to the border in twenty-three hours. That's when Jerry's phone, charging in his cottage, will send its scheduled messages to Len Byrne, Trevor P, Chad Nicholls, and "Bones."

I climb into the passenger seat of the van and drop my backpack into the foot well.

"Did you file all your toenails?" I ask.

"Bank didn't open until nine."

He releases the parking brake and eases the van into the morning traffic. Although he's changed his clothes, there's still a splatter of dried mud on the back of his neck. It occurs to me that Mark's primary bathroom is the one at the gym.

"Want to shower at my place before we hit the freeway?"

"No. Thank you."

His eyes stay fixed on the road, his jaw locked tight, the blue vein on his right temple terrifically embossed. While our dustup with Jerry was a carousel ride compared with what I saw in Beijing, it seems to have disturbed painful recollections within him.

Do you have any idea what it's like to live with that? Having killed someone?

As we merge onto I-5 South and Chinatown disappears into the distance behind us, I'm not getting a discuss-our-darkest-secrets vibe from the Mark-shaped pressure cooker in the driver's seat. So I click on his radio, which is tuned to KZOK Classic Rock, as usual. I roll up my sleeves and treat the cuts on my wrists with alcohol pads. Antibiotic ointment. Gauze and tape. Thank you, Anhui aunties.

Mark finally breaks the silence when I start eating my congee.

"Smells like heaven," he says.

"I got you one," I say. "Shiitake mushroom and barbecue pork. Want it now?"

He sizes up the shallow plastic spoon in my hand. "Maybe when you're driving."

"Yeah. About that."

He hears it in my tone. "*What* about that, Lao?"

"Victor."

"Right."

"I don't have a license."

Mark stares at the road and grips the steering wheel even tighter. "When you proposed the twenty-hour drive instead of the three-hour drive," he enunciates, putting a little extra pop on his consonants, "I thought that just maybe you'd be able to take a few turns at the wheel."

"I looked up the address. It's in Mexico City," I say. "So, twenty hours to Tijuana, and then twenty-five more from there. I should be okay to drive while we're still in Washington and after we get to Mexico. But in between, well. Even if I had a license."

It feels easier to leave the threat unspoken: an overzealous cop could crush our timetable with a thorough search. And these days, Highway Patrol is likely to devote extra attention to a Chinese-looking dude driving a rickety van with out-of-state plates through the middle of the night.

Mark punches the hazards and swerves onto the shoulder. He keeps both of his hands on the steering wheel, his knuckles turning white even after we've screeched to a halt.

"Every mile we drive south is a mile farther into this country," he says. "So tell me again why we're not headed north."

"You know this, Mark. A painite without papers is worthless in Canada."

He jerks his hands upward, fingers splayed. "Yeah, well, it's also worthless if we never cross the border because we're too busy getting cavity-searched in Chico."

I pull Song Fei's notebook out of my backpack and hold it up to him, open to the dog-eared page with the address and the per-carat price.

"Burmese gem. Chinese seller. Mexican buyer. What does that tell you? Even if this address is a dead end, we have a much better chance of selling it in Mexico. Ever since we built the border wall, Mexico has started to align with the Chinese. You know about all the money Mexico is borrowing from China, right?"

He looks back and forth between the notebook and me, giving me a face like we're sitting in a canoe and I just asked him where the bathroom was.

"Duì niú tán qín méi yòng," Dad would say—*There's no use in playing the lute for a bull.*

I put the notebook back in my bag and rephrase my argument in Mark's terms. "Okay. Yes, it's forty more hours on the road. But for each of those hours, you're making an extra three grand to spend in a country where a beer costs fifty cents."

He drags a hand downward across his face. "If you don't have a license, how do you plan to cross the border?"

"I have a Chinese passport under a different name. It's a forgery," I admit. "But it got me through immigration at the Beijing Capital Airport twice. So I expect it to play at San Ysidro."

He stares at me for a moment, cupping his chin in his palm. Then he unbuckles his seat belt. "You can explain that to me later. For now, *I* eat. Then *I* sleep. *You* drive."

When we cross the Columbia River into Oregon three hours later, Mark's still snoring. It's the middle of the day, and there are plenty of cars with Washington plates on I-5 South, so I decide to let him sleep. I keep the van in the second lane, locked into cruise control at the speed limit. Whenever my eyelids get heavy, I stab my fingers into the welts on my torso from Jerry's air gun until I'm wide awake with the pain.

Mark finally stirs about halfway across the state.

"Mother," he groans, rubbing his eyes with his knuckles. We switch seats in the parking lot of a burger place in Sutherlin, and I promptly fall into a deep, dreamless slumber of my own.

When I wake some five hours later, the sun is freshly set, its rays still glancing off the waifish cirri in the western skies, igniting them a thousand hues of creamsicle and crimson. The interstate is flat and wide here, lined on both sides by endless geometrical arrangements of almond trees.

California.

Mark is humming to himself. He drums his thumbs on the steering wheel in time with a Kinks song playing on a local FM station.

"My head," I manage to grumble.

He hands me a paper sack containing an energy drink, a bag of Corn Nuts, an empty water bottle, and a bottle of painkillers. I chew three pills to powder before washing them down with a slug of Monster.

"My hero," I say. "Where'd we stop?"

"Shasta."

"Can we pull over?"

"What do you think the water bottle's for?"

"Silly me."

As I relieve myself, the Kinks intone their final chorus before ceding the airwaves to the Police. Water, sugar, and caffeine filter into my bloodstream. And the events of the previous evening flood back to me in a slideshow of nauseating images.

"We should've left Jerry one of these." I screw the lid back on the warm water bottle and stow it under my seat. Roll down the window, stick my swollen face into the dry, dusty air. A flock of Harleys thunders by, the roar of their drilled-out baffles cascading through the Doppler shift as they weave around the van. The first freeway sign I see is Exit 610. Artois. Bluegum. I check the dash clock: 8:52 p.m.

Twelve more hours to do six hundred more miles. Not too bad.

"So," Mark says. "Chinese passport."

"Oh. Yeah." I take another sip of the energy drink. I hadn't expected Mark to follow up on that little detail. Now that I've slammed one door closed for him and opened another, has he decided that he wants to know a thing or two about me? Perhaps he spent some of the past hours wondering what happens if our plan works. We make it to Mexico City. We sell the stone. We split the dough.

But then maybe we decide that it's nice to know another soul when you're all alone in a foreign land. So we start a new security firm together. Or we open a beach bar in a surf town on the coast. And once a year, midway through June, we sip tequila and reminisce about when we drove forty hours from one life into another.

"What the hell," I say. "I guess we have the time."

I give Mark the long version, starting with Dad and his restaurants. How I'd had no idea about his criminal past until he was murdered in the home I grew up in. I tell Mark about Sun Jianshui, how Dad had taken him off the streets as a kid and raised him as a son and a slave, trained him in violence and deception. And I tell him how Sun tricked me into going with him to Beijing, how he tried to wash Dad's blood off his hands with the blood of Dad's old partners.

Mark doesn't yawn or interrupt. He doesn't turn up the radio and say, *Great tune.* He nods along, glancing over at me now and then, asking a question or two to clarify what the hell I was thinking. I talk for an hour, almost two, as twilight gives way to dusk, and dusk gives way to a moonless night lit bright by the Milky Way.

I'm getting to the part where I shot Sun Jianshui in the leg at that house in Pasadena when Mark holds up his hand and tips his head to the side. Then I hear it, too: a high whine from somewhere in front of us.

The van's engine.

And Mark's starting to say something about maybe giving the old gal a breather when the whine intensifies into a scream and the chassis starts to shudder like an old roller coaster.

10

We spend ten nerve-shredding minutes riding the shoulder in first gear before we reach the next exit: the Elkhorn rest stop, fifteen miles outside Sacramento. The van howls and shakes all the way down the off-ramp. We sputter into a parking spot by the bathrooms, and the ancient engine promptly shuts itself off with a shudder and a sigh.

Mark unleashes a barrage of f-bombs and palm strikes at the steering wheel. Then he presses his thumbs into his eye sockets for a full minute.

Finally he says, "How much cash have you got?"

"Hardly any," I say. "I keep my savings in crypto."

"Absolutely lovely," he says. Then he dives into the back of the van. I watch him dig through his canvas duffel bag and extract a roll of hundreds from a sock. Next he snatches his laptop out of his backpack, flips it open while chanting "Wi-Fi, Wi-Fi, Wi-Fi" under his breath.

"What are you doing?" I ask.

"Wi-Fi, Wi-Fi, yes! Don't talk right now. Don't think, either," he snaps at me. "No more of your bright ideas."

He pecks and squints at his laptop for another minute, then slaps it shut and shoves it into my hands.

"Search for limo services in Sacramento," he says. "Start with the ones with the worst websites. See if you can get someone on the phone, but don't say a word about Mexico. If they send a car, we'll negotiate in person."

"Um, okay," I say. "What are *you* going to do?"

"Fish for rides." He scampers around the back of the van, tossing things into his duffel. "Big fish, I procure a vehicle. Little fish, I get us a lift as far south as possible. If they've only got room for one, I'm taking it. I don't see that I have a choice. So if that's the case, I wish you the best of luck."

A fat tentacle of despair coils up my spine from tailbone to skull.

"But Mark—"

"Save it! No time!" He snatches a greasy rag off the floor and darts back to the front seat. He takes one of my phones from my backpack, tosses the rag into my chest, and commands me to wipe the entire van, inside and out, for prints.

Then he slings his duffel over his shoulder and saunters off to affect maximum cool on the bench by the bathrooms.

I stare at him for a moment, my eyes wide and tingly, my throat hollow and dry. Then I open the laptop. The last item in the search history is "casinoes near sacremento." I do as he asked, calling all six of the local limo services. Two of them answer the phone, but to no one's great surprise, neither will send a car to an interstate rest stop for someone unable to provide a credit card number.

So I put the laptop aside and wipe the van like Mark told me to, wondering all along why it matters. Then I return to the passenger seat and watch him through the windshield. He stands up to accost a guy in a baseball cap. The guy turns around and says something back to Mark, who smiles, gestures with his hands, and does a shrug like, *You know how it is.*

I peer at him through the darkness, parsing his body language for a signal that he's still my friend. Is he negotiating our escape, or just his? Half an hour ago, he listened intently as I spilled my life story. Back then, I was useful: the guy with the painite and the plan. But now? *I wish you the best of luck.* I'm dead weight.

The guy in the baseball cap shakes his head and walks away. Mark watches him for a moment, then kicks the ground and slumps back onto the bench.

I check the time: five minutes to midnight. Nine hours left to make the eight-hour drive to Mexico. Don't think about it. *No more of your bright ideas.* Don't think about what happens if those nine hours dwindle to seven. Or if Mark catches a ride with a teamster and leaves me stranded fifteen miles outside the capital of the state where I'm wanted for murder.

I punch on the map light, and my reflection springs up in the windshield. Then I pull my backpack into my lap. I'll focus on Song Fei instead. Because doing nothing will fuel the tempest of fear in my guts, and because hey, maybe I'll still make it to Mexico, with or without Mark.

And if I do get to Cerrada 5 de Mayo 17, my best play with the buyer will be to associate myself with Song Fei. So I need to figure out why she was flying around the United States with a giant gemstone locked in a puzzle box.

The first thing I do is use a phone cable to connect Song Fei's hair clip to the laptop's USB port. But of course, the contents are password-protected. Next I open the notebook to the page with the price per carat in Chinese. And this time, I notice a few characters written in pencil on the back of the page. 买方, the word for buyer, next to a character in brackets: [砍]—kǎn, as in kǎnjià—*to bargain or haggle*. Right beneath that character, she'd written 假名—*alias*— and four Chinese characters from the subset used for phonetic transliterations: 伊莎贝尔—yīshābèi'ěr—written large and circled twice.

Yīshābèi'ěr. Isabel. The buyer's alias is Isabel.

The following pages contain the list of dates, names, and cities. Atlanta, November 12, 艾莉森-外丝—àilìsēn wàisī. Who could that be? I open up Mark's laptop again and type "Alison Wise" into Google. "Allison Wise." "Alyson Whise Atlanta." None of my searches turn up anything helpful.

The next entry is Seattle, November 16, 艾登-布莱尔—àidēng bùláiér. Eden Blair? My pulse quickens when Google asks me if I'm searching for Aiden Blair. Senior senator from Washington. Chairwoman of the Foreign Relations Committee. Could she have something to do with the Burmese gem boycott? I do a few more quick searches for Aiden Blair, Myanmar, China, painite, sanctions, Rakhine refugees, genocide—but there doesn't seem to be any connection.

I shut the notebook and dig all ten fingernails into my scalp. What am I doing? What's the point? None of this matters if I never get to Mexico. I look through the windshield to the bench, where Mark is thumbing around on the burner phone like he hasn't a care in the world, even though it doesn't have an internet connection. Each time someone walks out of the bathroom, I see him lift his head and speak, but hardly anyone so much as turns to acknowledge his existence.

I hate him, I need him, I hate myself for needing him. I press my face into my hands for a minute. Then I turn back to Song Fei's notebook. The next page is the poem in classical verse.

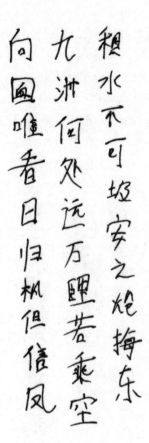

The ancient seas are vast
Who knows how far across?
You'll travel beyond the nine lands
Farther than the sky is deep
Your home lies to the east
Your sail must trust the breeze

Baike.com informs me that the verses are from an eighth-century poem by Wang Wei, a poet, musician, painter, statesman, and all-around stud nerd of the Tang dynasty, who wrote it to say farewell to a Japanese diplomat named Abe no Nakamaro. Thanks to my long hours on Huayiwang, I know enough about the written language to notice something unusual about Song Fei's transcription. The strokes in her characters have the distinctive look of those written by a southpaw, like me. This makes Song Fei rather extraordinary—much rarer than the average lefty—because most left-handed Chinese people are forced from childhood to write with their right.

But that's not all.

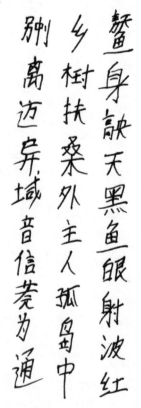

The shadows of great sea monsters
Will darken the sky and dye the waves red
You'll return to your lonely isle
The forested land of the sunrise
Such distance will lie between us
Could it be that you'll still hear my voice?

Each Chinese character is made up of components called radicals, and some of the radicals in Song Fei's characters are out of place. 木 (*wood*) for 巾 (*cloth*). 血 (*blood*) for 玉 (*jade*). Yes—I run my finger down the lines—her mistakes are numerous. Careless. No, not careless. Nobody carelessly dots an *e* or writes a *g* upside down. The misplaced radicals must be intentional.

A code.

I'm hunting around for a pen when I notice that Mark isn't sitting on the bench anymore. I click off the map light. Blink into the night.

This is it, I'm thinking. *Now I'm truly alone.*

Then I see two people smoking under the eaves of the bathroom, silhouetted by the glow of the yellow wall lamps. Mark. And a colossal man in a cowboy hat.

The cherry of Mark's cigarette dances through the air as he talks with his hands. The other man stands still, his head tipped down and forward, his weight in one heel. Then he turns around and, following Mark's outstretched hand, looks in my direction. He starts walking this way, his long strides purposeful yet unhurried. After a few steps, he turns to say something over his shoulder.

Mark, following behind him, stops in his tracks. He watches the man for a few more seconds, lets his cigarette drop to the grass. Then he walks back to the bench where he was sitting before.

I shrink down in my seat.

The man tries the driver's door, finds it locked. He taps on the window, gives me an expectant look. I tug on the handle to pop the latch. He pulls the door open, levers his big body into the seat, and sets his Stetson on the dash.

He punches the map light back on, allowing me to get a better look at him: a ponytail of thick dark hair, a craggy face with large features, and a beard that covers his chin. His flannel shirt is tucked into his light blue jeans. He's got a big silver belt buckle engraved with a filigree bronco. The only discrepancy from his cowboy thing is the pair of black-and-red Air Jordan 13s on his feet.

He's so tall sitting down that I'm not sure if he took his hat off out of some sense of propriety or because it's the only way he fits into the van's airspace. He takes his time looking me over. Then he speaks in a voice that's deep and slow.

"What's the deal with your homey?" he says. "He some kind of junkie or chiseler or what?"

"Who, Mike?" I remember to use his latest nom de guerre. "He's cool."

"Bull*shit* he's cool," the sneaker cowboy retorts, the bass of his voice reverberating in my skull. "First he's asking me for a light. Okay. Next he's singing some crazy tune about how y'all hit a hot run at craps over at Cache Creek and lost track of time. Now he's late to his cousin's wedding and he wants to buy my truck for five grand, and I can report it stolen in the morning. Shit! I haven't heard that much nonsense with the television off for months."

He scoffs, a low rumble.

"So you guys in some kind of jam or what? You trying to hit the border?" He narrows his eyes at me. "I don't trust your pal any farther than I could bowl a rooster, and no way am I selling my rig for some insurance scheme. But I am driving south tonight, and I'd be lying if I said I couldn't use a cash infusion. I don't mind helping a couple fellas out if you ain't gonna act like total sleazebags."

As he talks, the fear in my gut subsides, replaced by bewilderment and the urge to giggle. I look from this genial mountain of a man back to Mark. He's dropped his cool act, sitting now on the bench with his elbows on his knees, his head in his hands.

"What did you tell him to get him to sit there like that?"

"I told him that I'd consider his offer, but I needed to talk to both of you first. Dude looks like he ran out of meth two days ago." The sneaker cowboy jerks his head back toward Mark, then juts his big chin forward to examine me more carefully, his eyes lingering on the bandages on my wrists. "You look like a scared kid. Is he abducting you, or did you guys knock over the world's dumbest bank? I don't want any heat."

I study the sneaker cowboy's eyes, orange-brown like amber, framed by deep crow's-feet and the sharp arcs of his dark brows. Nothing I see makes me feel more paranoid than usual. I wonder if I shouldn't trust my trusting instincts—the same ones that led me to follow Sun Jianshui to Beijing. To send those parcels to Nogales. To tell Mark about the gem.

But when I glance at Dad's Casio, I know I don't have a choice. Mark needs to be headed south within half an hour or he'll be stuck on the lam in the land of law and order. This slow-talking behemoth in Jordans is his last chance.

And even though I know that I can't count on Mark, I'd still rather run together than hide alone.

So I tell the guy the truth. Nothing but the truth. But not the whole truth. Only as much as he needs to know.

11

The deal we strike with the man who introduces himself as Arturo is that he'll drop us off at PedWest, the faster of the two southbound pedestrian crossings at San Ysidro, by nine in the morning, in exchange for thirty of Mark's crisp one-hundred-dollar bills.

My first offer was fifteen hundred. Arturo countered with twenty-five. He pointed out in his calm, steady manner that he held every inch of the leverage, and could easily relieve us of every cent in our pockets, so we should be glad that he's a decent guy.

It was hard to disagree. Nevertheless, Mark was pissed.

"Three hundo an hour for a drive he's doing anyway? You call that a fair price?" he hisses at me after I catch him up by the bathrooms.

Arturo is punching buttons on one of the vending machines. He scowls at Mark as watery coffee splatters into a paper cup. "Damn me if you ain't a squealer," he says, and then spits onto the grass twelve feet away. "Guess what, math man: your price just went up to three Gs. Wanna complain some more? Shit. Last time I checked, you ass-clown desperados weren't rich in options."

He takes a sip from his coffee and makes a sour face. "You're lucky I don't ask for all of it. Used to belong to my people anyway, didn't it?"

Mark looks from Arturo to me, hands on his hips, forehead creased with disbelief. "You told him how we got the money?"

I shrug. "We got a ride, right? Think of it this way: you save half of your cash, and you don't have to drive, either."

Mark glares daggers at Arturo, who is dialing up another coffee, and then casts a mournful gaze back at the van.

"Shit McNuggets," he murmurs, shaking his head, and though I can barely see his face in the darkness, it sounds like he's on the verge of tears. It gives me some vindictive pleasure to see him get schooled. But I also recognize that Mark is running on nothing but congee, cinnamon rolls, and energy drinks since Jerry shot him up with wasp-waisted lead pellets. He's still clinging to the shreds of a life to which he'll never return.

I know the feeling.

"There's a crypto ATM in Mexico City," I say. "I'll pay you back half when we get there."

Mark shoves his hands in his pockets and paces three turns around a four-step circle. Then he pulls out his roll of cash, counts out thirty bills, and holds them out to me with a grimace on his face. After I take the money, he jogs to the van to repack his duffel one last time.

Arturo walks over, following Mark with his eyes, holding two cups of coffee in one giant palm and two bags of black licorice in the other.

"Dontcha just love it when white dudes talk about fairness?" he asks in his deep, flat cadence.

"Yeah, about that. I told you why we're in a hurry," I say. "So maybe it'd be 'fair' if you tell us why you're driving to the border in the middle of the night."

He purses his lips and nods his head.

"I'll tell you on the road."

Arturo's truck is a hulking affair with a high suspension better suited to dirt roads than the highway. There's plenty of room for the three of us in the crew cab. Mark crawls into the back with his duffel and falls asleep sprawled on top of it before we've made it two miles.

Me, I only woke up a few hours ago. The painkillers are wearing off, and I can feel my pulse throb in the side of my head where Jerry whacked me with his shotgun. But the relief of escaping from the Elkhorn rest stop has emptied me out and opened me up to the dry California night.

In Seattle, the sky is always near at hand, bearing down, making problems feel bigger. But here in the Central Valley, the starry void humbles me with its hugeness. As we cruise through the convergence of arterials in Sacramento, my eyes trace the cars in the other lanes: cheap cars, fancy cars, new cars, crappy old jalopies like Mark's van. Entering and exiting the freeway. Appearing and disappearing from my field of view.

Arturo doesn't say a word until the traffic thins out and the road goes straight on the other side of the city. When he does speak, it's the same low rumble.

"Most people call me Art, by the way."

"Okay. Art."

"You asked why I'm on the road tonight," he says. "I'm driving to Salamanca. State of Guanajuato. My pops lives there."

I look over at him. His eyes stay fixed on the road. I let the silence expand until he fills it.

"Pops likes to play the ponies. I got a call from him around noon today. Guess it's yesterday by now. He's in a bad way. Dudes he owes, they're, you know. Impatient types. I've been working at this ranch outside Arbuckle. Finished my shift and packed up. Gotta make it to down there by Sunday night, or he ends up in a body bag."

Art pops a piece of licorice in his mouth, washes it down with a sip of coffee. I want to ask how much his dad owes and what he's going to do about it. But Art promised me an explanation of why he was driving through the night. He didn't promise to share every painful detail of his family problems.

Still, his words left a heavy silence in their wake, so I change the subject.

"You were working at a ranch? This is, like"—I tip my chin to indicate his outfit—"a thing?"

"You mean, do I drive cattle? Nah," he says. "I'm a chef. Specialize in plant-based cuisine."

I raise my eyebrows. "Not my third guess."

"I grew up in ranch life, worked cattle outfits all around el norte and the border. Chihuahua, Oklahoma, West Texas, you name it. Loved that stuff when I was still a skinny kid. Big dudes aren't good for horses, though. When I filled out, it was always, 'Hey, Artie, how about you unload those hay bales while we saddle up and burn the breeze?'" He chuckles.

"Anyway, I got into cooking healthy after my gran had a quad bypass. Couldn't get her to quit smoking cigarillos, but I improved her diet by means of culinary deception. After she passed, I started working the kitchen at a spa down by San Miguel de Allende. Guy who owns this dude ranch up here, he comes in and orders the seitan asada. Calls me out of the kitchen and says, 'Name your price.'"

He catches the look on my face and shoots me a smug smile. "I'm that good, man, you better believe it. People in California are accustomed to meatlessness. Serve you seaweed sprayed with mustard, that's five stars on Yelp. In Mexico, that's an insult. You want mexicanos to eat vegan, you'd better be inventive. Especially norteños. We like our cows."

"I don't believe I've ever had seitan asada."

"It's all about grill temp. And cumin." Art shifts into the left lane to pass an RV. Then he glances over at me. "You like licorice?"

He holds out the bag. I hold out a hand. He shakes a few pieces into my palm.

"So you quit your job just like that," I say. "You must be close with your dad."

Art scoffs, a deep, staccato *hnuh*. "Ol' Rafa can't help himself, man. Not the worst guy, not the best. What am I supposed to do? Let these vatos flay him 'cause I'm too busy smoking jackfruit for the Pixar off-site? Pops hasn't got anyone else to look after him."

"Can you cover his debts?"

"Nope."

"But you gave up your salary."

"I gotta be down there to keep him in line. If I send money and he keeps borrowing, nothing changes, right?" He shakes his head, a tectonic motion. "I'll figure something out," he says, his voice dropping even lower and quieter than usual.

"Family is messy," I say.

"Yeah, well. What's that shit they say about Einstein's desk? Better messy than empty, right?"

My smile must look as forced as it feels because Art puts his left forearm on the steering wheel and peers into my face. "*What*, kid? Why the heck do you look so sorry for yourself?" he says, somehow keeping the truck in its lane. "You some kind of murder-suicide survival story?"

I open my mouth, then close it again and glance from the man I just met to my only friend, snoring in the back. *Everyone has their secrets*, I think to myself. *We're all just trying to survive our personal tragedies. So why do I feel so sorry for myself?*

Maybe because my desk's much more empty than messy.

"My dad was Chinese and my mom was white. When they got married, their families cut them off. They died pretty young. My mom, cancer. My dad, murdered. The only one left is my sister," I say, opting for the extra-short version, which is still enough to draw Art's caterpillar eyebrows together in a wince.

"Your sister someone you talk to?"

"We used to be close. I haven't seen her in a couple years. And now"—I gesture with my hand, indicating Mark, the truck, the southbound highway—"I don't know."

Art lets it sit for a minute. Then he says, "She up in Seattle, too?"

I shake my head. "She's in LA. That's where we're from."

"What part of LA?" Art says. "Asking for a friend."

I study his face, but his impassive expression reveals nothing.

"She lives downtown," I say.

His eyebrows lift a millimeter. His eyes stay on the road. "Interstate goes right through it."

Taken aback by this turn in the conversation, I say nothing.

He downs the last of his second coffee, folds the paper cup into a trapezoid, and flicks it into a plastic bag in the foot well.

"We'll see what happens," he says.

We chat for another hour or so, moving on to lighter subjects. The landscape goes flat and featureless for hundreds of miles before the freeway hits the Grapevine above LA. Art seems pleased to have someone to help him pass the drive, especially once I get him going on the subject of soy cheese. My eyelids flutter closed as he drones on about phytotoxins and xenoestrogens.

And then I'm waking hours later, my head nestled against the flaking Naugahyde of the passenger door. Sour taste in my mouth. Stiff ache in my neck. I blink my eyes open and look through the windshield at the beige tones of a shy dawn, inching across the beat-up and worn-down freeways of Los Angeles.

I rub sleep from my eyes with my index fingers. Mark, in the back, is still profoundly unconscious in the same posture as the last time I looked. That's Mark for you. A good sleeper in all circumstances. Arturo also remains as he was before, except that he's donned a pair of drugstore shades, and he's no longer talking about soy.

I check my watch: a few minutes after six. I clear my throat. "What was that you were saying?"

Art grins, revealing stained teeth bigger than my fingernails. "So this Jerry dude," he rumbles. "You said those text messages go out at nine, right? Maybe he's out of there at 9:30. Talks to the cops, when, ten at the earliest?"

"Sounds about right."

"Looks like you got a little room to wiggle." He cuts his eyes toward his phone, which shows light traffic en route to an 8:24 arrival at San Ysidro. "Might be a while before the next time you pass through."

I meet his gaze, then glance back at Mark, who's still doing a great imitation of a sack of rocks. I'm sure he'd be furious if he knew that we made any unnecessary delays. If we did anything that compromised his best interests.

Quite the contrast with Jules's attitude over the past year. Lying to the cops on my behalf. Offering to send me money. Calling me even when I was cold to her, even when it meant breaking the law herself.

"You'd stop?"

Art does his mountainous shrug. "Your dime," he says. "Your call."

"We could take 110 in a couple miles," I say. "I could keep it quick."

"Don't worry about me. Worry about your bean-counting pal."

"He'll be fine."

I sit up a little taller, take in the brightening concrete that surrounds us. We're passing Elysian Park on the right now. Dodger Stadium. The police academy. The temperature instantly rises when the sun peeks over Mount Washington to our left. Will Jules pick up her phone? Where could we talk? What would I say? And what if cops are watching her apartment?

No—one unsolved murder isn't enough to warrant someone

monitoring Jules around the clock. Nonetheless, as we navigate off 110 and coast to a stop across from Jules's apartment, I scan the block for unmarked vans. Dodge Chargers. Ford Crown Vics. Any excuse to turn around and get back on the freeway.

I see none.

Jules's building is a new one, all plate glass and aluminum, one of the posher specimens of DTLA revival. Doorman. Balconies. Hardwood floors, I imagine, and brushed-nickel appliances, and a washer-dryer combo stacked in a closet off the kitchen. I already knew, in abstract, that Jules has been living off Dad's money. But the reality of this luxury apartment on Pershing Square stirs up a swirl of resentment in my gut.

I close my eyes for a moment, calm the bile and the phlegm. Remind myself that this will be the first time we see each other in a year and a half. And perhaps the last time for many more years to come.

The thought plunges me into a blue sea of loneliness, but then it occurs to me: it doesn't have to be the last time. I could get out of the car and never look back. Turn myself in like she's been saying. Keep my head down in prison—maybe it'd only be a year or two. Remorse, good behavior, and then parole. No more living underground. Free to talk to my friends and visit my parents' graves. Free to use my real name.

I look back at Mark again and frown. I could leave this dickhead with the painite and the notebook and call it quits. He can see how he likes it on his own.

I'll test the waters, I tell myself. *I'll talk to Jules and see how it feels.*

Maybe this is what was supposed to happen all along. Maybe I'm facing the music. Maybe I'm coming home.

I'm retrieving my second-to-last burner phone from my backpack when Art points through the windshield and says, "That her?"

I follow his finger to a balcony on the third floor, where a woman sits at a café table, writing in a notebook. *Is* that her? That *is* her. I hadn't expected Jules to be out of bed at six, but there she is, wearing pajama bottoms and a tank top. Her hair is cropped into a pixie cut. And even from across the street and three floors down, I can see that her shoulders and arms, once rail-thin, are now muscular and toned.

I knew that Jules was taking kickboxing classes. But I didn't know that she'd cut her hair off or that she no longer slept until nine. When we talked, we mostly talked about me. Was she the one who steered the conversation that way? Or was it me?

"Kid?"

"Yeah," I say. "That's her."

I punch in her number, then look back up to the balcony as her phone rings. She doesn't move. Maybe she left it inside, and it's on silent. Maybe I'll have to go in and talk to the doorman.

That's when the balcony door slides open. A man steps through and holds out a phone to her. And every hair on my body stands up ramrod straight as Jules takes the phone from his hand and says something to him with a warm smile on her face.

Then she presses a key on the phone and says, "Hello?"

The man steps back inside. He was wearing black sports shorts, a black tank top, and flip-flops, looking as Angeleno as a chili cheese from Pink's. His face was obstructed by the railing, but nonetheless, I recognized him instantly. I know his movements. I've replayed them in my mind a million times. His efficiency. His lethal grace.

I'd recognize Sun Jianshui a thousand yards away at the bottom of the sea.

12

ello?" Jules says again. "Victor, is that you?"

I snap the phone shut.

Art is looking at me with one eyebrow cocked. Mark stirs and groans in the back seat.

"Where are we?" he asks.

Jules is standing at the edge of the balcony now, facing us. Thumbing her phone screen, holding it to her ear with her right hand as she chews the thumbnail of her left.

The flip phone starts vibrating.

My face burns hotter than a jet engine. My head rings with panic like a smoke alarm. I decline the call and turn off the phone.

"We have to get gas," I say to Mark, then turn to Art. "Take a left up there. There's a Chevron on Sixth."

He shoots me a look like, *If you say so*, and eases the truck back into the street. As we drive past the building, I duck out of sight and shove the phone into the bottom of my backpack.

Sun Jianshui living with Jules. I stare at my clenched fists, unable to believe what I saw. What the hell was he doing in Jules's apartment, walking around like he owned the place? Was he holding her hostage? Extorting her inheritance? Luring me back to LA so he could kill us both?

No—I know Sun cares nothing for money, and if he wanted to kill us, we'd long since be dead. Besides, the cozy dynamic between them was evident from their body language on that balcony. Jules had opened her guilty heart to the orphan assassin whom Dad had indentured so that he could start a new life in California.

Dad was a cruel person—I've accepted that much by now. But Jules living with the man who killed him, who lied to us both, who dragged me to Beijing and ruined my life—that was taking compassion to a perverse extreme.

I put my palms over my ears and press them inward as hard as I can.

"We stopped for gas in downtown Los Angeles?" Mark pokes his head forward to look at the fuel meter. "That quarter tank ain't enough to get us to San Diego?"

Art doesn't answer him, and neither do I.

"Well, whatever," Mark sniffs as the truck bounces up the curb and into the station. "It's not life and death, just a few years of hard time. I need the gents' like my eyeballs are floating."

He hops out while the truck is still rolling and jogs into the convenience store.

Art pulls the e-brake and cuts the engine.

"Breathe, kid," he says. Then he opens his door, steps down to the pavement, and pulls the pump from the dispenser.

I talk myself down as the truck gasses up, wrestling my rage into a box, sealing it hermetically, and burying it deep in the recesses of my spleen. *Get across the border. Sell the gem. Survive in the shadows and figure out the rest later. Forget about Jules and her deception. Her depravity.*

Trust no one.

When Art is tightening the truck's gas cap, Mark emerges from the c-store with a tray of coffees and a fistful of pepperoni sticks. Nobody speaks as Art pilots us back onto the southbound freeway. Then Mark hands forward the Styrofoam cups with a sly smile on his face.

"Black for the cowboy. Cream and Splenda for the kung fu kid. And these fine processed meat products are also sharesies." He deposits the Slim Jims into the drink holder in the center console.

"I don't eat animals," Art rumbles. "But gracias for the gargle."

"More for the rest of us," Mark says, plucking one up and peeling off the plastic wrapper. "It's Arturo, right? Okay, I acted like a chump last night. Off my game, and I guess you know why. Truth is we were way up shit creek and completely sans paddle. I apologize."

Art glances at Mark in his rearview mirror. "We're cool, rock star," he says. "Three Gs is a lot of money, but you're not the only one in a spot right now. You played your cards, and I played mine."

Mark dips his head and says, "Well said." Even with a mouthful of dehydrated beef, he manages to affect a specious amiability. Has he regained his elastic charm as Jerry fades further into yesterday? Or is he wondering what Art and I might have discussed while he was sleeping?

His van is gone, after all. And the gem is in my pocket. Lies. Conspiracy. Betrayal. Scratch hard enough on any surface and you'll find something ugly beneath it. But I'm not like Dad, or Jules, or Sun. I told Mark we'd sell the gem together, and I'll honor my word. Even though I doubt he'd do the same.

Art reaches into the licorice bag in his cup holder and finds it empty. He clicks a rhythm with his tongue as he fishes his soft pack of Pall Malls from his shirt pocket. After extracting one for himself, he holds out the pack to us.

I shake my head.

"No, thanks," says Mark.

Art rolls his window down a few inches, then braces the steering wheel with his knee while he lights up.

"You know so much about living healthy," I say. "How come you still smoke?"

"Got used to it pretty young. Learn to cook tempeh right, you'll never miss chicken. But vaping doesn't quite scratch the itch." He takes a drag, then holds the cigarette in front of him between his thumb and forefinger. "I guess there's some things you can replace, and some things you can't."

I turn toward the window and sip my saccharine coffee as the city of my childhood floats away from us. We spend the remaining two hours of the drive in silence. Traffic's fine. Weather's fine. *Everything's perfectly fine.* There's no line at PedWest when Art pulls up to the curb at half past eight.

"You been to DF before?" he asks me, pronouncing the letters in Spanish, *de efe,* as Mark and I unload ourselves from the truck. Testing me with Mexico City's old nickname.

I shut the door and stick my head back through the open window.

"El Distrito Federal? Yeah, a while back." I aim for casual confidence, not saying that I only spent three nights there with my high school Spanish class.

"Might be a little different than what you remember. DF is Longdai's town now."

I raise my eyebrows. *Longdai's town.* I hadn't guessed that the growing Chinese presence in Mexico City was a matter of concern to the vegan chefs of Arbuckle.

"I'll be fine," I say.

Art produces a pencil and pins the gas station receipt against the steering wheel. He jots down a number, fold the receipt in half, and holds it out to me. "You can call me if you get in a jam. Salamanca's not that far."

"Three hundo an hour?" I say, one corner of my mouth inching upward as I tuck the receipt into the side pocket of my backpack.

Art chuckles again, all timpani and tuba. "Plus expenses, punk," he says.

I step away from the truck as he drives off into the growing heat of the San Diegan day.

Mark and I split up as we enter the PedWest facility, taking separate lanes through passport control and customs. I remain calm when the Border Patrol agent punches Li Xiaozhou into the National Suspect Database, because it's Victor Li who's wanted for murder. But I start sweating profusely as she spends a full minute examining the B1/B2 tourist visa, replete with entry stamp, that I bought from the Anhui aunties for two weeks of wages.

"You've been in the United States for five months," the agent says, looking me up and down, taking in my rumpled clothes, my dusty backpack, my bruised face. "What was the purpose of your visit?"

I smile and bob my head.

"Sir? What was the purpose of your visit?" She speaks more loudly this time, her tone impatient and harsh.

"Toolism," I exclaim, bobbing my head some more.

Her narrowed eyes cut back to my passport. Stealing jobs, selling knockoffs, and spreading diseases, that's what she's thinking. But the detention centers are already full to bursting. And anyway, this nobody is on his way out.

She stamps the passport and hands it back to me with her eyes still narrowed. "Have a nice tool of Mexico," she deadpans, her tone as dry as the sand on Imperial Beach.

I bob my head a final time and walk out of the United States.

13

As planned, Mark's waiting for me at the cab stand in front of the Plaza Viva Tijuana mall, standing there like a trapped twig in the river of gringos flowing toward the restaurants, dentists, pharmacies, liquor stores, massage parlors, and other providers of goods and services that cost half as much on this side of the border. His thumbs are tucked into his belt loops. His fingers drum on his jeans. His eyes are hidden behind the pair of polarized Clubmasters that he found in Bin Thirteen.

"Finally sunny enough for you to wear those," I say.

He grins. "South has its perks."

We debate the idea of resting here before the thirty-eight-hour bus trip to the capital.

"I'd pay a toe for a hot shower," he says.

"A night in a bed doesn't sound so awful, either," I say.

But then he wrinkles his nose and points out that we're only a few hundred yards from the United States. Law enforcement has become the last bastion of cooperation between the United States and Mexico. Gone are the guest worker programs, the free trade pact, the developmental aid. All that remains are the DEA agents who "advise" the Mexican federales and the US Marshals who comb the country for American fugitives.

So we take a taxi to the bus station and purchase tickets for the next departure to Mexico City. With an hour to kill, we meander down the narrow lanes nearby and duck into a crowded mercado.

Stark fluorescent lights line the market's vaulted ceilings. The narrow aisles force us sideways through stalls overflowing with dry goods, kitchen supplies, toys, candy, candles, costumes, ceramics, and piñatas. After a dizzying quest to find the food hall, we settle onto plastic stools at a counter selling blue-corn quesadillas.

"Just order double of whatever sounds good to you," Mark suggests after squinting at the menu painted on the whitewashed wall. So I order two chicken, two mushroom, and two prickly pear. They come out fast and hot, steaming up the plastic bags that cover the plastic plates. No dishwashers needed here.

"What did Arturo mean when he said Mexico City is Longdai's town?" Mark asks between bites. "Longdai is a construction firm, right?"

"Kind of," I say, dabbing salsa out of my wiry stubble. I'd read a lot about Longdai's controversial projects on Huayiwang. "They do everything, but mostly infrastructure. They're a Chinese state-owned company."

"So what are they doing here?"

I give Mark a bug-eyed look like, *Do you really not know?* He returns it with a blank stare.

"What?" He speaks around a mouthful of blue masa and melty Oaxacan cheese.

I close my eyes and give my head a shake. When I followed Sun to Beijing and learned about Dad's syndicate, I'd seen how global flows of money formed the fabric of our daily lives. For every Victor Li growing up carefree in the Land of Opportunity, there was a Sun Jianshui halfway across the planet, living in semi-slavery, wallowing in the effluents of our affluence. In Seattle, my long nights at the internet café confirmed to me that the world was locked in a resource war between massive corporations, criminal masterminds, and ruthless governments—a war in which people like us were cannon fodder.

But Mark, well, evidently he isn't paralyzed by the imbalances that have made his life possible. He's just trying to survive, to get ahead and dig his own niche a little deeper. And maybe he's the smart one. Because all my time staring at the wet underside of every stone hasn't changed a single thing for anybody.

"China's not just the world's factory anymore," I explain. "They're the world's bank. Say you want to go to war in Iraq and Afghanistan at the same time. Rack up a couple trillion in extra military spending. How do you finance that deficit?"

"Okay, I'm not a complete moron," Mark says. "I attended those wars, remember? I know China's the main buyer of American debt."

"They've been lending to other countries, too. Especially for infrastructure projects. Pipelines through Central Asia, deepwater ports on the Horn of Africa. They funded a whole light-rail network in Caracas, and when the bolívar crashed, the Venezuelans had to give China ten thousand acres for their first naval base in the hemisphere. China will loan to anyone, even if they were elected by their dad and they live in a pink palace with a private zoo. And if the country defaults on the loan, that's fine."

"Because then China takes control of the port or the pipeline or whatever."

I nod. "And the money never leaves China in the first place. The borrowers have to hire Chinese firms to do the work."

"Slick play." Mark raises his eyebrows. "I'm guessing that Longdai's one of those firms."

"They got the contract to build the Amistad Airport in Mexico City. It'll be bigger than O'Hare."

"Okay, another guess: China's mining illegal painite in Burma."

I tap my nose with my index finger. "You mean Myanmar, but yeah," I say. "Even CNN knows that China is the only country still doing business there. That is, ever since the junta started gunning down their own people."

Mark whistles low.

"So how big is the loan for this airport in Mexico City?"

"I dunno. Several billion?"

"Hell's bells," he says. "What kind of hornet's nest are you dragging us into, Victor?"

"Who said anything about hornets?" I chase my last bite of food with a swig of tamarind agua fresca.

He leans toward me and lowers his voice. "You think we can waltz into a Chinese cash-a-palooza in Uncle Sam's backyard, hock a conflict stone for a quarter mil, and not encounter any friction along the way?"

I shrug. "Mexico's not a backyard. If they want to take money from the Chinese, that's up to them. Fact is, the United States has screwed up its relationship with Mexico, and China's stepping into the void. This stone is all we've got. The only market for it is in the Chinese sphere of influence. Seems pretty straightforward to me."

Mark's watch starts beeping. Time to get back to the bus station. He drops his crumpled-up napkin onto his plate, stands up, and slings his duffel over his shoulder.

"For someone with an encyclopedic knowledge of all the dark plays in the world, you are bizarrely blasé about your own chances of pulling off moon shots. Lucky for you, I'm here to watch your six." He seizes my shoulders to square me up and stare me in the eye. "But no more hotdog stunts like sending stuff to Nogales, all right? No surprises."

I snap off a mock salute.

On our way out of the mercado, I pick out a trucker cap with the UNAM Pumas logo on it and pull it low over my eyes. We keep an eye out for feds as we make our way back to the bus station. But the other passengers—mostly men traveling solo, lugging big suitcases, tote bags, and cardboard boxes—aren't studying us. On the contrary, they're studiously avoiding us. Mark is wearing combat boots and cargo pants along with his dark glasses. Me, I've dressed all in black ever since Beijing. We're the ones who look like narcs.

As the driver pilots us out of the station, Mark's words echo in my head. I don't feel bizarrely blasé, but I like the sound of it. Our plan entails risk—I know that, and I have no objection. If I die tomorrow, so be it.

The world wouldn't miss me. And the feeling is mutual.

The bus trundles out of the city, huffs onto the toll road to Mexicali, and gathers speed in the direction of the rising sun. We climb hairpin turns into the craggy, tan mountains, and then we descend again, coasting down vertiginous switchbacks, a cycle that repeats itself throughout the next two days as the bus traverses the arid center of the country.

The driver disgorges us to stretch our legs at bare-bones stations in Caborca, in Santa Rosalía, in Torreón. Dried out by heat and altitude, we piss bright yellow in men's room troughs, wolf down tacos de canasta sold roadside by grandmas in rebozos. Our bodies are mending, our minds acclimatizing to a new reality in which this land is home. And my Spanish skills are tuning up, thanks to the marathon of shrilly dubbed *Malcolm in the Middle* episodes playing on the bus's drop-down screens.

Mostly, we eat and sleep to languid excess. Recovering, preparing. Focusing our minds on the yet-obscure hinge of our fates. Cerrada 5 de Mayo 17. 伊莎贝尔—yīshābèi'ěr. Isabel.

14

Early on our third morning in Mexico, we coast down a valley freeway into a mile-high basin of twenty million people as the hot light of a new day seeps across the eastern sky. The endless city yaws away from the bus windows: an ocean of smallish, blocky buildings. Many glow with colorful paint, many more hunker dingy white. The hilly outer neighborhoods are pocked with rugged street trees, webbed by tangled networks of power lines, shrouded in a gray haze of particulate matter.

Like Los Angeles, Mexico City is neither tall nor dense, and the bus crawls through the great range of the place like a blind beetle on an epic rug. But unlike Angelenos, the people here use their roads for more than driving cars. Street life comes into resolution as the bus descends from the freeway into the neighborhood of Magdalena de las Salinas. Breakfast stalls offering tortas and tamales occupy every corner. Men, women, and children wash cars as they wait at red lights, or do magic tricks, or juggle, or eat fire. They dash from car to car, collecting five-peso coins from outstretched hands before the signal goes green. If I could open the bus window,

I could buy breakfast, or a tabloid, or a dozen roses, or a kaleidoscope, but nothing I saw inside of it would match the vivacity of the streets of el Distrito Federal.

We snag a taxi from the line of pink-and-white Hyundais in front of the station, and I ask the driver to find us a hotel in el Centro Histórico that accepts cash. The buildings grow older and the streets narrow as we approach downtown. We're one car back from the stoplight to cross Avenida Paseo de La Reforma, the skyscraper-lined central boulevard, when a big white pickup comes roaring through the intersection from the left and screeches to a halt in the crosswalk.

"Hijos de puta," mutters the cabdriver. He presses his wrist against his receding hairline, then cuts the engine.

Four men with assault rifles stand in the bed of the truck, holding on to a rack of black steel bars. They're dressed in gray-checked flannel shirts, with black cowboy hats on their heads and red bandannas covering their faces. My eyes go wide as they sling the rifles off their shoulders and take up positions like a military platoon, pointing their guns back and forth on a swivel, one facing each direction.

"Uhhhh," says Mark.

"Lo siento, muchachos," says the driver. "Tenemos que esperar aquí un ratito."

"¿Qué está pasando?" I crane my neck to see around the car in front of us. The traffic is draining out of La Reforma, and there's another truck in the opposite crosswalk, blocking cars on the other side.

"Hay una manifestación. Tenemos una casi todos los días."

"¿Manifestación de qué?"

"Pues, contra el Chinopuerto."

Mark elbows me in the upper arm.

"There's a protest," I explain. "Against the airport."

"Awesome," he says, shifting in his seat. "Can you tell them that I haven't crapped in three days?"

Heralded by a cacophony of car horns, the front line of protesters appears in the street. La Reforma is some eight lanes across, with wide sidewalks and a tree-lined median, and the great breadth of the boulevard quickly fills with hollering, fist-pumping pedestrians. There are students in thick-rimmed glasses and green canvas jackets, paunchy yuppies with children balanced on their shoulders, and plenty of working uniforms: gray coveralls, blue blazers, aquamarine scrubs. I can't understand the chants amid all the honking horns, but I glimpse some of the homemade signs as they pass:

#NOCHINOPUERTO

NUESTRO PAÍS, NUESTRO TRABAJADORES

CHINA NO ES BIENVENIDO

¡CHINOS VÁYANSE Y NO VUELVAN!

Go away, Chinese, and don't come back.

I ask the driver about the guys in the white truck.

He glances back at me with his head tipped to the side. "¿No ha oído hablar de la Nueva Generación de Almas Prehispánicas?"— *You haven't heard of the New Generation of pre-Hispanic Souls? That's what they call themselves,* he explains. *—NGAP. They claim to be a patriot organization, but they're narco-traffickers, that's all they are.*

—A cartel?

—More like a figurehead for cartels. They take money from the syndicates and spend it in the capital to influence people. And politicians.

—Like a trade association, I say.

The driver smiles sardonically. "Más o menos," he says—*More or less.*

I translate into English for Mark without taking my eyes off the men brandishing their rifles in the truck bed.

"What about these dudes?" Mark says, a lively smile on his lips as he tips his chin at the group of a few hundred men bringing up the rear of the protest. Most of them are wearing nothing but wide-brimmed straw hats on their heads and printout photos of someone's face covering their crotches. They sing loudly, raised voices bellowing forth from the round O's of their lips, and dance to the music of handheld boom boxes.

"What cool gang are they?" Mark asks. "And can I join?"

I interpret his question to the taxista.

"Es el Movimiento de los Cuatrocientos Pueblos," he explains: the Movement of the Four Hundred Villages, a die-hard group from Veracruz that formed thirty years ago when their feckless governor, Dante Delgado, appropriated their lands and sold it to developers right out from under their homes.

Ever since, they've been disrupting traffic on La Reforma with a photo of Delgado taped over their dicks, dancing and chanting and repeating their demands to have their lands restored to them. Their complaints have never been addressed, and Delgado was appointed ambassador to Italy. But they still don't return home because their homes are gone.

"Nada cambia nunca," the taxista sighs—*Nothing ever changes.*

I ask him what they've got against the airport.

The driver shrugs. "Son como manifestantes vocacionales"— *They're vocational protesters now.*

The honking of the horns dies off as the last few naked men straggle across the intersection. The gunmen sling their rifles back over their shoulders and grab hold of the steel bars. The white truck pulls into the road, tracing S-curves across the boulevard behind the massive crowd.

"Ask him what he thinks of the airport," Mark suggests once we've started moving again.

The driver nods to himself for a moment before answering. "Es una monstruosidad, ¿me entiendes? Como signo del Apocalipsis."

Mark rolls his eyes. "Seems a little dramatic," he says, "coming from the guy who just said that nothing ever changes."

The driver pulls up in front of a baroque colonial building of gray stone: Hotel el Paraíso. He catches Mark's eye in the rearview and responds in English.

"I suppose I could say, 'Nothing ever improves.'"

Then he opens his door and steps out to unload our bags from the trunk.

The hotel is immaculate and snug, all stone tiles and worn wood. At reception, we pay cash for two nights. Then we take the loose-jointed elevator up to our third-floor double, where Mark promptly locks himself in the bathroom.

I fish his laptop out of his duffel, clear the top of the narrow desk, and get to work on Song Fei's notebook. The anti-airport protest along La Reforma made me realize that Mark was right about the peril in our plan. It doesn't feel like the best time to be a Chinese person in Mexico City, let alone one trying to sell a gemstone from Myanmar, another country wriggling under China's thumb.

We need to know more about what we're getting into.

A quick internet search reveals that there's no jeweler anywhere on the alley named Cerrada 5 de Mayo. The street view of No. 17 shows a squat stone building sandwiched between two taller ones, with an arched red door and a worn wooden sign: PULQUERÍA LOS TRES PIRATAS.

A bar. Great. Could we find the buyer there? Would we need some kind of password? Is "Isabel" enough?

I flip forward to the Tang dynasty poem, make a list of all the incorrect radicals that Song Fei used in the first stanza:

田土火手水
臣人血木又
Tián tǔ huǒ shǒu shuǐ.
Chén rén xuè mù yòu.

Field, earth, fire, hand, water. Surrender, man, blood, wood, repeat. Whatever this means, it doesn't sound nice. I reconnect the hair clip to the laptop and enter the first letters of the romanizations of these radicals—tthsscrxmy—in the password field. Long shot. No dice. Incorrect Password.

Mark emerges from the bathroom, hair wet, a towel wrapped around his waist. He falls onto the bed with a wan smile on his face.

"That toilet's gonna remember me," he says.

I ignore him, move to the second stanza.

天高白王
立巾辶元

Tiān gāo bái wáng.
Lì jīn chuò yuán.

Sky, tall, white, king. Stand, cloth, go, first. Or *eminent.* Or *dollar.* 元 is a tricky one.

I double-click on the hair clip's icon again and enter tgbwljcy. **Incorrect Password.**

I flip back to the page with the address on 5 de Mayo. Sixty-five thousand dollars per carat. 买方—*buyer.* 砍—*bargain.* 假名—*alias.* 伊莎贝尔—Isabel.

I press a palm to my forehead and heave a sigh of frustration.

"Okay, okay." Mark levers himself off the bed, walks over, and plants his hands on the edge of the desk, hunching forward to look at the notebook and the laptop screen. "What's with all the agony?"

I tell him about the address, the poem, the hair clip. As he listens, his lips draw into a tight line across his face.

"You've gotta simplify, dude," he says when I'm done explaining. "We've got one option: go to this Tres Piratas place, get a drink, scope the scene. Ask the bartenders if they know where one might unload a stone. Or if they know anyone named Isabel. Nothing so hectic about that. If we don't get anywhere, we start hitting up sketchball jewelers mañana. All right?"

He rests a hand on my shoulder. His other hand is still braced against the desk, and I contemplate the mottled skin grafts on his forearm, the knots and whorls of hardened tissue, before looking away.

"All right," I say.

"You're overstraining that big ol' brain. Bad for your ticker," he says. "How about you scrub yourself for a solid minute and then we step outside and get our bearings? Locate that crypto ATM like you promised me, huh? C'mon." He yanks my chair away from the desk. "Look lively."

I shuffle into the bathroom to do as he says, knowing that he's probably right about our options and definitely right about my blood pressure. And as Mark predicted, I feel less glum about our prospects once I've showered and donned fresh clothes.

I'm sweating again within moments of our emergence into the midday sun, but after sixteen months of Seattle's constant moisture, I don't mind the dry heat. The world looks brighter and sounds crisper in the thin air up here, more than a mile above sea level, and the streets pop with so much stimuli that my mind can't stray into the future or crawl back toward the past.

We weave our way southeast through el Centro Histórico. The ornate buildings cast stark shadows over canopied street markets, surly organilleros cranking dissonant melodies out of ancient barrel organs, curanderos cleansing auras right there on the sidewalk with salt, lime, and chant. And then we pass between a ruined Aztec temple and a sinking baroque cathedral and arrive at DF's central plaza, the Zócalo: a huge, flat square disrupting the cityscape with its sheer quantity of void.

The crypto ATM is located a few blocks south, behind a photo booth, at the back of a vintage store dripping with hipster charm. Mark browses the comic books while I withdraw enough pesos to repay him half of Arturo's fee.

Twenty minutes after that, we're sitting in plastic chairs at a long table set up in the middle of a sunny side street, washing down braised barbacoa tacos with a savory broth of onions, chickpeas, and cilantro. Mark watches raptly as a fellow customer disappears into a corner store, returns with a bottle of Modelo Especial, and garnishes it with a lime wedge from the tray of condiments in the middle of the table.

He hops up without a word. I check my watch: just past noon. He's back with a six-pack within a minute.

"Five bits a pop." He grins. "To Mexico."

We tap the bottles together. The Lost and Found, the busted van, Jules and Sun, the airport protest—it all feels light-years away from this sunny table in the middle of the street. Despite Arturo's cut, we've reached freedom with the lion's share of our loot still in our pockets. Including the painite.

"What do you say we swing by Cerrada Cinco de Mayo on our walk back?" Mark says as he pops the tops off two more beers.

"You want to check this place out after three rounds?"

He eyes the last two unopened Modelos.

"Maybe we take those to go," he says. "C'mon, let's do it. We can't rent a tandem bicycle or hit a museum right now with this question mark hovering over our heads. And if we go back to the hotel, you're just going to crawl around on the ceiling."

"Fine. I don't see why not." I lean back, cross an ankle over a knee. "What'll you do? If we can sell the stone."

He looks at the bottle. "Think they sell these by the truck?"

"Would you run a security firm down here?"

He gives me an irritated look. "We've been in town, what, two hours?"

"Just curious." I take a sip, watching him over the top of the bottle.

"I don't know about security." He frowns at a couple of lavender blossoms fluttering onto the checked tablecloth from a nearby jacaranda tree. "I'm sick of scrounging for gig work all the time. Passive income, that's how you do it. Maybe I could own a shop. Like that place with the crypto ATM. Or"—he snaps his fingers and punches his palm—"an arcade! All old machines. None of those newfangled five-dimensional games that you can't pee straight after playing."

A dreamy smile drifts across his lips. "Pinball, air hockey, and Pac-Man. I'd curate a heck of a tap list. People knock back a couple of cold ones while playing the games they grew up with. Except I'd turn off all the sounds and pipe tunes through the place on audiophile speakers. Classic rock till eleven, Motown till close."

Each "I" smacks me like a pellet from Jerry's air gun. Mark sits there enjoying his beer in the sun, making his plans for his future in Mexico without me, and all I can think is, *Fine by me, jackass. I could use a fresh start. I fell into your thrall for a minute, just like I fell into Sun's. But I'll be better off on my own. Counting on nobody and taking care of myself.*

"Sounds great," I say. "Fun and games."

"Yeah, well." He downs the rest of his Modelo and sets the bottle onto the table. "Let's go get this money before we talk any more about spending it."

The sun feels much hotter as we walk north along Calle Simón Bolívar, a narrow one-way lined with stores selling musical instruments. Music Depot. Cosmic Music. Karma Music. Blankets spread with patterned textiles and handbags crowd the sidewalks, the stoic vendors mostly indigenous women from the southern states, shy-eyed children tucked into their bright cotton skirts. Mark weaves through the foot traffic, striding ahead of me, then stopping abruptly to give his pocket change to a paraplegic girl playing a dirge on her accordion.

A right and a left later, we find ourselves on the pedestrianized alley of Cerrada 5 de Mayo. The walls of the tall buildings on either side are covered in murals and graffiti. More tables shaded by canopies line the cobblestone street. Cocina Rosita, Café del Jardín. And of course, because we're still on planet Earth, a Chinese buffet. Restaurant Kamling has four red lanterns out front, each painted with the characters 吉祥. Jíxiáng—*good fortune.* But even though it's lunch hour, the big metal shutter is closed.

Directly across from Restaurant Kamling, the arched red door of Los Tres Piratas is open a few inches. Mark and I exchange a glance. He gives the door a push with his palm, and it swings open, disgorging a rush of cool, musty air. Revealing an uneven staircase that descends into an interior so dimly lit that I can barely see inside.

Mark steps in, and I follow behind.

15

The pulquería is little more than a semi-basement den, divided into alcoves by columns and low archways. The furniture is mismatched, but all of it looks sticky. A trough urinal occupies one corner, half hidden by a sheet tacked to the ceiling. Incongruous art covers the walls: a bright diorama of the Virgin of Guadalupe; a sepia photograph of masked revolutionaries arrayed in some dusty pueblo plaza; a cubist mural of a faceless woman, curvaceous and nude in a psychedelic palette, facing away.

All of the denizens are men. Two of the three are playing dominoes in the near corner. They're dressed in matching gray-checked flannel shirts. They manage to clock our entrance by rotating their eyeballs without moving their necks.

The other drinker, an elderly man in a felt kettle cap and a Servicio de Transportes uniform, stares toward the only window, which offers a view of shoes clopping along the alleyway outside. He doesn't seem to notice us. It looks like he hasn't noticed anything in weeks.

"Does this place scream big money, or what?" Mark whispers as we walk up to the counter, a folding table that holds several jugs of milky liquid in pastel colors. There's also a sack of tortillas, a plastic bag of pork rinds, and a bowl of salsa.

The bartender is a teenage boy with pale eyes and wispy whiskers. He sets his phone down on the counter as he rises from his stool.

"Buen día, señores. ¿Algo de tomar?"

I ask if they serve beer. He shakes his head and says, —Only pulque. He points from jug to jug and lists the flavors: —Pineapple. Mint. Coffee. Banana. Coconut. Pistachio. Oat. Natural.

It seems most appropriate to pretend we know what pulque is. I choose coconut. Mark opts for mint. As the kid ladles the viscous liquid into plastic cups, I ask, as quietly and casually as I can, if there's someone around here named Isabel.

I watch his eyes dart around the room before returning to mine.

"¿Isabel?" He repeats, then shakes his head. "Nadie con ese nombre, señor."

We take a table and sip our drinks, glancing around us, struggling to act comfortable within the surreal stillness. There's no music playing, no sound at all except the clack of dominoes and the street noise filtering through the sole window. The two dudes in flannel play without talking, and the old man in the felt cap gazes at the dust motes floating in the window's corridor of light.

Mark inspects the art, the corners, the knickknacks on the shelves, which are bolted into the stucco walls at askew angles.

"Cameras?" I ask in a whisper.

He shakes his head. "Don't think so."

I sit back in my chair, sip my pulque again, will myself to taste it this time. Sour, fruity, a faint hint of ferment.

"Refreshing," I say.

Mark takes a sip of his own. "It's something," he says.

Minutes stretch long, the silence as relentless as summer sun in my eyes. Disappointment settles over us like a sodden quilt. An address in a notebook. What exactly was I expecting? A lonely princess with a suitcase full of cash?

Mark drums his fingers on the table. Sees me notice and shoves his hands into his pockets. Gives me a flat look and deadpans, "I love this place."

I've got nothing to say. We make short work of our sweet, thick drinks. Once our plastic tumblers are empty, we get up to pay.

"¿Cuánto te debemos?" I ask the teenager.

"¿Les gustó el pulque?"

"Sí," I reply, without bothering to feign enthusiasm.

"¿Quizás les gustaría probar algún otro sabor?"—*Perhaps you'd like to try another flavor?*

My hand's already in my pocket, reaching for the rumpled bills there, when the tremor in his tone catches my attention. That's when I notice the forward tilt of his head. The beads of perspiration on his upper lip.

"¿Qué recomiendes?" I ask.

A minute later, we're back at our table. Pineapple for me. Oat for Mark.

"Your instincts are priceless, you know that?" he says. "I'm so very glad we came here, and I can't wait to try all the flavors of jizzy juice."

"You can leave," I say.

He sticks out his lower lip and shakes his head. "I want to die here."

I'm working on a snappy comeback when the door swings open. Footsteps sound on the creaky stairs, and then the guy appears: a compact man in a fitted leather jacket and a black beanie. He's got a cigarette tucked into the cuff of his hat, and his forearm is threaded through the face of a motorcycle helmet. He strides in with purpose, radiating the heat of recent activity into the cool basement, his presence so palpable that it feels like I'm holding a stethoscope to his chest.

He skips the bar and heads straight for our table. Pulls up a chair and studies us without saying a word. The teenager comes over and sets an ashtray and a cup of pulque on the table in front of him.

Brown. Coffee.

The guy takes a sip without ceasing to inspect us. I can't see his hair because of the beanie on his head, but the wiry whiskers of his neat goatee are black and straight. His irises are dark brown, his brows and lashes sparse, his sockets shallow. He could be thirty, he could be forty-five. He could definitely be Chinese.

A fuller silence pervades the bar now, interrupted only by the clacks of the dominos, until Mark says, "Well, *hel*-lo."

The guy looks from Mark to me. "You. I need to hear you talk," he says.

"What do you want me to say?"

"American." He nods to himself, studying my face. "How tall are you? Speak Chinese?"

"Uh," I say. "Maybe?"

"Sorry. Small talk first. Do you like the pulque?"

Mark and I look at each other.

"It's new," Mark says.

"Pulque is old. *You* are new." He plucks the cigarette out of his beanie and lights it with a chrome Zippo. "It's made from the sap of the maguey. They say it enhances virility. And lowers cholesterol, repairs kidneys, and prevents diarrhea. They say."

His English carries some blend of accents that I can't quite place.

"Dude." Mark opens his hands above the table like he's holding two halves of a grapefruit. "Who the hell are you?"

"You asked about Isabel," he says. "Do you know Isabel?"

The air deadens when he asks this question, and I sense that our response will have consequences—I just don't know what they are. I glance at Mark, at the bartender, at the dudes in flannel shirts. The clack of dominoes has slowed.

"We'd like to speak with her," I say.

The guy's eyes narrow, and the corners of his mouth curl upward. The air between us seems to shift. I think to myself: *Wrong answer.*

"Isabel left town months ago," he says. "Where did you hear that name?"

Mark makes a dismissive gesture with his hand, batting away the guy's question like a pesky fly. "We have something to sell," he says. "It's that simple. That's why we're here."

The guy's eyes light up. "You have a stone? A red one?"

Mark leans back in his chair, folds his arms across his chest, and nods his head.

The guy peers into Mark's face. "How did *you* get a stone? From Isabel? When?"

"Hey, dickweed, we don't know you from Adam," Mark says. "Did you come to play marbles, or what?"

"Marbles are nice," the guy says. "But information is nice, too."

Mark shakes his head. "I hate gossip. Nice chatting with you, pal. I think I hear our mommy calling? And it's almost time for milk and cookies."

He starts to stand. The guy reaches out and grabs his arm. "Show me the stone."

Mark is halfway out of his chair. He looks at the hand on his arm. He sits back down. The hand comes off. Then Mark says, "Why should we?"

"You heard that you could sell your stone at this place. I'm the buyer."

"No, you're not."

"I represent the buyer," he says. "You can call me Ken."

Wait—*Ken?*

I extend two fingers at the level of the table, a gesture to forestall Mark's next hardball retort, because the guy's name has triggered my memory of Song Fei's notebook. The address, the

price, and that Chinese character in brackets: [砍]—kǎn, as in
kǎnjià—*to bargain or haggle*. But what if 砍 were a name? Ken is
usually rendered in Chinese as 肯—kěn—but maybe Song Fei was
being sneaky with her language once again.

The old guy is still staring into space. The bartender is looking
at his phone. The dudes in gray flannel intently stare at their dominoes, pretending not to eavesdrop.

"Can I speak with you for a moment?" I say to Mark.

We retreat across the pulquería to another niche, confer in
hushed tones as Ken stabs out his first cigarette and lights a second.

"He's the buyer in the notebook," I whisper. "It says that exact
name: Ken."

"What the fuck are you talking about?" Mark hisses. "You said
the buyer's name was Isabel."

"I read the Chinese all wrong," I say. "I think Isabel was the
name that Song Fei was using."

"Great work, numbnuts! No wonder he's sneering at us like it's
frickin' amateur hour."

"I'm sorry, okay? I made a mistake. But look, he's the guy," I
whisper back. "It's still our best shot. We have to take it."

Mark presses his lips together, glances around the room again,
then nods his head at me once.

We return to our seats. Ken rests his elbows on the table and
knits his fingers together, a posture of anticipation. I produce the
velvet bag from my jeans pocket, untie the drawstrings, and set the
stone on top.

Ken leans forward and squints at it, tipping his head side to
side. He scoots his chair closer, reaches into the pocket of his jacket,
and pulls out a jewelry scale. After calibrating it with a tiny chrome
cylinder, he uses a pair of tweezers to place Song Fei's painite in
the tray.

I watch his face as he reads the LED display. A gleam in his eyes and a twitch at one corner of his mouth suggest something like recognition. Like a suspicion confirmed.

The scale shows 0.803 grams. A hair over four carats.

Ken looks back and forth between Mark and me. "How did you get this stone?"

Mark shakes his head. Then his hand moves rapidly across the table, and the stone goes back in the velvet bag, and the bag goes into the breast pocket of his shirt.

"No more Q&A, Jack. Make an offer or don't. We're walking out of here in thirty seconds either way." He slides his hand into his pocket, grips his balisong. "And if you and your lumberjack pals try to make a play, you'd better be prepared to bleed."

Ken smiles, but his eyes remain narrowed. He folds his arms across his chest. "Those two are not with me," he says. "But yes, I have an offer for you."

And then he leans in and lays out terms. Sixty-five thousand US dollars per carat, paid in gold-tethered crypto, transferred when the gem changes hands.

Tomorrow morning. Nine sharp. A white Chevrolet Suburban at the southwest corner of Plaza de la República.

No weapons. No wires. No phones.

"And one more condition," he says, producing a pen and an index card. "Write down your names. Your real ones."

"Why should—"

Ken interrupts Mark with a sharp gesture of his hand. "Like you said, no Q&A. The terms of the offer are not negotiable. If you accept, leave the card with your names with the boy at the bar. And remember this: you will not find another buyer for that stone in this hemisphere."

Then he stands up and walks out of the bar without paying, leaving the index card, the pen, and the cup of coffee pulque between us on the table.

16

It wasn't a thorough discussion. It felt impossible to speak in the pulquería without being overheard. Ken had boxed us into a corner.

So we decided to keep our options open. We wrote down our names. Then we snuck back to Hotel el Paraíso by a circuitous route, splitting up and backtracking to make sure that we weren't followed.

Now I'm lying on my bed in the hotel room, holding the gem up to the lamp on the bedside table. Tipping it this way and that, exploring all the greens and pinks that the light reveals at certain angles. Painite. 红硅硼铝钙石—*red silicon boron aluminum calcium stone.* Sixty-five thousand dollars per carat. Were these little rocks the reason that China was shielding the murderous Burmese generals from UN sanctions? Why Song Fei was flying around the United States, talking to senators like Aiden Blair? Could these four carats be our big break, or were we about to get all four of our legs broken?

The curtains are drawn. The room is dark except for the bedside lamp and the screen of Mark's laptop. He's pecking furiously at the keys, researching the gem boycott, the Amistad Airport, the Chinese mines in Myanmar.

"Why, Ken, why?" he chants. "Why do you want our names?"

"It could be a sting," I say. "Local enforcement of the gem boycott."

Mark shakes his head. "Ken's no Mexican cop. Those dudes playing dominoes were dressed like the narcos at the protest. What was it? MMMBop?"

"NGAP. Nueva Generación de Almas Prehispánicas."

"Right," Mark says. "Enemies of the Chinese, right? Ken wanted to know if you're Chinese, didn't he?"

"So what are you saying?" I put the stone back in my pocket and sit up against the headboard. "The cartels are pretending to buy painite?"

"Oh, they buy the painite all right." He hops up from the desk and starts pacing back and forth, gesturing with his hands. "But instead of paying us two hundred and thirty fat ones, they feed us to their crocodiles."

"Okay, maybe," I say. "Or maybe Ken represents some eccentric billionaire."

"Then why does he want our names?"

I study the ceiling, probe my imagination. "So he can run a background check. Make sure *we're* not cops on a sting."

"Or make sure that nobody will miss us if we disappear."

More pacing. More conjectures. Ken said Isabel left town months ago. His name was in her notebook, so that meant she'd been in Mexico *before* she went to the United States. And he asked if we'd gotten the stone from her.

"I think he'd seen this exact stone before," I say. "When he saw what it weighed, he had this look on his face, like, 'I knew it.'"

Mark nods. "I saw that too. So let's say our Isabel tried to sell it to him."

"So why didn't she? What went wrong?"

"I don't know. She got cold feet?" Mark shrugs. "We know that she moved on. She somehow snuck into the States and then got deported, presumably to China. Ken didn't bury her in an abandoned quarry."

I hear the strand of hope in his tone. If Song Fei survived the buyer, maybe we can, too. Ken seems about as trustworthy as a scorpion in a ski mask. But his offer is tantalizing and immediate. All our other prospects are vague and bleak.

We talk in circles like this for hours, ending up more confused than when we started. We can agree on one thing: if we get into that Suburban tomorrow with the gem, then we'll have no defense, no leverage, and no witnesses. The likelihood that we walk away with a quarter million dollars seems impossibly slim.

"So we go," I say. "But we don't bring the gem."

"You'd leave that thing here? There's not even a safe in this room."

"Then one of us goes. The other waits in a public place. You get the money, then bring them to me, and I hand over the gem."

Mark scowls. "Why am I the one who has to cha-cha with the T-Rex while you stroll around eating churros?"

The first answer that comes to mind is: *I'm the one who found it. I'm the one who got us here, too. You say you're watching my back, but all you want is to take your money and run.*

But that line of argument won't get me far, so instead I say, "You're the better negotiator. I can't lie without sweating through my shirt."

"Bull*shit*, Victor!" Mark halts his pacing and wheels around to stab his finger at me. "You pulled off that Nogales stunt right under my nose. You lied about your name on the day we met. And now you're saying, 'Oh, Mark, help me, take the risk, I can't lie.' And every goddamn minute with you, my life is circling the toilet!"

These words hang in the air, suspended from the end of Mark's index finger, as silence fills the room like a fetid gas. Then he drops his hand and slumps into the chair by the desk.

"The Lost and Found was *your* hustle, Mark," I say. "You were already on this road when we met."

"Maybe so." He speaks to the wall in a dulled monotone. "But at least I had it to myself back then. Without you nipping at my heels like a needy puppy."

Ire rises in my throat. "Hey, *I* didn't hire *you*, asshole. I didn't sign up to be your sidekick just so you could blame me every time we hit a speed bump. What's your problem, anyway? Where do you get off treating everyone like a disposable napkin? What's your precious secret reason for hating the world?"

He keeps his voice low, his eyes on the wall. "I have no idea what you're talking about."

"The hell you don't! You've never said a single word about yourself since we met each other." I'm shouting at him now. "Everything's a big joke! Everybody's just here for a laugh and a beer! What's the truth, Mark? I told you that my dad was knifed to death and that I'm wanted for murder, didn't I? So maybe you could tell me how the fuck you got those burns on your arms!"

Silence returns as he continues to stare at the wall on the other side of the dark room, enough silence for me to become aware of the clench in my jaw, the fury burning behind my eyes. And I wonder: Did I go too far? Do I really want to know?

Then he speaks again. "I killed my best friend. Feel better now? Want details?"

A beat. Two. Three.

"Tariq was my interpreter," he resumes, speaking in the same flat tone. "A Shiite from Makhmour. Before the war, his family was Iraq's only importer of Ryukyu glassware. Tariq spoke English with a Japanese accent. All his *L*s were *R*s."

The ghost of a smile passes over Mark's face.

"We trained half of northern Iraq to upkeep satellite dishes.

Tariq could make a statue laugh in English, Arabic, or Kurdish. We worked together for two tours, had a real thing going. Support. Funding. Gear. After a decade of screwing the pooch, the army was finally getting it right over there. Then, all of a sudden, political winds shift in the Rust Belt, and it's drawdown time. Everyone out of the sandbox, and that program you're acing? Nix." Mark slices his hand through the air, chest-high.

"Tariq wanted out. He applied for embassy work, academic scholarships, refugee status—everything he could find, and he didn't get a sniff. So he comes to me. 'You gotta help me, Knox. You leave me here after I worked for the Joes, it's a death sentence.' Like I had any pull."

Mark snorts indignantly. "I'd never promised him anything. It's not like I taught him English and signed him up for his job at the base. But I tried anyway. I gave him my sidearm so he could protect himself. He wanted a recommendation letter for the Special Immigrant Visa list, so I pestered the fuck out of my CO to ask *his* CO to write one. All I get is 'Can't bring your boyfriend home, Sergeant.' Like giving a shit about the lives we were ruining was *gay*."

Now he turns and looks at me. "Wanna hear about our bluegrass act? How his cute son taught me how to play the oud? Would that bring it to life for you, Victor Li? When ISIS found out Tariq was working at the forward operating base, they kidnapped his family and handed him a bomb. Best friends, right, but he didn't tell me that key little fact. He just begged me for one last favor. 'My brother, Knox, *please*. Let me talk to the captain myself.' So who do you think brought him into the officers' club with the bomb and a hundred frickin' Japanese tea glasses in his guitar case?"

Mark squeezes his eyes shut. His fingers float to his face, hover over the pizza-slice scar on his cheek.

"Who do you think had the privilege of jumping him while he was literally on fire, shooting up the place with my standard-issue

M9? Yeah, my best friend killed my CO and two other officers before I choked him to death. And I *still* got court-martialed. You think I'm proud of that? You think I keep that secret because it's so goddamn precious to me?"

Silences aren't freestanding. They've got beginnings and endings. Some silences are like wakes: marking what is missing, what cannot be replaced.

After a minute of silence like that, I say, "I'm sorry."

Still facing the wall, hands clenched into fists, Mark says nothing. Another minute limps into the fathomless black past. Then he stands up and walks out of the room.

I don't move an inch in the hour that follows, just sit there with my head tipped against the wall as the sun sets outside, as the dying light abandons its assault on the polyester curtains. Mark didn't want to tell his story, but it does explain a lot. Why the VA won't send him disability checks. Why broken glass triggers his gag reflex. Why he builds walls, pushes people away, and tries to make himself as small as possible—so he'll never be vulnerable again.

Is that what I've been doing, too? Is that how I've ended up so far from home, on the verge of losing the last friend I've got?

I skip the elevator in favor of continuous motion: trotting down the stairs to the lobby, pushing through the revolving door to the street, pacing to the corner as I flip open my last burner phone. But the *X* on the screen indicates no service. My prepaid minutes don't work in Mexico. Back in the lobby, I ask if I can make a long-distance call at the front desk.

"Sí, señor, from the phone in your room," the man in faded livery tells me, and he gives me the code to dial out.

This time, Jules picks up on the second ring.

"Victor?"

"How'd you know it was me?"

"What's going on with you? Did you call and straight up breathe on me like a stalker a few days ago?"

"What? Maybe. I'm fine, though."

"Okay, sure. But what's up?"

It takes me a moment to work up the nerve to say it. "I know I've been walling you off," I say. "And I'm sorry."

For a long moment, Jules says nothing, the sounds of her breath isolated in the silence. When she finally speaks, I hear the flush of her cheeks, the tears in her eyes. "Thanks for saying that. I understand that it's been a really hard time for you. It's been hard for me, too."

"You're not the one wanted for murder."

"Okay, but my dad died, too, remember? And it'd be nice—" She pauses, sniffles. "It'd be nice if we could go through that together."

"Is that why you're always telling me to turn myself in?"

"No! I mean, okay, partially. You're the only family I've got. But I want what's best for you. You're not exactly flourishing in the fugitive life, right? You work for a con man, scaring people into buying fancy locks and security cameras. You're lying about your identity. And your main hobby is getting beat up by random meatheads."

She pauses, and I sense her moving the phone from one hand to the other, pressing that first hand to the back of her neck. "It's like you're caught in a feedback loop of violence and lies. If you turned yourself in, even if you went to prison, I could be part of your life again. And eventually you'd get out. You wouldn't have to live a lie. And you wouldn't have to carry all that baggage on your own."

My mind is blank and function-free. Her words bypass my brain, proceed directly to my chest, pry open great barrels of hazmat stored there. But when I squeeze my eyes closed, I see Sun Jianshui, calm as a Hindu cow, stepping through her balcony door in his tank top and flip-flops. My face goes hot. *She* says *I'm* living a lie?

"What about you, Jules?" I say. "Are you carrying your baggage on your own?"

I hear her press her lips together. Furrow her brow. Carefully choose her words to deceive me.

"Sometimes it feels that way," she finally says. "Not a lot of people can understand what happened."

A long moment passes as I try to reconcile the painful truths she's spoken with this glaring lie by omission. What perverted game is she playing, telling me how traumatized I am by Dad's murder while she shacks up with the man who slit his throat? I flash back to that moment sixteen months ago. Arriving home from Beijing. Standing with her at LAX baggage claim while Sun tried to persuade us to drive him to that house in Pasadena.

Jules threw her car keys at me and said, "I'm done with this shit."

My thoughts are interrupted by the eerie drone of a scrap metal truck coming down the street, playing a recording on a loop.

"Se compran . . . colchones . . . tambores . . . refrigeradores . . . estufas . . ."

—*We'll buy . . . mattresses . . . bed frames . . . refrigerators . . . stoves . . .*

I peek through the curtains at the street, spot a smallish gray pickup truck heaped with rusted appliances. A teenage boy in a Pumas hat stands in the bed, his elbows resting on the roof of the cab, his face cradled in his palms.

The loudspeaker falls silent as the truck pulls to a stop. A second boy hops out of the cab and vaults into the bed. The two exchange a few words and an elaborate handshake, and then they switch roles and the recording starts again.

"Refrigeradores . . . estufas . . . lavadoras . . . microondas . . . o algo de fierro viejo que vendan!"

—*Refrigerators . . . stoves . . . washing machines . . . microwaves . . . or anything of old iron that you'll sell!*

"Victor, what's that sound? Where are you?"

Resolution fills the vacuum in my head like a drumbeat.

"I'm nowhere," I say.

"You're acting strangely. Even for you."

I know you're not alone, I want to say. *And neither am I. Not as long as I don't betray Mark like Tariq did. Like how Sun betrayed Dad. Like how you're betraying me.*

I've never won an argument with Jules. Big sis has always been the better talker. She's got me all figured out. She thinks she can fool me and school me in the same breath. Well, not tonight.

"Have you got a pen handy?" I ask her.

"Um. Yeah. Why?"

I recite the account number and password for my crypto wallet. I tell her how to use it.

"If you don't hear from me within the next week, use whatever's in that account for a good cause. Your first documentary or something." I take a deep breath, let it out. "I'm sorry for the way I've been acting."

"Victor, what the fuck are you talking about?"

"I'll explain later, I promise. But if I don't. Thank you."

And I hang up the phone. I'm sitting in the dark, coming to terms with my decision, when it rings. My palm rises to my face. *Stupid.*

"Hello?"

"Victor? Are you in *Mexico*? What is—" I set the receiver down and yank the cord out of the wall.

I lie motionless on the bed as light bleeds from the sky and the room falls dark. My pulse pounds in my ears. My tongue feels thick in my mouth. I realize that I might be dead by lunchtime tomorrow. But at least I'll have shown one person what it means to be trustworthy.

Around nine, I hear a key in the door.

Mark walks in, turns around, and closes the door behind him with a deliberateness that suggests extensive intoxication.

"Gotcha tacos." He drops a greasy paper bag into my lap. Then he redirects to the bathroom and pees with the door open for longer than seems healthy.

After that, he falls face-first onto his bed, his arms at his sides.

"Did we have a drink or two?" I say.

"That stuff I told you earlier. None of it's true." He speaks with his eyes closed. "I just made it up to make you feel sorry for me."

"Okay," I say.

"Forget I said it. Did you forget?"

"Sure."

"I'm actually a bareback barbecue wrangler. It's a Montana thing. That's how I got the marbling." He wriggles his forearms back and forth at his sides.

"I'll go in the morning to meet them," I say. "I'll do it."

He opens one eye, runs it around my face, closes it again.

"I owe you," I say. "You've been a good friend to me, and I screwed you over by sending that stuff to Nogales. I know it. I'll take the risk."

Both of his eyes open now, and I detect increased neural activity behind them as he studies me for a long moment. Then he levers himself upright and staggers out of the room.

He returns a few minutes later with a cup and saucer in each hand. Coffees. After setting them on the desk, he goes to the bathroom and runs the cold tap over his head. Then he sits down at the desk with a towel draped over his shoulders and brings his cup up to his mouth with one shaky hand, holding the saucer beneath it with the other.

He takes a sip, closes his eyes, and says, "Eat your tacos. Let's do this right."

We spend the subsequent hours consulting maps, gaming out scenarios, memorizing code words. Cues. Contingencies. What if they're Mexican law enforcement. US Marshals. NGAP, the cartel reps. Or Longdai itself, buying back its errant treasure. What cards do we hold? What are our plays? The Logistical Solutions team, trying their hands at a new game, the stakes higher than ever.

It's well past midnight when we're satisfied with our preparations. I set an alarm on Dad's Casio for eight. That will give me enough time to grab a torta before I make the half-hour walk to Plaza de la República.

Mark jabs his toothbrush around in his mouth for thirty seconds before collapsing on his bed and immediately beginning to snore. I lie awake, studying the trapezoid of streetlight cast by the window onto the ceiling. Wondering why I feel so much better now that I've got a plan in place to risk my neck. Am I a sick fool bent on self-destruction? A scared runaway who's finally sprouted a spine? Or simply a loner who needs someone to need me? I'm no closer to an answer when I finally fall asleep as the room begins to brighten with the dawn.

I'm awakened an hour later by a knock on the door.

17

Mark's on his feet, darting on his tiptoes to the peephole in the door, while I'm still blinking my vision into focus.

He flies back across the room. Yanks his pants on. Snatches his balisong out of his pocket and twirls it open.

"It's Longdai!" he hisses at me. "They found us!"

I jerk upright and find the floor with my feet.

Another knock. Then a voice. Not just any voice.

"Hello, hello! Anybody in there?"

Mark freezes in space.

I fall back onto the pillow, cover my face with my hands, and rub sleep out of my eyes with my pinkies. "You see black hair, you think Longdai? Really?"

Mark's face is blank. "Am I missing something?" he whispers.

"It's my sister."

"Open up, Victor," Jules hollers. "I can hear you."

Mark's eyebrows draw together as his jaw drops open.

"Your *sister*?"

"I called her last night while you were out. She must have found the hotel address from the phone number." I pull on my shoes and socks. "And flown in on a red-eye. Jesus."

He looks at the disconnected phone on the end table, then back to the door.

"She's not alone."

"Oh, shit." I dash to the door, look through the peephole at their fish-eye forms. Right then, the alarm on my watch starts beeping. "Shit shit shit shit shit," I say, clicking it off.

"I know you're in there." Jules puts her hands on her hips. "I'm not going anywhere."

"Please tell me what is happening," Mark says.

"The guy is with her," I whisper. "The one I told you about, who used to work for our father."

His eyes go wide. "The one who *killed* your father?"

"Just let me handle this," I snap at him. "Put your knife away."

I pull the door partway open and fill the gap with my body, and there she is, sitting on the floor with her elbows resting on her knees: Juliana, Juju, Jiějie, the only living person who's known me since birth.

I can barely see her because her current self, some newborn adult sheathed in muscle tone and athleisure wear, appears through the layered filters of Juleses past. Twelve-year-old skater Jules. Sixteen-year-old preppy Jules. Twenty-year-old art-school Jules. Each of them teasing me, ignoring me, casually rearranging my notions of cool and right like a fickle dictator. Recruiting me into fleeting rebellions. Deconstructing my musical tastes. Messy-tucking my T-shirts.

A shoulder bag sits on the stone floor next to her, and next to that, Sun Jianshui. He wore only black clothing throughout the week we spent together, but now he's mixed up his wardrobe with a daring gray T-shirt. There's a new crease in his forehead, a spray of silver in his clipped hair, and a crinkle of crow's-feet extending outward from the very white whites of his eyes.

He looks at me with the slightest of smiles.

"Well," I say.

Jules gets to her feet and takes a tentative step toward me.

"Sun and I are friends now," she says in a matter-of-fact tone, like hanging out with our father's killer is the equivalent of taking up embroidery or selling a chair. "I never told you because I thought you wouldn't understand. Now that you're dealing with some kind of crisis, maybe you can put the past behind you and prove me wrong."

"Who said anything about a crisis?"

"You called me last night and gave me access to your bank account 'just in case.' You think I'm going to read a magazine and go to sleep after that?" She folds her arms across her chest. "You need me, so you called me. Here I am."

"What? No!" I shake my head emphatically. "I wanted you to answer a question, not hop on a flight. Everything's fine. In fact, I have to go. Why don't we meet up later and talk"—I shoot a glance over her shoulder at Sun, who's watching me with his customary expression of extreme attentiveness—"just the two of us."

Jules takes another step forward and lowers her voice.

"Victor, I crashed hard after Dad died, just like you did. And I couldn't talk with you about it because you were too busy searching for someone to strangle you to death. I dropped out of school. I lost my appetite. I had vivid nightmares all the time. When Sun got in touch with me, I was terrified at first."

She raises her eyes to meet mine.

"But he didn't mean me any harm. We started talking. He was the only person who could understand my loss."

"Jeez, Jules, do you think maybe that's because *he caused it*?"

Sun gets to his feet. "I am sorry, Xiaozhou. I brought a lot of trouble into your life. I apologize, and I want to help you now to make a compensation for my errors."

In a year and a half in the United States, Sun has managed to learn some fifty-cent words and shed his accent. Now he's speaking in the affectless English of a newscaster. And I know from experience that he can mimic the voice of anyone he's ever met.

"Your 'errors'? You're 'sorry'?! You promised to leave us alone."

He tips his head to one side. "I only promised to not kill you."

Jules turns from him to me with an expectant look. "Victor, can we start living in the present? Or do you want to keep clinging to your grievances?"

But I'm staring at Sun's left hand. The thin silver band on his ring finger. The one that matches Jules's.

"Well!" I say again.

"I'm helping him get a green card. Nothing more," she says in the wary tone of a dogcatcher. "Think we can come in?"

I don't budge. "You two are *married*?"

"Whoaaaah," Mark exclaims from somewhere on the floor near my feet.

"Was that Mark?" She eyes the rings of scabs on my wrists from Jerry's handcuffs. "How about you tell us what's going on?"

"You need to turn around," I say. "And walk away."

She shakes her head. "We're not leaving."

"Holy donuts." Mark pushes me aside and yanks the door open. "I thought I was finished with this kind of conversation after I got expelled from kindergarten. Hi! I'm Mark!"

"Stay out of this," I say. "It's got nothing to do with you."

"It does if it lasts another nine minutes because we've a car to catch. Anyway, the hallway is no place for this Jerry Springer show. If you please." He waves us all into the room.

I step inside with a sigh and sit down on my bed. Mark pulls out the sole chair and offers it to Jules. Sun sits cross-legged on the floor beside the desk. Mark stays on his feet.

"Allow me to offer my take," he begins, raising his eyebrows and splaying his hands open. "Victor, you first. These people are here to help you. How nice. I know you love bitching and moaning, and there will be plenty of time for that later, but for now? Eyes on the prize."

He turns to them with the same professorial demeanor. "Juliana and Sun, right? What a pleasure, given the circumstances and yada yada. Here's the score. Our beloved client Jerry entrusted us with a package that we need to deliver"—he checks his watch— "in forty-two minutes. Thing is, the recipients turn out to be a bit tetchy. Perhaps prone to an excessive covering of their tracks. Follow me?"

Jules looks from him to me and back, brows furrowed. "Kinda?" she says.

"You've got the nifty close-combat skills, right?" Mark says to Sun. "So if you tag along with Victor to the meet, his odds go up. Juliana, you can accompany me to the drop, play bystander, and record the handoff. In case anything untoward transpires."

"Okay, wow, that sounds like such a bad idea," Jules says. "How about we drop off this package with the local authorities and go sit somewhere that sells caffeine? And talk about getting you guys jobs that don't involve mortal danger?"

"Well, see, these recipients, they might own the authorities, and they also might *be* the authorities. Trust me, we've considered all the options. You can help us, or you can pass. Or you can wrap yourselves around Victor's legs and prevent him from doing what we came here to do. But if you do that, you might be signing his death warrant. One thing's for sure"—he glances at his watch again—"we have no more time to discuss it."

"'Hēishǒu lànquán, tiān gāo huángdì yuán,'" Sun says.

We turn as one to look at him. He's got my notebook in his hands. He's looking at me.

"Excuse you?" Mark says.

Sun hops to his feet, picks up my pen, and circles the first three radicals on the list I'd made of Song Fei's mistakes: 田土 火. "Tián tǔ huǒ. Stack them vertically. That's hēi. *Black.*" He writes the character—黑—and holds the notebook out to show me. "Shǒu stands alone. *Hand.* Hēishǒu, *black hand.* The next four go together. Shuǐ beside chén and rén, above xuè." He circles 水, 臣, 人, and 血, and then writes another character next to them: 濫. "Làn. *To overflow.* Then you have mù and yòu left. That's quán. *Power.*" He writes 木 to the left of 又: 权. "Lànquán, *the abuse of power. The black hand abuses its power.*"

He looks at us as if seeking corroboration. Nobody says a word. He shrugs one shoulder and then turns back to the notebook.

"The second part is more simple. Tiān and gāo stand alone." He circles 天 and 高. "*The sky is high.* Bái and wáng make huáng." He circles 白 and 王, then writes 皇 next to them. "Lì and jīn make dì." He writes 帝 next to 立 and 巾. "Huángdì. *Emperor.*"

Mark looks from Sun to me. "What is he talking about?"

I stand up from the bed, take the pen and notebook from Sun, and combine 辶 and 元 into 远. "Chuò and yuán make a different yuán. Not *primary* or *dollar.* It means *far.*"

Sun nods. "It's a common expression. 'Tiān gāo huángdì yuán.'"

"*The sky is high,*" I recite. "*And the emperor is far away.*"

"An old saying. It means that the central authority is weak when you are in a distant land," Sun explains to Mark, then turns to catch my eye. "So mischief is possible."

"That's all very groovy, but Victor," Mark says, "we need to go. Now."

"I will do it." Sun stands tall and sticks out his chin. "You need my help."

Jules frowns as she looks from him to me. I can tell that she's unimpressed by Mark's spiel. But she's also out of her element, and the clock is ticking. The masterstroke of his bullshit performance was giving her no time to think.

She speaks to Sun.

"If you say it'll be okay, I'll trust you. So. Are you sure?"

He pauses, then nods his head once. Her mouth sets in a grim line. She looks to me.

"You really have to do this?"

I look from her to Mark and back, try to remember the truth beneath the layers of deception he just caked onto our situation. Is this what I want? It's not too late for me to change my mind. But if I do, I'll be hanging Mark out to dry.

"Yeah," I say to Jules. "I really do."

"All right! Same plan, more people. Let's move!" Mark claps his hands. "Come with me," he says to Jules. "I'll explain more on the way."

18

Your father had more money. Cash assets from his remittance scheme," Sun explains as we walk through the plaza in front of the Palacio de Bellas Artes, past the monument to Beethoven, onto the paved pathways that divide the leafy park beyond. "I brought it to her, and I apologized for what I have done. I told her that you chose not to kill me when you had the chance. After that, my perspectives changed."

"I'll bet," I say.

He ignores my tone or doesn't catch it. It's hard to gauge how much more fluent in English he's become. And the extent to which he's learned to decipher human emotions.

"She wanted to understand what happened. Once she did, she wanted to help me." He turns to me with a blank look that nonetheless feels laden with accusation. "She felt that your father harmed me for her benefit."

"And whose idea was it for you to get married?"

"It was hers. I attempted other methods first. She assisted me.

We made some progress toward making asylum claim before the State Department froze all applications from mainland Chinese."

I shake my head. "To get a green card through marriage, you'd need papers. A birth certificate or a residency permit. Proof of your identity." I knew Dad had never acquired such things for Sun after pulling him off the streets.

Instead of replying, Sun looks at me with his slight smile. Of course. He knows how to forge, and he knows who to bribe.

"You're using her," I say. "Just like you used me."

"I cannot say a thing that will stop you from thinking like this," he says. "But perhaps I can change your view with my actions."

"How do you intend to do that?"

He shrugs. "You will tell me."

Now Sun Jianshui wants to be my helper. Repay his debt. The same sick relationship he had with Dad. "Qiánrén zài shù, hòurén chéng liáng," Dad would say. Then he'd leave Jules in charge for a couple of weeks while he went to Beijing to attend to his business.

—*The parents plant the trees, the children reap the shade.* His words keep proving true, but not in the ways he intended.

"Remember when those ketamine dealers cornered us behind that nightclub in Beijing?" I ask him. "And you scurried up a drainpipe and left me there, with a tracking dot on my collar?"

For a moment he is silent. Then he says, "I have learned many things since then."

I say, "So have I."

We arrive at the back of the crowd waiting to cross Paseo de La Reforma. On foot, I have a better view of the great expanse of the boulevard, as well as the angular towers that dominate the sky above it. Most of Mexico City's streets scream *Mexico City*, but La Reforma feels more sinister and bland. If I unfocus my eyes, I can imagine that I'm waiting to cross Fifth Street in Los Angeles or Finance Street in Beijing. The same pinstripe suits and silk ties, the same sterile chain eateries, the same jagged buildings with the letters—BBVA, HSBC, CITI—that spell the same thing in every language: power.

As we flow with the herd across the grand avenue, heads around us turn left, glimpsing the tail end of this morning's anti-airport protest. A pair of white NGAP trucks are still visible behind the mass of chanting marchers. A printout of Dante Delgado's face lies in the crosswalk, marred by footprints.

Above our heads, whipping the polluted air into sonic thumps, is a sleek orange helicopter with two giant Chinese characters painted on its side in black.

龙带. Lóngdài. *The Dragon's Belt.*

After a few more blocks, we arrive at Plaza de la República, fifteen minutes early for our pickup at nine. I lead us down an adjacent street to a cart shaded by a red-striped umbrella. We order two servings of the only menu item, Dorilocos: grated carrots, cucumbers, and jicama, sprinkled with peanuts and gummy candy, and tossed with a bag of Nacho Doritos, lime juice, and hot sauce.

As we sit eating on the flagstones that slope upward to the enormous Monumento a la Revolución, I give Sun some need-to-know details of our predicament. He'll surely abandon me without hesitation when it suits him. But for now, his goal of becoming a legal American by guilt-tripping Jules seems to mean that he'll employ his inventive brand of violence on my behalf.

"Just try not to kill anyone," I conclude.

He nods agreeably. "I have promised Juliana that I will avoid fights," he says. "Killing is on her list of 'deal-breakers.'"

"Oh, super," I say.

A cloud passes over his symmetrical features as he says, "I do not think that you should rely on Mark. My interpretation is that he will act opportunistically."

"Thanks for the tip," I say. "Coming from you, that means a lot."

He lowers his eyes. "I apologize again for the harm I have caused you."

You can apologize yourself blue in the face, but that won't give me my life back, I want to scream at him, but what's the point? Sun's right: there's nothing he can say to change my mind. So I allow silence to settle between us. I focus on chewing and swallowing and breathing. Try to paper over my fear with a facade that might help me survive the day.

Play it cool, I tell myself. *Be like Mark.*

A minute before nine, a mutant Chevy Suburban arcs into the loop that runs around the plaza. It glides to a stop, hazards on, at the southwest corner. The windows are tinted black, and the stretched chassis, about thirty feet long, rides low on its suspension.

The rear door swings open and disgorges a brawny man in khaki pants and a snug olive green T-shirt. There's a bushy red beard on his face and Chuck Taylor high-tops on his feet. He puts on a pair of mirrored aviators, crosses his arms across his chest, and leans his hips against the gargantuan vehicle.

"American military," Sun whispers, giving voice to my thoughts.

I stand up and start walking. Not who I expected, but not necessarily a problem, either. If the military is in town, they have bigger fish to fry than me. They can buy our stone at a premium and still afford to wage three or four simultaneous nuclear wars.

And the ostensible details of their operation—this muscleman stepping out of an armored limo, letting us see him first—suggests that we may possess an advantage in subtlety.

As we draw close, the soldier pulls off his shades, revealing flecked green eyes that shift from Sun to me and back.

"Which one of y'all is Knox?" he says.

"Plans changed," I say.

The python arms remain folded over the barrel chest. "I'm picking up one Mark Knox, one Victor Li, and nobody the fuck else. You Li?"

"Yep." I nod. "This is Sun. He's with me. Mark has the item. We can go pick him up once we've received the payment."

His freckled features screw up into a frown, and I can almost hear the grinding of giant gears in his head. But before he can formulate a response, an inch-thick window rolls down, and a clean-shaven, toffee-colored head pokes out.

"Street's no place to conversate, Mr. Pabst," the head says in a Brooklyn accent.

"Cargo don't match the manifest," Pabst protests.

"We'll work it out en route."

Pabst directs his frown back at us, then pulls open the door. "In you go," he says, gesturing with a hand like a catcher's mitt.

The thick door of the Suburban says, *We laugh at your puny rifles*, but the interior says, *omg prom nite!* Pleather seats curve in arcs around ice wells and cup holders. Round speakers lit red by LED tubes pock the roof.

The man sitting at the far end possesses a musculature as imposing as his colleague's. He's wearing the same outfit, except his tight shirt is black. As the limo begins moving, he introduces himself as Mr. Miller.

"And the full name of our unexpected guest?"

Sun spells it out for him. Miller taps the letters into a phone. Then he tosses a couple of towels to us and orders us to strip.

"You can have your clothes back after we search them for recording devices," he says.

A minute later, we're sitting naked and barefoot with the towels around our waists, and Pabst is searching our clothes one item at a time, pinching every hem and seam. I notice that Sun, despite claiming to no longer be the person I saw end three men's lives with razor-sharp blades, remains as svelte and sinuous as a welterweight contender.

Miller's phone rings. He answers it and says, "Miller." A minute later, he says, "Copy," and ends the call. Then he turns back to us, leaning forward, resting his elbows on his knees.

"Mr. Sun is welcome to tag along, but we can't proceed to your meeting until we have Mark Knox in the vehicle."

"Okay, but look at it from our perspective," I say. "If Mark gets in with the item, we're completely at your mercy. So that's not going to happen."

Miller casts a look at Pabst, who looks up from massaging my socks and shrugs.

"Put him on with Keystone," Pabst says.

Miller fires off another text. Sun and I are mostly dressed when his phone rings again. He answers it as before, and then hits speakerphone and places it on the seat between us.

"Mr. Li," says a calm voice with a slight southern accent. "Mister" sounds like *mistah*. "How do you do?"

"Peachy," I say, affecting nonchalance. "But lite beers? Really?"

Keystone chuckles. "Let's say that they're easy to remember."

"Okay, Operation Keg Stand. How about that crypto?"

"You are businesslike, Mr. Li," Keystone replies. "I appreciate that. But I need to speak with you and Mr. Knox in person."

"That can happen if you want to buy this stone someplace nice and public."

"Paranoia's the fad these days, ain't it, Mr. Li? Rest assured that I share your interest in self-preservation. That's why you're in the vehicle: to be searched prior to our meeting. I am in fact waiting for you in a public place. So perhaps you should tell my men where they can pick up Mr. Knox, and then we can, as they say, get this show on the road."

"Your plan still involves that stone getting into this car before it's been paid for."

"Very astute, Mr. Li," Keystone drawls. "You won't disclose Mr. Knox's location until you've been paid, and I won't pay you until we meet in person. It seems that we've reached an impasse."

My armpits are sweating. My guts clench like a fist. Keystone's logic is hard to defy, but his vibe is very crocodile.

Do not cave, Mark said last night. Remember, you have what they want.

"It seems that you have grasped the situation, Mr. Michelob," I reply.

Pabst snickers. Miller shoots him a disapproving look. On the phone, Keystone chuckles again. Mirthful, but not warm.

"Perhaps I can change your perspective, Mr. Li," he intones. "You are aware, I suppose, of the outstanding warrants for yourself and Mr. Knox?"

I feel my face flush hot. "You have access to the National Suspect Database?"

"You have grasped the situation, Mr. Li," he deadpans. "Now, glance around your surroundings with those keen eyes of yours. Would you surmise that Operation Keg Stand, as you have so amusingly dubbed it, is concerned with your past infractions?"

"You people have mobilized more firepower for dumber reasons in the past," I retort.

"A critical citizen, I see. Allow me to set your mind at ease, Mr. Li. My colleagues and I are not here to enforce domestic laws. Nor are we particularly interested in rare gems. You'll just have to trust me on that"—another gentle chuckle—"which clearly isn't your predilection."

I glance from Miller and Pabst, who are watching me intently, to the nearest tinted window, through which the Monumento a la Revolución is still visible. The Suburban is driving in circles.

"You're telling me all about the things you're not interested in." The cool evaporates from my voice. "If I'm not selling painite, why the hell am I sitting in this ridiculous car?"

I seem to hear a smile spread across his face. "Mr. Li, there's a drama unfolding in this city. You've surely noticed. I believe you and your friends have a role to play."

"We're not keen on drama, Keystone." I shake my head, fighting the sensation that the car is shrinking around me like a crypt. "No matter how much cash is on the table."

"Not a man to be bought! I appreciate that, Mr. Li. Perhaps you'd consider other incentives," Keystone drawls. "Those warrants in the NSD, for example. What if I could make them disappear?"

19

The invisible driver slides the limo to a halt on Avenida Mazatlán, a tree-lined boulevard of shops and cafés in the posh neighborhood of La Condesa.

"Remember, fifteen minutes and that's it," Miller says.

"I heard you the first time," I snap back at him. Then I turn to Sun. "If they try to follow me, break their legs."

Miller and Pabst exchange a scoff.

Sun looks at them, then back to me, and says, "All right."

As I walk to the restaurant that Mark and I selected as our drop spot, electricity courses through my body, crackles in my ears. The glass doors into the restaurant are propped open. The place is full of natural light, patterned pastel tiling, and well-heeled yuppies. Mark's seated on the ground floor with a carafe of coffee and half an enchilada in front of him.

When I sit down at his table, his eyes flit behind me before settling on mine.

"New developments," I say.

He clears his throat, reminding me to use the nonverbal codes we devised last night. Two blinks for *all is well*. Three for *we're being watched*. Four for *fight or flight*.

I blink five times. *Change of plans.*

Then I look up to the second-floor mezzanine. There's a jazz trio up there, easing through a samba set, as well as a huge skylight and a cascade of cacti suspended in macramé hangers. At one of the two-top tables, with a clear view of Mark, is Jules.

I wave at her impatiently. She scuttles down the spiral staircase and snags a chair from a neighboring table.

"What's going on?" she says. "Where's Sun? I thought I was pretending to not know you guys."

"Sun's waiting with the buyer." I glance over my shoulder at the door as I talk, search the big windows that overlook Avenida Mazatlán, scanning for the lite beer grunts. "They're some kind of American paramilitary outfit. They're insisting on meeting us both in person. They've got access to the NSD."

"Chief, slow down," Mark says. "If you stroke out before lunch, no one wins."

"These people want more than the stone. They want us to do something for them. And they're offering more than money: they're claiming that they can wipe our warrants. SeaTac, Pasadena—everything!"

"Okay, wow, way too much," Jules says. "What say we mosey over to the embassy instead?"

"We might end up in the same hands," I say. "But with no leverage left."

"Feels like we're switching planes mid-flight," Mark says. "I like the old plan, where we get paid today and get lost tonight."

I press my hands flat on the granite tabletop. "Listen to me, both of you," I say. "These people are for real. They can clear our names."

"How could they do that? Who are these guys exactly?" Mark says. "Like, S.H.I.E.L.D.?"

"They look like military. They talk like CIA. But they're riding around in an armored party limo that must've been custom-built for a drug lord."

Nobody says anything as this information sinks in, our silence making room for the lively sounds of the café. People drinking coffee, eating cute foods, living nice lives.

"All they want is the gemstone and a few days of our time," I say. "They'll pay us double the original price. Half a million and a clean slate. No more running, no more hiding."

Mark purses his lips and raises his eyebrows like, *Doesn't sound too bad to me.* But Jules folds her arms over her chest. "This feels exactly like last year when you followed Sun to Beijing. You thought you were making things right, but it turned out to be a total disaster."

"I thought you came here to help me."

"I did," she says. "But not to enable you to make more bad decisions. What do these people want you to do, anyway?"

"They won't say what until they have our confidence. But it doesn't involve violence," I say. "Sun was particular about that. He's following your rules for him."

"What's he got to do with it?"

"They want him, too, and he wants to do it. He says he owes me."

"Victor, how do you know these people won't screw you over?"

"I don't," I admit. "That's where you come in. They're stingy with information, but they don't know you're here. If you can figure out who they are and what their game is, then maybe we can get an edge on them."

I take our room key out of my pocket and put it on the table in front of her.

"Call this guy Arturo. His number's in my backpack. He'll want some money, but he'll be willing to help. Tell him we need a safe house."

And I tell them what Keystone said: a drama unfolding in this city, a role for us to play.

"Something to do with the Longdai airport," Mark interjects, his face bone-white. "It has to be."

I stay focused on Jules. "See if Art knows anyone in the police or the army. And get online, comb the message boards, look for rumors about US military operations in Mexico. I'll find a way to contact you. A few days, that's it. *Please.*"

Jules stares at the room key on the table, pressing her fingertips against her temples. Then she lifts her chin again and fixes me with a look sharper than a diamond saw.

"Tell me I should trust you," she says.

I squeeze my eyes shut, take a deep breath, open them again.

"Maybe you shouldn't, Jules. But I'm taking this chance whether you help me or not. I'm tired of fake names and shell games and surviving in the shadows." As the words come out of my mouth, conviction braces me like a plunge in the ocean, and for the first time in sixteen months, my mind is clear as polished glass. "I want to go home."

20

We walk around the rim of the larger artificial lake in Chapulte-pec Park, toward the bench where the man called Keystone awaits us. The bench faces north, offering him a view of our approach. Behind him, towering above the park's lush treetops, are the austere ramparts and parapets of Chapultepec Castle.

Keystone sits cross-legged and casual. He's wearing wrap-around shades, an Oxford shirt tucked into olive slacks, and the kind of chunky white sneakers favored by sciatica sufferers. His pale hair is parted and moussed. His jaw is square and tan. His wristwatch is big and shiny.

He looks like an advertisement for multivitamins or boner pills.

"Mr. Knox." He stands up to shake our hands. "Mr. Li. Mr. Sun."

"Call me Mark," says Mark.

Keystone looks past us to Pabst and Miller, trailing some fifty feet behind, and makes a gesture with his hand at belt level. They disperse into the throngs of families and tourists as Keystone starts walking around the perimeter of the lake, and we fall in beside him.

"Let's see this stone, then," he says.

I look at Mark. He shakes his head.

"Buy me dinner," he says. "Take me dancing."

Keystone smirks. "No matter. Ken assured me that it was the one we did not buy from Isabel."

As he speaks, he inclines his head ever so slightly across the lake. Following his gaze, I see the man from the pulquería on the other side: Ken, dressed in the same leather motorcycle jacket, pretending to watch birds through a pair of binoculars.

Then I look back to Keystone, see him watching me notice Ken with a slight smile of approval on his face.

"Wanna explain to us what this is all about?" I say. "What's the military doing down here, buying Burmese conflict stones?"

"I am not the military," Keystone replies in his gentle drawl, "I" sounding like *ah*. "I have told you what I can do for you: clear your records and pay you well. And I'll do it if you can do something for me. But before that happens, I need to know I can depend upon your competence. So."

"So?"

"So you know that the Chinese are in town, leashing up Mexico with this mammoth airport loan. You know that Ken and I are buying uncertified painites at Los Tres Piratas. What else do you know?"

Mark chews his lip. "The Chinese are mining painite in Myanmar, right?"

Keystone inclines his head.

"They're using rare gems as currency. Why? Oh." I connect dots in my head. "The sanctions. Longdai can't access normal financial systems."

Keystone smiles without showing his teeth. "That's public information. The US Treasury has placed extensive restrictions on Chinese state-owned firms, including Longdai. We've gotten half of Europe to do the same. Of course, China's money can't be contained completely."

"The stones are untraceable." It dawns on Mark's face as he speaks. "Great way to put a million dollars in a sandwich bag."

Keystone's smile widens, producing a chin dimple, and he raises his blond eyebrows above his dark glasses.

"Let's walk this way," he says, leading us onto a brick path lined with vendor carts. Luchador masks. Hibiscus iced tea. Skewered slabs of peeled jicama, coated in chili salt and lime.

"So Longdai's using painite for what? Bribes to garner support for their airport project?" I say. "That doesn't explain why you're buying it."

"We'd like to know who's in Longdai's pocket," Keystone says. "Thanks to our front at Los Tres Piratas, we have an extended list of local nabobs with their hands in the cookie jar. It's simple: they send their gophers, we pay an extra slice on top, and we learn fer whom the gophers go. Thanks to Ken's hard work, we know that half the Mexican cabinet has a painite collection by now."

I roll my eyes. "Using taxpayer dollars to buy Chinese IOUs from corrupt Mexican politicians. That's rich."

"We're using taxpayer dollars to uphold the Monroe Doctrine." The chin dimple disappears as an edge drops into Keystone's voice.

"But what does that get you?" Mark asks. "A list of names?"

"The names are a starting point. We're looking for more than that. You've seen the protests? The airport is unpopular. With the right nudge, Mexico could turn against China."

"You want dirty laundry," Mark says.

"Someone taking bribes from Longdai who would expose their scheme," I say. "And make the Chinese look bad."

Keystone says nothing. We compress into a single file to pass between two clumps of lost German tourists on rented bicycles.

"You haven't found anyone," Mark says. "You haven't even come close."

Keystone shakes his head, but the smile stays on his face, takes on a rueful tightness. "We *did* come close. Isabel was a disappointment."

"So Isabel had some connection to Longdai? And you recruited her?" I ask.

"She came to us. Isabel was Longdai's ace security officer. But part of her job was attending galas in evening gowns and handing off painite to Mexico's sleaziest oligarchs. She developed an unfondness for it. So she got her hands on two large stones and came to see us at Los Tres Piratas."

He pauses to watch a bird flap across the cloudless sky, following it with his whole torso like he's drawing a bead. When it disappears behind the ramparts of the castle, Keystone resumes talking in the same casual tone.

"We asked Isabel to blow the whistle on Longdai. She corroborated our list of corrupt locals, but that's as far as she would go. So we paid her for one of her stones and helped her escape to her chosen place of exile, which was the United States. She said she wanted to see the Grand Canyon." He shrugs his shoulders like, *None of my business.* "Naturally, we suggested to some friends back home that they keep tabs. It seems that they saw fit to have her deported. She was the first candidate for the job we'd like to discuss with you."

"She wouldn't wear a wire," Mark says.

The dimple returns when Keystone does his gentle chuckle. "Gentlemen, you're no fools," he says. "Our intel from Beijing indicates that Longdai's on thin ice with the Communist Party leadership. As they see it, Longdai is generating image problems. Acting a little big for their britches, one might say."

Sun's stab at Song Fei's encoded message replays in my head: *Hēishǒu lànquán, tiān gāo huángdì yuán.* I flip the order of the clauses. *The sky is high, and the emperor is far away. The black hand abuses its power.*

So that's why Song Fei defected and fled to the States. She didn't like being the black hand.

"So the party leadership isn't so keen on the Amistad Airport," I say.

"The airport's all right," Keystone replies. "It's all the protest movement that has the general secretary losing sleep. China wants to look like the savior of the world's downtrodden. Not just a new colonial villain."

"And you want to vilify them a little more. Expose the bribery and the corruption. Fuel the local outrage in order to pull Mexico away from China," Mark concludes.

I shake my head in disbelief. "Just so that Washington can keep using this country as a scapegoat."

"Washington ain't got a thing to do with it," Keystone snaps at me. "Son, we play a longer game than the blowhard demagogues who spend all morning in hair and makeup. Mexico's been a good friend to the United States for centuries. Farming our produce. Cooking up some damn fine recreational drugs. Number two market for our exports. Mexico's a pillar of the American empire, and we all know it. It appalls me, the way our politicians disrespect these fine people." Keystone's lips twist into a sneer. "Like a jockey who loses a race and tortures his horse."

"But you're smart. You torture the other guy's horse." Mark grins.

"I'm serving the greater interests of the American nation."

"And that gives you the right to stick your fingers in Mexico's affairs?" I say.

Mark jabs his elbow into my ribs.

Keystone stops walking, heaves a sigh, and puts his hands on his hips. We've arrived in a spacious plaza, tiered with wide brick steps, dominated by six marble columns.

"See this monument? Los niños héroes." Keystone's Spanish pronunciation is flawless. He gestures to the columns, each of which is topped with a statue of a black eagle. "The boy heroes. Six cadets who gave their lives defending that castle in 1847. The last of them, they say he leapt from the ramparts wrapped in a Mexican flag. You know who built that castle? The Habsburgs, my friend. Spaniards with Austrian kings. And who was invading in 1847? You know that, smartass?"

Keystone pulls off his sunglasses and squints at me. His eyes are steel gray.

"We were. The good ol' U. S. of A. Won that war, too. Mr. Li, Mexico has been a vassal state ever since Cortés. Longdai's just the latest jack in town. They're the ones doing the meddling. We can't let our main competitor set up shop down here." The veins in Keystone's neck thump with his pulse. "That airport is a thumb in Uncle Sam's eye and you know it."

"Yeah, look, we got sidetracked somewhere." Mark shoulders in front of me. "Nobody here is trying to defend Chinese bribes. Transparency, accountability: all for it." His hands go up, palms out. "But what is it exactly that you think *we* can do about that? You know about our warrants, so you know we got the stone in Seattle. Nobody's bribing us. We have no access to Longdai. We can't wear a wire for you."

Keystone's posture softens, and the good humor returns to his face. "The wire is an antiquated concept, Mr. Knox," he says. "Longdai's entire operation is embedded with smart surveillance. We don't need to make recordings because they already exist. We just need to steal them. And we need to do it without getting burned."

"You want to hack Longdai," Mark says. "From the inside."

Keystone lowers his chin half an inch.

"So why us? Haven't you got your pick of white hats and ghosts from the Pentagon? Or do they only send you beefcake?" Mark cuts his gaze toward Pabst and Miller, who are standing at the back of a large crowd across the plaza, watching a clown with a mobile PA system entertain several dozen rapt children.

Keystone studies Mark for a moment. Then he raises his chin and looks past him to Sun, who's staring upward at the monument to the boy heroes. The black iron eagles cutting sinister silhouettes into the cloudless blue sky.

"Mr. Sun, you've been awfully quiet."

Sun turns to face Keystone with his blank, observant gaze.

"Do the words 'plausible deniability' mean anything to you?" Keystone says.

The slight smile appears on Sun's lips. He does his one-shoulder shrug.

"So?" Keystone says.

"We don't work for you. No paper trail," he says. "And we look Chinese."

21

Mark, it must be acknowledged, does not look Chinese. For this reason, Sun's arrival was a boon for Ken Saito, the man we met at Los Tres Piratas, who turns out to be the architect of the scheme into which Keystone recruited us.

"After I got your names and researched you guys, Keystone and I drew up a three-man infiltration op. Li and me at Longdai's offices, passing as Chinese, and Knox driving," Ken explains to us after lunch. "Four is much better. More elbow room. And I get to drive."

We're sitting on lounge chairs on the roof of a pool house. The pool house is on the grounds of a mansion in the Las Lomas neighborhood. Keystone deemed us fit for the job, so he confirmed the terms he'd made over the phone: he would wipe our warrants from the NSD and pay us double the original price in exchange for the stone and four days of our time. After we accepted, he beckoned to Miller, who jogged over and handed him a tablet computer. Then he transferred me nine OroCoins on the spot, each one tethered to a kilobar of gold worth sixty thousand dollars.

After that, right there in Chapultepec Park, Mark barfed up a tiny Ziploc bag containing the painite. He rinsed the stone in a water fountain and handed it to Keystone, who barely looked at it before slipping it into his pocket. We rode the limo to the mansion, where a quartet of Mexican marines stood guard at a tall iron gate. Keystone escorted us to the pool house with Miller and Pabst in tow.

He told us that the pool house would be our home for the next three days, and we were not to leave under any circumstances. He said that Ken would be along later to brief us on our operation. Then he walked across the lawn toward the mansion without waiting for us to respond, his hands in his trouser pockets, whistling a Rat Pack tune in the warm June breeze.

This pool house was not a shack containing a filter pump and a net on a pole. It was a full-sized guesthouse with an open floor plan and a gourmet kitchen. Pabst showed us to our room, which was right across from his. Before the mansion became a mysterious paramilitary stronghold, our room must have been the kids' room. There were two sets of bunk beds, a fold-up Ping-Pong table, and a fortune in Legos.

It didn't take us long to settle in. We didn't have anything to unpack. I helped Mark remove the duct tape from the small of his back, where he had concealed his balisong knife. Miller served us some very salty spaghetti and meatballs. Then Ken summoned us to the roof.

Now he's handing me three sheets of paper. The first says POINT BRIEF at the top, followed by about a hundred bullet points in tiny handwriting. The second is a black-and-white photo labeled LIJIA NU'ERHACHI—a glum Manchurian man with rimless glasses and a mole on his upper lip. On the third, a trio of detailed maps:

MEZZANINE

ATRIUM

CORRIDOR

"I don't know, and I don't need to know, how you got into the picture," Ken says to Sun as he hands him a sheet of paper. "But you're gonna make things a fuckton easier."

I tip my head to look over Sun's shoulder. His sheet is labeled GREASE BRIEF.

"'Relay Brief,'" Mark reads aloud. He squints at the myriad tiny bullet points on the page, then looks up at Ken with a pleading look on his face. "They say I'm more of a kinesthetic learner."

Ken levels an intense stare at him. "Do exactly as I say, and you'll be fine. You played shortstop, right? Three years All-State in Montana?"

Mark's eyes go wistful. "My salad days."

"It's this simple," Ken says. "Longdai's local operations are headquartered in the Baoli Tower on La Reforma. Underneath the Baoli, there's a secure corridor that leads to the maglev train platform. And along that corridor, there's a server room. Check your map."

He stands above me and points to a square highlighted in pink on the map labeled CORRIDOR.

"In that server room, there's a computer terminal. And when you, Point"—he gestures at me—"upload spyware from a USB drive onto that computer terminal, Keystone will gain backdoor access to the smart surveillance network that runs through the Baoli Tower like a central nervous system."

Ken explains that they know from Isabel that painite changes hands on camera in Longdai's offices. "Once we have access to their internal surveillance, we can expose their whole bribery scheme. Leak the vids to the media. Half of Mexico's political class will be implicated."

"Fueling the protest movement," I say. "Undermining Mexico's alignment with China."

"And Uncle Sam leaps in for the rebound!" Mark does his basketball commentator voice.

Ken nods curtly.

"In four days, there will be an opening ceremony for the maglev train at the airport site. Longdai's security will be focused there. The Baoli will be quiet. It's a perfect moment for us to make our move."

"I'm missing something." I look up at Ken, using the paper to shield my eyes from the sun. "If Keystone releases the footage of bribes being paid, Longdai will know they were infiltrated. They'll go back and find the surveillance footage of us planting the spyware. It's an act of war."

"Yeah, but by who?"

"Everyone will suspect the United States."

"'Suspect' isn't enough to start World War Three," Ken says. "They can't identify us. Two out of three Asian faces would've been enough. Three out of four, even better. Longdai can't release the surveillance and say 'Look what the Americans did' because we don't look like what people think Americans look like. Our Americanness is debatable."

"Plausibly deniable," says Sun.

Ken nods again. "Even if we were caught, identified, tortured into confessing, Longdai couldn't make it stick. We're slanty-eyed freelancers, paid in untraceable crypto. It's like a Zen riddle: if a bunch of Asian nobodies break into a Chinese office building in Mexico, who gives a fuck?"

"Like Natalee Holloway," I say. "But the opposite."

"You're getting it. In terms of war-justifying video evidence, if you ain't white, you ain't American."

"Let's go back to 'tortured into confessing,'" Mark says.

"Purely hypothetical. My plan is airtight, especially now that we're four. Like Keystone said, Isabel was Longdai security. She gave us the rundown of their protocols before she split for the States. And we've been cultivating another asset on the inside: a Longdai engineer. His name is Lijia."

Ken takes the black-and-white photo out of my hands and holds it up.

"The only tricky part is getting the spyware into the secure corridor beneath the Baoli. Point here impersonates Lijia to get through the security checkpoint in the atrium, and then Relay passes him the bug through the air. That's you, Mark—think of it like throwing out a runner at first. Then you join me in the vehicle and run a comms dispatch while Point uploads the bug. Sun here has the easy role: Grease. He creates a diversion in the atrium so that Relay can make the pass without anyone noticing."

My guts hollow out as I realize I've been assigned the riskiest role. "Can't this Lijia guy just upload the bug himself? Why do I have to impersonate him?"

Ken shakes his head. "Their security is too strict. Even employees like Lijia can't bring a random USB drive into the secure area of the building. It will take a pinpoint throw and a perfect catch to sneak the bug in. Lijia can't do it. He won't even try. He says his eyes are screwed up from staring at screens ten hours a day."

Mark wrinkles his nose. "So what will *you* be doing while we execute this 'pinpoint throw and perfect catch'?" he asks. "Eating Cheetos?"

"I'm Wheels. I drive." Ken tips his chin up. "And nobody in DF is better at that than me."

Ken's buzzed black hair is neatly lined at his temples and the nape of his neck. You can tell just from his goatee that the guy can drive. Only an intensely present person, with a sure hand and an eye for detail, could maintain a goatee that symmetrical. He says he's one of us: a plausibly deniable nobody. He grew up in Houston, relocated to Mexico City thirteen years ago after plowing a modded-out Acura TL into the dining area of a Buffalo Wild Wings. It took him a few years to learn his way around DF's underworld, but eventually he found a niche working as a fixer for yakuza junkets. He'd been moonlighting as an informant when Keystone recruited him to infiltrate Longdai.

"Just 'cause I got 'black hair and almond-shaped eyes,'" he says, "or whatever polite way Keystone would say that I look like an alien to him. This is my affirmative action, fellas. Don't fuck this up for me."

We spend the next three days prepping Ken's plan. Pabst takes our measurements and procures our disguises: tourist garb for Mark, suits for Sun and me. Every time he comes back to the pool house, Ken sends him out again with another shopping list. Hair clippers, prosthetic moles, the biggest sombrero you can find. White spray paint, large number stencils, a poster-size vinyl decal in pink.

Sun hangs out with Miller in the pool house, watching videos on his tablet computer and rehearsing the diversion. Within a day, he's seen every epileptic seizure on the internet. Studied the convulsions. Mastered the grunts.

Mark and I have the tricky part, which is the pass. Ken hasn't found the right container for the USB drive yet, but he promises us that it will approximately match the weight and size of a chicken egg. So we devote long hours to practicing with eggs on the big lawn between the pool and the mansion, breaking several dozen in the process. During the hottest part of the afternoon, we take breaks to cool off in the shade of a palm tree and speculate about the constant bustle of un-mansion-like activities at the mansion. Coming and going and standing and sitting and barking into satellite phones at all hours are severe men with glossy hair, clad in a staggering variety of uniforms, saluting each other and signing enormous documents, screaming at each other in English and Spanish, bombarding each other with interminable PowerPoints at the card tables in the window-lined salon.

Meanwhile, Ken works on the vehicle. On the outside, it's a pink-and-white Hyundai, identical to a hundred thousand taxis on the streets of Mexico City, down to the big white registration numbers painted on the roof. Under the hood, though, he's making plenty of custom modifications.

"What's that?" Mark asks him on Friday afternoon, our second full day at the mansion. We're walking back to the pool house after several hot hours of throwing eggs in the sun. Ken's putting a black rubberized case in the cab.

"Med kit," Ken says without looking up. As he bends over the passenger seat, the hem of his pants rides up, exposing the barrel of a handgun in an ankle holster.

"Bullshit," Mark says. "Med kits are white or clear, and half that size. You forget I served."

Ken fixes Mark with an irritated glance, then pulls the black case back out of the car, lays it on the hood, and pops it open. It's filled with gauze, tape, scissors, pills, and syringes, all individually wrapped in plastic.

"These guys aren't active-duty military, dumbass." Ken jerks his thumb at the mansion. "They're contractors. Of course they have better equipment than you did in Iraq."

"Contractors," Mark repeats in a nonchalant tone, poking a finger through the medical supplies. "Why do we need a med kit? You said your plan was airtight."

"My plan *is* airtight. Grease requested it." Ken tips his head toward the pool house. "He says he has basic medic training. The guards in the atrium only carry stun wands, but we know from Isabel that there's a gun locker downstairs in the security center. And I sure as hell am not dropping you at a hospital if you fuck up your jobs. Any more stupid questions?"

Mark raises his hands and steps back. "Nein, Überkommander."

Ken shifts his laser gaze to me. "Why is there egg on your shirt?"

"It's from yesterday. I only have one shirt," I say. "We just went fifty for fifty."

"Pabst has the real egg now. Get that from him and practice more. In your disguises."

Mark and I exchange a look. Then he snaps off a salute and we head inside to change.

"Such a dick," I mutter under my breath.

"Suck it up. Two more days," Mark replies. "Does Sun really have medical training?"

I nod. "I saw it firsthand when I shot off one of his fingers in Beijing."

Each night, the three of us convene in our en suite bathroom, open all the taps to ensure we're not overheard, and sit on the edge of the tub to pool our information.

"They're contractors, not military," Mark says that night. "Ken let it slip."

"This is what I thought," Sun says. "Miller and Pabst have luggage tags printed with the same logo. 'APEX.'"

"APEX Corporation?" Mark says. "They're enormous. They took over half the army's logistics in Iraq and Afghanistan."

"That explains the mansion and the drug-lord limo. They're probably consulting the Mexican military on poppy eradication or something like that," I say.

Mark's eyes spring wide open, and he slaps himself in the forehead. "I *knew* I recognized that smarmy prick."

"Who?"

"Keystone. He's Whitney Pearce!" he hisses.

Whitney Pearce. Whitney Pearce. *Whitney Pearce.*

"Wait. *The* Whitney Pearce?"

"Uh-huh," Mark says. "His title at APEX is senior board adviser or something, but he's the guy running the show. I saw him twice in Mosul. From afar."

Makes sense. Whitney Pearce isn't a man you see up close very often. He's the guy boarding the private jet in the tuxedo, the guy whom heads of state have on speed dial. I'd come across his name in the dark corners of the internet, posts by conspiracy theorists citing unverifiable rumors and redacted intelligence reports.

Now that Mark's connected the dots for me, it all clicks into place. Keystone has the bearing of a lifelong shot-caller. A man with a ranch in Wyoming, a private college in St. Louis, and a brother in the Senate. A man who took silver in skeet shooting at the Athens Olympics.

"This painite thing," I say. "It's below his pay grade."

Mark and Sun exchange a look.

"What?" I say.

"Nothing," Mark says. "Look, forget that you know who he is, okay? Act dumb and maximally compliant. No more of this 'What gives you the right' stuff. These contractor types, they like kicking ass and getting paid. Not answering questions."

The next day, our last at the pool house, Mark and I nail the pass one hundred times in a row. Sun and Miller paint white numbers on the pink decal and attach it to the roof of the cab. Ken cuts my hair to match the photo of Lijia Nu'erhachi. When he's done, he rotates me to face the light, holds my shoulders at arm's length, and chews his lip.

"I'm gonna fuck with your eyebrows," he says.

He's wearing a tank top that reveals a muscled torso with a diverse collection of scars: dark lines from blades, spongy skin from abrasions, little pink moons from cigarettes. As he peruses his array of trimmer attachments, I ask him, "Ever wonder if you should've been a hairdresser?"

"Fuck you," he says.

I shrug. "Or a mechanic, then."

"Don't talk." He uses his thumb to pull the skin of my forehead taut, then strafes my eyebrows with a dozen precise movements. In the next room, I hear the *thock, thock, thock* of a Ping-Pong doubles match between Sun, Mark, Miller, and Pabst. They're all done with their preparations. Ready to tie one on and quell their nerves. But Ken takes his time, repeatedly checking my eyebrows against the photograph.

By the time he answers my question while he's packing up his gear, I'd forgotten that I asked it.

"I wonder that shit all the time. Truth is I've tried square life before. Never could commit to the day-to-day."

"Why not?"

It's Ken's turn to shrug. "Ever get a report card in grade school that said something like, 'bores easily'? 'Demands intense stimulation'? 'Most at home on the playground'?"

I flinch. "How'd you know?"

Right then, I hear the sounds of a Ping-Pong ball being smashed. Cries of frustration from Mark and Pabst. Miller screaming "That's how you debate!" in his thick Brooklyn accent.

Ken levels me with a sardonic stare. He holds up the photo next to my face one more time, nods once with satisfaction, and says, "C'mon, let's get a drink."

We have a few, the icy Modelos cutting right through the grease of Miller's very salty sloppy joes. After dinner, Ken produces a bottle of his preferred tequila reposado and blends up a chaser of tomato, orange, and lime juices seasoned with onion and chili: sangrita, the little blood. Shot glasses in hand, we repair to the roof to go over the plan a dozen more times. After an hour of grilling us like a fascist game show host, Ken says, "All right, you guys are solid."

He kicks his legs up on the table and lights a Newport.

"It's DEA, right? The contracting agency," I ask him. "They're paying these guys to help the Mexican military fight the cartels."

"No shit, man," he says. "They've been on this contract for a decade. Where d'you think these digs came from? Used to be a pied-à-terre for the last two Beltrán-Leyva brothers."

That was before they were annihilated, along with their body-guards and families, at their oceanside hacienda in Nayarit, Ken explains. Their vanquishers were Mexican marines in an Apache gunship. Designed in Culver City; assembled in Mesa from components manufactured in San Diego, Incheon, and Yeovil; named for a decimated indigenous nation. Lighting up that sultry Pacific midnight with six thousand minigun rounds per minute.

"Mex government used to buy Apaches from Boeing for fifty mil a pop," Ken sneers. "Now they're switching to Chinese birds for thirty-five. Only business around here bigger than dealing drugs is hunting dealers."

"So what does the DEA have to do with Longdai?" I ask. Mark kicks my leg beneath the table. But Ken doesn't seem to notice.

"I don't know, and I don't want to know," he says. "Long as I get paid."

"How much do you get?" Mark asks. He doesn't look up from the object that he's holding between the tips of his index fingers: a glass saltshaker in the shape of an egg. Yesterday, Miller coated it in matte silver paint that rendered its curved surfaces as reflective as a frosted mirror. "Bet it's more than the rest of us combined."

"I'm getting my rocking chair money," Ken says, crushing out the butt of his Newport in an ashtray he carved from a beer can. "Haven't made a buck this big my whole life. Just in time, too. Too many people know me around here. Guadalajara, that's where I'll go. Maybe Veracruz. If I spend another year in DF, I'll end up a red streak on the pavement."

He shoots the last of his tequila and follows it with a sip of sangrita. Then he snaps open his Zippo, lights another Newport, and exhales with a sigh.

"I wish someone had told me about federal contracts back when I was still boosting Subarus in Sugar Land."

By my count, Ken is four beers and six tequilas in. He's reclined in his lounge chair, smoking with his face tipped up toward the giant cypress tree that overhangs the pool house from the other side of the compound's north wall.

I touch my shot of tequila to my lips, then take a slow sip of sangrita. Tangy, spicy, sweet. I catch Mark's eye over the top of the glass.

He blinks twice: *Proceed.*

"Ken," I say, "we need to make a phone call."

Ken cuts his eyes to me without lifting his head. "You know that's a no-go."

"Crypto accounts, you can't list a beneficiary," I say. "If something happens to me tomorrow, those nine OroCoins are lost forever."

"Who do you want to call?"

"My uncle," I say. "I won't give him any details. Just my account number, my password, and an email address. He's a corporate lawyer. He'll understand."

"Whose email address?"

"My ex-wife," Mark says. "I haven't been able to get online to create my own account, remember? That's fine, but arrangements must be made."

Ken's face is dark but for the undulating glow of the purple and pink LED globes floating in the infinity pool beneath us. He takes another drag of his Newport and blows smoke up at the stars.

"Keystone said no outside contact."

"One call," Mark says. "Or we walk."

"You think you can walk?"

Mark sets the mirrored egg on the table. "This is us insisting," he says.

Ken sits up and fixes Mark with a cool stare. His bloodshot eyes are wide open and alert. And as Mark's hand inches down his leg, toward the cargo pocket that holds his balisong knife, I see Ken remembering that we've already been paid. Noticing that he's outnumbered three to one. Calculating whether the five feet between him and Mark would give him enough time to draw his handgun.

And we're all thinking about Pabst and Miller, playing backgammon some fifteen feet beneath us. The Mexican marines posted outside the heavy gate at the front of the house.

Tension spreads through the silence like a fetid gas until Sun drawls, "It appears we've reached an impasse."

His imitation of Pearce's southern accent is uncanny. Our eyes snap to him, perched on his lounge chair with his arms folded over his knees. He directs his neutral gaze at Ken, who seems to suddenly recall that he only gets his rocking chair money if he plays nice with the viper.

"Jesus." Mark shakes his head. "That is spooky."

"Don't do that shit," Ken snaps at Sun. He unclips his flip phone from his belt and tosses it to me. Then he reaches down to his ankle holster and produces his handgun, which has the distended barrel of an integrated silencer. He chambers a round, cocks the hammer, and sits back in his lounge chair with the butt of the gun resting on his thigh, the barrel aimed at my chest.

"Make it quick."

I flip open the phone and dial Arturo's number, silently thanking fate that his area code is Sacramento and not Salamanca.

He answers on the third ring. "¿Bueno?"

"Auntie," I say. "It's me. Victor."

"Uh," Art says. "Okey."

"How are you?" I keep my tone even, my eyes on Ken.

After a beat, Art says, "I guess you just called me 'auntie,' so you're being listened to, and I'm not. Well, your sister reached me two days ago. I drove down and found her a quiet place to hole up. I hope you and your sleazy buddy know what the heck you're doing."

"That's great. I'm glad you're well. Can you put Uncle on? I have to ask him something."

Art clicks his tongue. "Momentito, kid."

The line goes quiet for a moment. Then I hear my sister's voice.

"Victor? My God, finally. Are you okay?"

"Hey, Uncle. Can you do me a favor?" My eyes flit from Ken's keen gaze to the empty black eye at the tip of his pistol. And then I tell Jules some random numbers and ask her to repeat them back to me: code for her to tell me what she's learned in the last few days.

"Yeah, look, we've done some poking around," she says, and I hear the crinkle of paper in the background. "There's still loads of US law enforcement in Mexico. DEA, FBI, US Marshals, NDIC—whatever that stands for. And the Merida Initiative is funded for three more years."

"That's five, eight, *zero*, two. *Zero*," I say. "Sure, repeat it again."

"The scary thing is this, V. Art's dad knows a bookie who says that there's a lot of buzz from the Mexican military recently. And this is a bookie in Salamanca—not Mexico City. People are getting ready for something. But he has no idea what."

"Okay." My voice is going higher, my throat tightening up, and I blink rapidly. "Yeah. You got it."

"Anyway, we're staying at his cousin's restaurant in the Iztapalapa neighborhood. It's closed for remodeling," she says. "Pozolería Urbana. The street name is Vicente Guerrero."

"The password is the name of Grandma's old cat," I say, trying hard to speak in a natural cadence. "The *gray* one."

Ken's eyes narrow. He sits forward.

"You've got ten seconds," he says.

I hold out a palm toward him as a trickle of sweat runs down my spine.

"Gray, gray." I hear Jules press her palm to her forehead, recalling the passwords we came up with before parting ways three days ago. "Tabby cat" means call the Mexican police and tell them everything. "Calico cat" means call the embassy. "Black cat" means run.

"Gray means a day," she says. "The day you'll be on the move."

Ken stands up and starts walking around the table toward me. I squeeze my eyes shut, turn away from him. *Sunny Sunday, Molly Monday, Teresa Tuesday* . . .

I tell Uncle to send three OroCoins to Mark's ex-wife.

"Her email is sunnyknox at Hotmail dot—" I'm almost through saying it when Mark and Sun both kick me beneath the table at the same time.

And I slap the phone shut and toss it into Ken's chest a split second before Whitney Pearce appears at the top of the stairs.

22

Pearce's gray eyes glide over each of us in turn, lingering on the handgun tucked into Ken's unsnapped holster, the phone held in a fist in his lap.

Miller and Pabst trail behind him. They stop a few yards from the table, hands clasped at the smalls of their backs, weight balanced in their wide stances. Like they're ready to shove us headfirst into trash cans.

Or perhaps, after a couple decades of conditioning, they assume defensive postures by instinct.

Mark smiles wanly at Pearce. "Grab a seat, Keystone," he says. "We're playing Truth or Dare."

Pearce speaks to Ken. "Your preparations are complete?"

"I need those contact lenses. And the spyware."

"I have them. Come with me, all of you."

He leads us down the stucco steps on the east wall of the pool house. Pabst and Miller fall in behind. In the middle of the lawn between the pool and the mansion, he stops and turns around.

"How about let's see that pass?"

Mark and I look at each other.

"It's dark," I say. "And we had a couple—"

"Pace it off," Mark interrupts.

I glare at him, then walk thirty steps to the north: about sixty-five feet, the distance Ken measured when he reconnoitered the atrium of the Baoli Tower. Broken eggshells crunch beneath my sneakers. I turn back toward the group, mere silhouettes in the light from the sconces on the mansion's colonnade. Sun has moved twenty feet west, toward the pool. Mark has turned to face south.

"Point is moving east between the security checkpoint and the down escalator," Ken says to Pearce. "Relay is visually shielded from security by the sculpture when Grease hits the floor by the information desk."

"I know," Pearce says. "When you're ready."

"Hut," Ken says.

I start walking away from them at a casual pace. A moment later, I hear Sun scream.

I pause for half a second, then turn my body toward the sound of his voice. I rotate my head about thirty degrees less, facing Mark, and spot the mirrored egg four feet off the ground between us, a blur of distorted reflections rocketing through the night air.

I catch the egg with my left hand, about six inches from my waist, and slip it into my pants pocket in a single, isolated motion, keeping the rest of my body as still as possible.

Pabst whoops. I jog back to the group, trying not to smile.

"Helluva throw," Miller says to Mark.

"Fine catch, too." Pearce nods at me. "But you're stiff as a robot. The illusion isn't that you're a mannequin. The illusion is that you're turning to look at the man who screamed. So you're alarmed."

"Okay. Alarmed."

He claps me on the shoulder, then resumes walking toward the mansion. The six of us follow behind. We pass through the brightly lit colonnade, trace the wraparound patio to a side door secured with a keypad lock. Pearce punches in the code, then leads us into a stone stairwell and up to the second floor.

We proceed down a dimly lit hallway with parquet floors and smooth bare walls the color of lemon pith. Pearce stops in front of a set of double doors. He unlocks them with a key from his pocket and strides into what was once a master bedroom, presently repurposed as his office.

The space is a disorienting mash-up of corporate gravitas, yoga retreat, and retro sex den. Glowing paper lanterns shaped like giant gourds hang from the vaulted ceiling. Exposed wooden beams radiate outward to a long, curved wall of multicolored glass bricks.

Pearce steps around his varnished maple desk and sits down in a swivel chair as big as a throne.

"Make yourselves comfortable." He begins tapping on his ergonomic keyboard.

Ken unfurls himself into a cream-colored recliner by a casement window. He cranks the window ajar and snaps open his chrome Zippo to light another Newport. Mark glances around before taking one of the chairs in front of the desk. After pulling the door shut behind him, Pabst stands beside it in his usual grim pose, while Miller lines up seven snifters on a glass bar cart next to an antique grandfather clock.

Sun sits cross-legged against the base of the curved wall, as far as possible from the center of the room. Where he can see everyone, and no one can see him.

I take the other chair in front of the desk. A single-bladed ceiling fan twirls above us, lazily stirring the smoke from Ken's Newport into the rich odor of the cigar butts resting in the abalone shell next to Pearce's mouse pad. Miller delivers the snifters around the room. He puts black leather coasters on the desk in front of Mark and me before setting down our glasses.

Mark shoots me a look like *whoop-de-do* and straightens an

imaginary pair of cuff links at his wrists. Then Pearce leans over his desk and rotates one of his dual monitors to face us.

"A screenshot from Tuesday," he says.

The monitor shows a web page with a chunky, dated interface. The banner at the top reads **National Suspect Database**. The interminable URL begins with justice.gov.

I shake my head. "The NSD is three years old. This looks like an AOL message board."

"Not the worst government website I've seen. Not even bottom three," Mark reassures me. "And they wonder why they're getting lapped by China." He leans forward to read the tiny, all-caps text next to his name on the screenshot. "*Aggravated* assault? Like my shoe was a deadly weapon?"

"You imprisoned a man in a shipping container for twenty-four hours. Here's now." Pearce hits a key to switch browser windows, and the charges beneath Mark's name vanish.

Awe spreads across Mark's face as he stares at the monitor. "Reload it," he says quietly.

Pearce hits a key, and the window clears, then repopulates piecemeal like a bad web page should. I watch the letters of my name appear in the search bar as he types. Then he hits enter, and my file appears. Victor Xiaozhou Li. Age: 24. Ethnicity: Asian. Outstanding warrants: none.

And a tingling sensation spreads from my solar plexus to my fingertips: my American liberty, an elusive memory once ordinary as air. Liberty to return to Los Angeles. To walk the streets without looking over my shoulder. To be Victor Li again.

"How did you do this?" I ask, unable to tear my eyes from the screen.

"It wasn't very easy." Pearce leans back in his swivel chair and cocks an eyebrow. "Nor was it very hard."

"Get thee behind me," Mark mutters.

Pearce picks up his snifter and lifts it in our direction. "Congratulations, gentlemen," he says. "You're almost home."

I lift my curved glass to my lips and sip the clear liquid. My eyes immediately water as intense vapors fill my sinuses. Mark tucks his head into the crook of his elbow as he sneezes, rapidly, twice. He sets his glass back on the desk.

"Got anything stiffer?"

"Not a mezcal fan, I see." The corners of Pearce's mouth turn upward. "This one is a hundred and ten proof. From the salmiana agave, which takes twenty years to reach maturity. A patient people, Mexicans. They appreciate complexity. Traditions that develop over time."

Mark turns to me and says, "Habanero and brimstone."

"We should get some sleep," I suggest, not feeling much appetite for Pearce's esoteric booze and arch stereotypes.

"There's something else I'd like you to see. A news program that aired today." He clicks around with his mouse, calling up another window to the monitor facing us. This one shows a groomed, poised woman in a pantsuit, standing on the familiar set of a distinguished American news show.

Pearce clicks play.

"And now we visit Mexico City, the site of the latest and boldest project in China's global lending initiative."

The woman walks slowly toward the retreating camera as she speaks, marking the rhythms of her words with little taps of her tented fingers.

"Currently under construction by Longdai, a Chinese state-owned conglomerate, the Amistad Airport will be the second largest in the world. Tomorrow, Longdai will host an opening ceremony for its magnetic levitation train. The maglev train, which will be first of its kind in North America, will eventually carry passengers to the airport at speeds upward of two hundred and fifty miles per hour. I sat down with Lai Yixun, the president of Longdai, for an exclusive interview in his Mexico City office."

The shot cuts to the skies above La Reforma. Video footage from a helicopter, closing in on the Baoli Tower: a ziggurat of plate glass tinted black against the sun, jutting into the sky, cuddly as a tiger shark in its killing prime.

The next shot shows the journalist perched on a club chair in an airy conference room. Behind her, floor-to-ceiling windows offer epic views of La Reforma. Across from her sits a fleshy man in a double-breasted suit, a red necktie, and a helmet of slick hair dyed black.

"Mr. Lai," the journalist begins, "your firm, Longdai, is handling every aspect of the construction of the Amistad Airport. Can you explain how this project came to be?"

"Thank you, Ms. Weiss. I appreciate you taking the time to speak with me," Lai says, his English deliberate yet fluid.

"No terp," Mark remarks.

"Harvard Kennedy School," Pearce speaks without looking up from the screen. "Master's in public policy, 2004. Top of his class."

"The Communist Party has built the world's most populous country from a poor, agrarian society into the leading engine of global growth," Lai is saying. "China has more roads, train tracks, airports, and solar arrays than any other country. Now we are sharing our expertise with other developing economies. The Amistad Airport will be the most advanced airport in the world. It is a symbol of China's friendly relations with Mexico."

As he speaks, the camera cuts to another aerial shot, this one of the airport construction site: a fenced perimeter in the desert, tended by an armada of elephantine construction vehicles, all of them painted Longdai orange. The four bow-shaped terminals join end to end to form the shape of a snake, jetways lining the outer arcs. The facade of Terminal One, a great comb of red and gold glass panels, resembles a monstrous crested head, and the maglev track extends from its mouth like a silver tongue. At the opposite end, more than a mile away, the air traffic control tower rises from what might be a snake's tail.

The journalist's voice: "According to Longdai, the snakelike design of the airport pays homage to Quetzalcoatl, a principal deity of the Aztec pantheon: the Feathered Serpent, the god of wind and air. But some critics of the airport project see a Chinese dragon, advancing on Mexico's capital and threatening to devour it."

The next shot is back in the Baoli: the journalist, head atilt, palms pressed in supplication, asks Lai to clarify the relationship between Longdai and the Chinese government.

"You're the president of the Longdai Group, but also a senior member of the Communist Party. How does that work?"

As Lai does his best to explain state capitalism in layman's terms, Pabst nibbles on his cuticles, and Ken lights his thirteenth Newport of the night.

"So you guys don't get Nickelodeon here?" Mark asks.

Pearce clicks ahead in the video progress bar. "Here's the part I want you men to see."

"—at a steep price for the Mexican people," the journalist is saying. "After all, Mexico now owes China more than eleven billion dollars. Meanwhile, the entire airport, including the security checkpoints, will run proprietary Chinese software. Personal data collected by that software will be processed by servers in Shenzhen."

A reaction shot of Lai Yixun: the president of Longdai maintaining a perfect poker face. His lips curl into a bemused smile, and he tips his head forward as if he's talking to a child.

"We have only followed the American example in this case, Ms. Weiss. Your National Security Agency has required tech companies to build secure back doors into consumer products for decades. Did you think that we didn't read the Snowden leaks?"

"Mr. Lai, I do not represent the American government, and

I assure you, we ask them the same tough questions. Right now, we're talking about the high price of the Amistad Airport. What would you say to the Mexican people who are calling for a more modest airport, with a lower debt burden, built by Mexican workers instead of Chinese?"

Lai's eyes narrow above his fixed smile.

"Are you sure it is the Mexican people who are calling for that? And not the State Department or the CIA?"

The journalist shifts in her chair and clears her throat.

"Thousands of Mexican citizens have marched in the streets for months now." As she speaks, still images of the protesters slide across the screen: mouths frozen open, fists held aloft. "Do you have any concerns at all about the popular opposition to your project?"

Lai lets the question hang in the air for a moment before he clears his throat and begins to speak.

"Who knows what incentives these protesters might have received in exchange for representing the American view of their country? No, I have no concerns. I don't think Mexico wants a more modest airport."

The hairs on my forearms stand up as Lai's smile broadens.

"Mexico has lived in the shadow of the United States for decades. In this sense, the Mexican people have much in common with the Chinese. While Americans have enjoyed the fruits of our labor, we have all remained invisible: in a factory overseas, or on the far side of a wall. America has always resisted challenges to this status quo. I believe the expression is 'Stay in your lane'?"

He squares up the camera with the intent gaze of a hypnotist. "I am here to say that China is building roads, not walls. In our journey to global leadership, we have learned much that we wish to share. We say that developing countries can help each other to stand on their own two feet."

His face twists into a grimace that manages to blend pity with disdain.

"It is natural for Americans to feel uncomfortable because their era of predominance is ending. Such is the fate of empires." Then Lai's smile returns as he says, "Perhaps you will learn to handle it gracefully."

Pearce taps the space bar, freezing the smirk on Lai Yixun's face, and leans back into his swivel chair with his arms crossed over his chest. The silence stretches long, marred only by the relentless ticking of the grandfather clock.

Then Mark picks up his snifter, gulps the rest of its contents, and twirls his finger in the air. "Hit me again, Charlie," he gasps. "And make it a double!"

"That was the biggest load of bullshit I've ever heard," Pabst exclaims.

"Rife hypocrisy." Pearce rises from his chair. "But was it not grounded in fragments of truth? Our politicians have insulted the Mexican people with their scapegoating, their fearmongering, their ridiculous wall. Thirty years ago, Americans loved their neighbors. Today, we fear them. The world needs our leadership! Yet we behave like petulant children."

He stops his pacing, puts his palms on the desk, and leans forward to loom over us.

"Well, China's not going to eat our lunch, not yet. Lai talks like he's helping the Mexican people, but all he's doing is lining the pockets of the powerful. It's not too late for us to set the record straight."

He scoots his chair back, picks up something from the floor by his feet, and sets it on the desk: a black box, ornate and sheenless, locked with a padlock. He opens it with another key from his pocket and starts placing items from the box onto the desk. A contact lens case. A thumb drive. Two felt bags—one empty, one full.

"This box was given to me by the first democratically elected president of Angola, in front of their first parliament. African blackwood. The original ebony. Hardest wood there is."

He keeps talking as he shakes the contents of the first felt bag onto the desk. Painite stones—more than twenty. He culls nine, examining them one by one before placing them in the second felt bag.

"Know a thing about Angola? A bloody mess for decades. Insurgencies. Islamists. Mass kidnappings. The Portuguese, the Soviets, the UN—everyone had their turn, and nobody improved the situation by one iota. Locals are mighty slick with a chisel, though."

Pearce pushes the box toward us. I dutifully examine the intricate carvings on the lid. Masks. Spears. Daggers. Snakes.

"I spent three years there on a contract for the State Department," Pearce continues. "Built them an ace army from the boots up. Recruited from every tribe in the country. Trained them, equipped them, made sure they were decently paid. Now it's the safest country in Central Africa. Top destination for foreign investment, too."

Mark puts the tip of his index finger on the box and slides it back toward Pearce. "Cool," he says.

Pearce stares at him for a moment, then shuts the lid of the box and replaces the padlock.

"Y'all think I'm a bag of wind," he says, his wry smile returning. "You want your payday and off you go. Well, you're temps. That's fair. But I still ask you to appreciate the import of your task. This is how the world works, gentlemen. You will free this country from a crippling debt to Chinese overlords as foolhardy and power-hungry as they come."

He directs a withering glare at the frozen image of Lai Yixun.

"He thinks he's already won. But this is still our continent. And we can still laugh last."

23

The two har gow are identical, each dumpling sealed with nine tiny pleats, a hint of pink shrimp visible through the delicate skin. I push one around in my saucer of chili oil and force myself to eat it. Chew mechanically. Swallow dry. I glower at the other childhood favorites on my plate: the egg tart, the fried taro puff, the lotus leaf filled with sticky rice and sausage.

The dim sum from the buffet at Canton Garden, on the mezzanine level of the Baoli Tower, shows exceptional attention to detail. On another day, I might be going back for seconds and thirds, but today, I'm only eating to remain inconspicuous. I set my chopsticks down and glance at Dad's Casio. 10:27. Thank God, almost time for the swap.

I steal another glance at Lijia Nu'erhachi, sitting alone by the windows that overlook the vast atrium of the Baoli. He's watching the hallway to the bathrooms. Making sure the men's is empty before he makes his move.

Lijia's dressed in the jumpsuit and white baseball cap that identify him as a Longdai worker. His jumpsuit is royal blue, the color worn by technicians and engineers. Orange for laborers. Security wears black. He has a pair of rimless glasses on his face and an ID badge clipped to his chest.

He hasn't eaten much of his food, either.

I pour myself more jasmine tea and look through the windows as I sip the fragrant brew. The atrium is quiet. Longdai built the Baoli Tower and occupies twelve floors of its offices. Working weekends is expected when you're building an empire, but today, most of the Longdai staff are at the airport site, seated alongside Mexican dignitaries on bleachers outside Terminal One. The temporary pavilion will offer them a spectacular view of the inaugural arrival of the maglev train in thirty minutes. A livestream will show the event to millions more, including the receptionists and security guards in the atrium, who are following along on the Jumbotron-size screen above the information desk.

At the moment, the Mexican interior minister is making his remarks, muted and subtitled in Chinese. Lai Yixun will speak next. There are a few hundred hard-core protesters there, too, bused by NGAP to the last public road before the airport site. Half a mile from the media cameras, on the outside of Longdai's high perimeter fence, they wave their signs and chant their slogans unseen, unheard, deniable.

Of course, Longdai's not the only company with offices in the Baoli. There are still people coming and going between the main entrance and the elevator bank, which is protected by unmanned turnstiles. The mezzanine level, home to an art gallery, a souvenir shop, and the restaurant where I'm not eating, is open to the public.

A wide staircase curves down from the mezzanine to the information desk. Between the desk and the entrance, there's a sculpture the size of a U-Haul truck. A celebrated Chinese artist received the commission to pay homage to Quetzalcoatl, the Aztec creator god. She used thermal lances to hew her design out of a block of Longdai's proprietary synthetic jade. The titanic result, a lumpy cyan coil, could pass for either a feathered serpent deity or a life-time supply of mint soft serve.

Close to the main entrance, there's another set of turnstiles that restrict access to the building's lower levels, including the under-ground maglev station. When the airport opens and the maglev starts carrying passengers, these turnstiles will accept tickets from a row of electronic kiosks. For now, they only open for select Longdai staffers whose irises have been scanned and entered into a secure database. On the other side of the turnstiles, there's an X-ray machine and a millimeter wave scanner manned by three guards in black jumpsuits.

The escalator beyond the checkpoint descends to the corridor that leads to the maglev platform. And I know from Ken, who knows from Lijia Nu'erhachi, that the first door on the left houses the security center, where more men in black jumpsuits monitor the building's smart surveillance network.

Lijia's domain is behind the next secure door on the left: the digital heart of the Baoli Tower. The server room that hosts Long-dai's computing mainframe.

As I think about it, the few bites I took of my breakfast churn in my stomach, and a mezcal-tinged belch rises to my throat. I close my eyes and think, *Do not puke. Do not puke. Thirty minutes and it's all over.*

Thirty minutes and I'm free.

When I open my eyes, Lijia Nu'erhachi is gone.

I jump up and walk to the bathroom, focusing on putting one foot in front of the other, sweat already beading at my temples. The brightly lit men's is empty except for the last stall, where Lijia has already stepped out of his sneakers. As I enter the stall next to him and lock the door, he hangs his jumpsuit over the partition.

I pull off my suit jacket and start undoing my shirt buttons, fumbling with them as sweat runs into my eyes.

"Gēmenr, nǐ néng bu néng zài kuài yì diǎnr?" he whispers through the partition—*Buddy, think you can move a little faster?*

I don't respond, stay focused on removing my clothes, noting the thick *r* sounds tagged on the ends of his words. A Beijing accent. Ken hadn't mentioned that, but of course, he doesn't speak Chinese, so he wouldn't have noticed. Hopefully it won't matter. If everything goes according to plan, I shouldn't have to speak to anybody while I'm impersonating Lijia Nu'erhachi.

"Gěi nǐ"—*Here you go.* I toss my pants over the partition. Then I don his jumpsuit, still warm from his body, and pull the zipper up to my neck. Put on his shoes and center his white baseball cap over my side-parted hair.

We step out of the neighboring stalls at the same time and look each other over. Lijia and I are about the same height. He's got at least five pounds and ten years on me, but with the clothes, hat, matching haircut, and prosthetic mole, which Ken adhered to my upper lip this morning in the pool house bathroom, fumigating my pores with his cigarette breath, we look passably similar.

"Wǒ de qián, ne?" he asks—*And my money?*

—*In your pocket*, I say.

He pats the suit jacket, extracts an envelope from one of the flap pockets. A grim smile appears on his face as he inspects its contents: twenty five-hundred-euro bills, a business-class ticket for a flight to Madrid, and the felt bag with nine uncut painites in assorted sizes. Stones worth about two million dollars. And now I see the merits of Longdai's payoff method: more tangible than crypto, less bulky than cash.

—*Don't forget these.* He hands me his glasses.

I slip them on, and the world gets a little bit bigger.

—*The server room will be empty?* I ask.

—*I only have one subordinate. I sent him to the opening at the airport site.* Then he points to my hip pocket. —*The authentication token is there. They won't let you through with anything else.*

—*We have a way to get our bug in*, I say. —*You're sure it won't trigger an alarm?*

—As long as it doesn't modify the existing software. I told your colleague many times.

—I wanted to hear it from you, I say.

We look each other up and down one last time. Two men of similar size and shape, similarly serving APEX's agenda. One headed to the heart of the building. The other headed out the front door.

And later today, I'll return home to the United States, while Lijia flees into exile, an enemy of the Chinese state for life.

"Wǒ zǒu le"—*Off I go,* he says, and starts past me, toward the door.

"Nǐ bu zěnme àiguó ma"—*You're not a patriot.* I blurt it out as he passes.

The Chinese word for patriotism is "àiguó": 愛國 in traditional characters. 愛, *to love.* A hand ⺥ that covers ⼍ a heart ⼼ walking slowly 夂. And 國, *country.* Territory 口 defended by a wall 一 and a battle-axe 戈, enclosed by borders 囗. Love: to walk on tiptoe. Country: land protected by weapons.

Lijia turns with his hand on the bathroom door. "Àiguó? Wǒ zǎo méi guó le"—*Love my country? I have no country,* he says. *—I've been here two years, working seventy hours a week. I put in a lot of time learning Spanish, too, but thanks to this Chinopuerto garbage, I can't walk down the street without being harassed. Before Mexico City, I spent three years in Venezuela, building the naval base for the Motherland. My girlfriend and I did video chats for the first year. Now she's married. She has a daughter.*

He pats his pocket. *—If I worked twenty more years, I wouldn't save half this money. You people are setting me free.* He sniffs hard, once, and then produces a pained smile. *—There's Chinese food everywhere in the world.*

And then he's gone, the door swinging shut after him, leaving me alone with my reflection.

I check the time: 10:44. Three minutes to spare before the pass.

I blot my sweaty brow and clammy palms with paper towels. Give myself one last look in the mirror. Dash into the nearest stall and retch out the contents of my stomach. Pinch Lijia Nu'erhachi's glasses out of the toilet bowl and wash them off in the sink. Rinse the sour bile from my mouth. Blot my face again.

Leave the bathroom and proceed down the stairs, a few steps behind Mark, as Sun walks in the revolving front door.

24

I tail Mark to the bottom of the stairs, where he heads toward the main entrance before pretending to notice the Quetzalcoatl sculpture and changing direction to check it out. As I cross the atrium toward the turnstiles that guard the lower levels, Mark strolls around the sculpture with his hands in his pockets, examining it like a tire kicker.

While Mark circles the sculpture, Sun walks right past me, toward the information desk. On my way to the turnstiles, I pause to look at the giant screen. Lai Yixun's giving his remarks now, and I read his signature sound bite in the closed captioning: 其他国家修墙时, 我们修路—*While other countries build walls, we are building roads.* The assembled luminaries deliver subdued applause. Then the livestream cuts to the maglev platform beneath the Baoli.

The station engineer presses a single button on a touchscreen panel, and the electrified loops of conductive metal along the track begin their alternating push and pull of the train's superconducting electromagnets, cooled to 450 degrees below zero.

As I walk up to the turnstile and remove Lijia's eyeglasses, all three guards are raptly watching the live feed of the driverless train floating out of the station, silent and sleek.

I close my eyes for a moment, dilating my pupils so that my irises retract behind the images printed on the contact lenses I'm wearing. When I open my eyes again, my field of vision is ringed by a brown haze. I swipe Lijia's ID badge over the RFID panel on the turnstile and then lean my face into the iris reader. After a moment, it makes a plinking sound, and an LED flashes green, and the glass barriers slide apart with a *shoop*.

On the other side, I put Lijia's hat, glasses, and authentication token in a doggy bowl for the X-ray machine. As I step into the millimeter wave scanner and raise my hands above my head, I notice that I've already sweat through the underarms of my jumpsuit. I curse myself for not doubling up on undershirts, but the guard waves me through without much scrutiny. As I collect my belongings, he returns his attention to the giant screen above the information desk.

All three guards wear garrison caps in addition to their black jumpsuits, lending their getup a military aspect. They're wearing the same black Li-Ning training shoes—emblazoned with the same swoosh-like logo—that I saw in Song Fei's suitcase. Their upright posture and fit physiques mark them as fine specimens of Communist Party 3.0: World Domination Edition. But they also look young. A little green. Like maybe they've never had to use the twenty-thousand-volt stun wands strapped to their belts.

Hope you don't lose your jobs over this, fellas. I silently thank them for paying me so little mind. And I decide to put Lijia's glasses in my pocket instead of on my face before walking to the escalator. Spotting a mirrored egg flying across a bright lobby will be hard enough without them.

That's when Sun screams.

When an epileptic suffers a seizure, they sometimes scream in a very specific way: tonic spasms force air out of their lungs, producing a garbled howl. It's a difficult sound to make on purpose, which is why Sun practiced that exact scream, while imitating the frenetic muscle convulsions that accompany it, dozens of times over the past three days.

But today, at 10:49 on the morning of our foray into the Baoli, instead of simulating a seizure, he makes a completely different noise. A scream that sounds more like a deranged battle cry.

My brain begins the process of freaking out—*What the hell is he doing?*—as my body follows the routine established through relentless rehearsal over the past seventy-two hours. I turn toward Sun, my head rotating somewhat less than my body, and search the air between Mark and me for the mirrored egg.

A larger projectile, one not coated in reflective paint, would be easier to catch. But it would also be easier for the security guards to notice. And it might trigger the smart surveillance cameras hidden throughout the Baoli, which are programmed by machine-learning algorithms to alert the security center of any behaviors that don't fall within the spectrum of observed patterns.

Fortunately, I've gotten pretty good at spotting that mirrored egg. Unfortunately, Sun's behavior has thrown off Mark's aim, and I don't see the egg where I expect it.

When I do spot it—a distortion of the lobby's light, flying through the air at fifty miles per hour—the trajectory is low and wide.

The egg clears the waist-high barrier around the turnstiles by an inch and zooms toward the ground in front of me. I dive without thinking, snatch it out of the air a few inches from the polished granite floor. In the same motion, I roll back to my feet, prepared to fight or flee, my heart thumping in my ears like a subwoofer.

But nobody's looking at me. All three security guards are sprinting across the lobby, drawing their stun wands as they rush the information desk.

Sun is standing on top of it, kicking a computer monitor,

throwing a clipboard, dancing away from the outstretched hands of the two receptionists.

"Xiānshēng, qǐng cóng nàlǐ xiàlái!"—*Sir, please come down from there!*

I watch, stunned, as they grab at his legs, yelling admonitions and entreaties. Then I snap back into my role. Slip the egg into my pocket, snatch Lijia's white cap off the ground, and return it to my head. Tear my eyes away from Sun's performance. Glance out the great glass wall and see Mark speed-walking through the plaza outside the main entrance. Replace Lijia's glasses on my face. Step onto the escalator down.

25

As the escalator carries me deeper into the building, the shouting in the atrium fades, making room for my frantic breathing, my racing pulse. *What the hell is Sun doing?* Why'd he deviate from the plan? If there's one thing I know about Sun Jianshui, it's that he always has a reason.

I take a few slow breaths, reassert control over my fritzing nervous system. Then I twist the egg open in my pocket. Keeping my movements as small as possible, I poke through the dried beans Ken used to match the weight of a chicken's egg and identify the three small devices: a thumb drive, a compact transmitter, and a tiny skin-tone earpiece.

I palm the earpiece into my ear with a motion like a head scratch, then press the power button on the transmitter in my pocket. After a moment's delay, the sound of Ken's outraged voice fills my head:

"—explain to me what the fuck just happened?"

"Is he on here?" Mark. "Grease online?"

"He's not on here, you idiot. If he were, we'd be able to hear the commotion in the atrium!"

"All right, calm the fuck down. Where are you? I'm on the plaza now."

I hear Ken exhale hard through his nose. See, in my mind's eye, his carotid artery pounding along his throat. "South side of the roundabout."

"I see you."

"Point online." I'm walking off the escalator, speaking through clenched teeth, eyeing the cameras hidden in little black domes along the ceiling of the bright white corridor that stretches in front of me. "What the hell is going on?"

"No idea," Mark says. "Your boy flipped the script and went berserk."

"He's not 'my boy.'"

"Yeah, well, anyway," Mark says. "I'm approaching the cab now."

"Did you plant the camera on the sculpture plinth?"

"Yep. You should be able to see the feed already, Wheels."

"I'm looking at it. Grease is handing out beatdowns on these security guards like candy. OH, SHIT."

"Tell me what's happening!" I hiss.

The great sterile tunnel feels interminable, like I'm an electron traveling the polished inside of an iPhone. The only visual exception to the glossy white tiles are the orange banners hung on the walls at eye level, printed with bold white characters. 凝心聚力　和谐共进—*Cohere in heart and join in strength to move forward together harmoniously.* 代表母国　做出贡献—*Make contributions to represent the Motherland.*

And at the far end, walking toward me, a cluster of people: the camera crew that just filmed the departure of the maglev, accompanied by another pair of security guards in black jumpsuits.

"They zapped Grease with one of those wands." Ken's voice. "Looks like he's having his seizure now."

I hear the sound of a car door close as Mark joins him in the taxi.

"They're binding his hands."

"What the hell was he doing?"

"Don't worry about him," Ken says. "You're through the checkpoint, that's all that matters. You need to upload that bug."

I'm walking past the first door on the left, then the long one-way mirror that runs next to it. Song Fei told Ken that there are three or four more guards in the security center, as well as a weapons locker. I keep my gaze fixed forward and try to walk naturally, which feels impossible as soon as I start thinking about it.

"Point? Do you copy?"

"I just passed security. Arriving at the second door now."

"Get in there," Ken says. "They're taking Grease down the escalator."

The steel door to the server room is protected by another iris scanner. I swipe Lijia's badge and present my face. After a moment, an orange light blinks, and six characters appear on the LCD display.

无法读取红膜—*Cannot read iris.*

"Shit shit shit." I close my eyes.

"Point, update."

"It's too bright down here. My pupils are constricted." I turn away from the camera crew, bearing down on me now, and count to ten. When I open my eyes, I see two of the guards from the lobby pulling Sun along the corridor, their hands gripping his upper arms. His head lolls forward as he stumbles between them.

I swipe Lijia's badge again and look into the iris reader as the camera crew passes behind me.

The orange light blinks. The same characters reappear.

无法读取红膜

"Shut 'em tight, Point." Mark's voice. "Lose the specs."

My heart pounds around my rib cage like a mad bat in a phone booth. I squeeze my eyes shut again, harder, until my field of vision goes from dark red to pitch black. Count to fifteen. Swipe Lijia's badge before pulling off his glasses and opening my eyes directly into the iris reader.

The green light blinks and the deadbolt slides out of the jamb. "Lijia xiānsheng, nǐ méishì ba?"

My hand is on the handle. My foot is one step through the doorway. I lift my head to see the two guards thirty feet away, at the door to the security center, Sun still sagging between them. One of the guards is looking at me with a concerned expression.

—*Mr. Lijia, is something wrong?*

I attempt a smile and a Beijing accent as I say, "Wǒ méishìr"— *Nothing's wrong.*

His eyes are narrowing, his head tilting to one side, when Sun falls to the floor next to him. The guard turns away to grab him by the arm again, exclaiming, "Wǒ cào, zhè ge guīdàn"—*Shit, this turtle's egg.*

I push through the door, shut it behind me, and fall back against it.

"Point? Anything? Point? Update."

After a deep breath, I say, "I'm in."

"Sweet heavens to Murgatroyd."

"What was that convo?" Ken says. "Were you IDed?"

"I don't know."

"Get this thing done and get out of there."

"Great idea. Thank you."

My fingers quiet their quivering as I slow my breaths and take in my surroundings. Based on what I'd seen of the Baoli, I expected the server room to look like the engineering deck of the Starship *Enterprise*. The corridor feels like the future, and the train itself resembles a UFO. Everything at the Baoli is bright, shiny, and clean. That is, everything outside the locked doors.

The control room is dark, low-ceilinged, and about half the size it would like to be. Racks bolted up with computers and servers fill the room floor to ceiling, packed in so densely that it'd be hard to access one without making love to another. The rest of the room is stacked with plastic crates containing bundled cords, cables, and power strips. There's a bucket with a mop and a couple jugs of cleaning products tucked in the corner by the door. They look dusty. Everything looks dusty.

A windowless space dominated by gadgets. It reminds me of our storage unit back in Seattle, minus all the human touches: the wall calendars, the turntable, and the cheap Swedish sofa. And when I imagine Lijia Nu'erhachi spending seventy hours a week down here, I see how he fostered such resentment toward Longdai.

I get to my feet and sidle over to his workstation: a desk with a keyboard and a couple of side-by-side monitors. There's just enough space in front of it for a metal stool. I jiggle the mouse. The screen wakes up and asks me to log in. A green LED lights up on a flat gadget above the mouse pad: another RFID reader.

I swipe Lijia's ID badge one last time. Then I pull out his authentication token: a sturdy little device like a pager. Its display shows a nine-digit code, which I type into the number pad on the keyboard.

It works. Both monitors come alive, displaying an incomprehensible array of data in boxy windows of various colors.

"I'm in. I have access to Lijia's computer."

"Load the software."

"Where are you guys?"

"Cruising Reforma. We're heading back to the roundabout to meet you there."

I check Dad's Casio. 10:56. Five minutes until the maglev arrives at the airport: the moment Ken described as "peak distraction" at the Baoli.

"How's the atrium?"

"Two guards back at the checkpoint now."

"And what about Grease?"

I hear Mark and Ken look at each other.

"They'll probably hassle him for an hour and then release him," Ken says.

"It's not that different than if he'd ended up in an ambulance, like we'd planned," Mark says.

"But he didn't follow the plan. Why?"

"Who knows? The man is strange."

"Don't think about that right now," Ken says. "It doesn't change what happens next. You need to upload that bug. Now."

I fish the thumb drive out of my pocket, turn it around in my fingers. One little device, half the size of a poker chip, capable of rearranging the global balance of power.

"We contracted top Israeli programmers to design this spyware," Pearce boasted. "It will embed itself into the local area network and transmit data to us through a back door. It's completely undetectable."

I crouch down and inspect the terminal under Lijia's desk, locate a pair of USB ports on its dusty top. After I insert the thumb drive and minimize the windows, a folder appears on the desktop. It contains one file: an application. I take a deep breath, and then I double-click.

A window appears. A progress bar rapidly fills and empties, fills and empties, above file names scrolling too fast for me to read. And then the window vanishes. Lijia's desktop looks as before.

I eject the thumb drive and put it back in my pocket, feeling numb. Check my watch again. 10:58.

"It's done," I say.

And that's when the alarm sounds: a shrill siren rising in loops, bleating out of speakers hidden who knows where, so loud I fall off Lijia's stool and bonk my head on the server rack behind me. The lights in the control room snap off, replaced by an orange halogen strobe above the door. Mark and Ken start talking simultaneously in my ear, but the shrieking alarm renders their words unintelligible.

And every square inch of my skin goes cold as one thought cuts through the shock: *I'm dead.*

26

quickly grasp the benefits of being dead. For one, I've got no more future to worry about. No more hope, no more fear. Just a head ringing with cacophonous noise and a belly full of rage like fissile plutonium.

Completely undetectable.

Pearce lied.

I scramble to my feet and snatch the mop out of the corner. Make it halfway to the door before skidding to a stop and going back for a jug of cleaning product. A projectile. Slippery. Probably stings the eyes.

I hear Mark and Ken barking like sea lions in my earpiece, but I can't understand a word that they're saying. I switch off the transmitter. Take several rapid, shallow breaths. Grit my teeth and rush out the door.

Orange lights are flashing in the corridor, too, the wail of the siren deafening as it reverberates off the tiles. One guard in a black jumpsuit has just emerged from the security center, thirty feet away, and another one is coming through the door behind him. I drop the mop to the floor, twist open the jug of cleaning fluid, and hurl it at the second guard's feet as hard as I can.

It explodes against the tile. The second guard balks and collides with a third guard, who's rushing out of the door with a shotgun in his hands. As the two of them tumble to the floor, I slip my toes under the mop handle and loft it back into my hands. The first guard is charging at me with his stun wand extended in front of him. Twenty thousand volts at the end of a two-foot baton: less than half the length of my gorgeous mop.

I take one step toward him, drop my hips, and twirl on my front heel with my arms extended, swinging the mop head into his chest with all the torque I can muster.

The wooden shaft snaps in half as he goes tumbling down. I leap past him and sprint toward the spreading puddle of blue fluid where the other two guards are clambering to their feet. I hurl the broken end of the mop handle at them, zigzag toward the wide end of the puddle, and dive into it, sliding a good twenty feet past them on my belly. As I spin onto my feet and start running again, I feel no pain.

Then a *BOOM* fills the corridor like a dynamite blast, and the floor tiles rush up and smack me in the face, and the sound of my own scream fills my ears even louder than the alarm.

And now I feel pain.

I'm writhing onto my ignited back, seeing the third guard pump his shotgun as he takes another step toward me, and thinking, *You better fucking aim well, you better kill me quickly*—when Sun flies out the doorway of the security center feetfirst, connecting with both heels against the side of the guard's head.

BOOM—the gun goes off again, spraying buckshot into the wall, as the two of them crash to the floor in a pile. Sun's up first, his hands still bound behind his back. He moves in a blur through the soap like it's not there, planting his heel on the stock of the gun and sending it sliding across the tiles toward me.

Ten feet behind him, a fourth guard emerges from the security center, another shotgun in her hands.

I'm scrambling toward the gun. The guard is turning toward me, taking aim at my head. Sun is hopping over the empty jug of cleaning fluid, clenching it between his ankles. He kicks his heels up to loft it into the air like a tennis serve, then plants his left foot for a spinning kick with his right—smacking the midair jug with the force of a baseball slugger, sending it rocketing into the face of the fourth guard.

The guard's head snaps back. She falls backward onto the ground, but she keeps hold of her weapon. I'm back on my feet, pumping the slide of my gun and rushing toward her as she raises hers to aim at me again. I dive to the side as she blasts the ceiling behind me, and I fire my gun at the barrel of hers, erring wide, trying to disable her weapon without blowing off her face. And my aim is true, mostly: the gun flies from her hands, clattering against the tile wall. But her scream is audible above the siren, and as she clutches her hands to her chest, I see where a pellet of buckshot tore a hole in her right wrist.

I spring to my feet and pump the slide again. Two of the others are back on their feet, but they raise their hands when I point the gun at them. The one Sun kicked in the head is still facedown on the tiles, his eyes closed, his breath blowing bubbles in the soap.

As I hold the guards at bay with the gun, Sun squats against the wall and fiddles with his left shoe behind his back. He extracts a slender metal object from under the insole: Mark's balisong. Twirls it open and slices the flex-cuffs off his wrists.

Then he pulls the shoe back onto his foot and tries to take the gun out of my hands, but my fingers are gripping it like a vise. He says something in Chinese that I can't discern. I shake my head, tear water blurring my eyesight, nothing in my head but wailing rage.

"You were hit!" he shouts in English.

The guards are cutting their eyes at each other, inching toward us. I steal a glance at my right shoulder, see my blood diffusing through Lijia Nu'erhachi's jumpsuit, staining it black in the flashing orange light. Pain rushes to my throat like a searing blade, and nausea blooms in my gut.

I choke back a gag as I pass him the gun, and he pushes Mark's knife into my hand. He aims from guard to guard as we backpedal down the corridor. When we reach the escalator, they stop at the bottom. The siren and orange strobes recede as we rise toward the daylight of the atrium. Sun keeps the gun aimed at the guards at the base of the escalator. But when I look up, I see the two remaining guards from the security checkpoint waiting at the top, looking down at us with mixtures of fear and menace on their faces, their stun wands held in front of them.

I drum on Sun's shoulder with my good hand. He spins around, aiming upward, and I get behind him, facing down, holding Mark's knife out in front of me. Not much of a deterrent. The three guards at the bottom of the escalator start charging toward us.

"Go!" I push Sun in the back.

BOOM—he fires over the heads of the guards above us, driving them back, then pumps the slide and starts running. I follow, sprinting now, and—*BOOM*—he fires again as we burst into the security checkpoint, blinking and bloody like crazed animals.

Sun flings the shotgun at the guards with plenty of spin, catching one in the gut as the other jumps backward. He dives over the barrier around the turnstile, rolls onto his feet, and sprints toward the entrance. Mindful of my damaged shoulder, I try to hurdle the barrier, but my right foot catches on top and I crash to the granite floor before bouncing up and chasing after him.

The atrium is stunning in its bright silence, the two of us blazing through it like stray demons on a hall pass from hell. A smattering of people lie prone on the floor, one surreptitiously filming us with her phone.

As we hit the revolving doors, I look back to see four guards halfway across the lobby, slowing their steps. A fifth farther back, holding the spent shotgun aloft.

And I come back to life with the realization that they won't leave the building. Days that aren't today, places that aren't the flashing orange corridor, and people who aren't trying to kill me rush back into existence like hailstones from a dark sky. As we spin into the hot mid morning, the last thing I see in the Baoli is the giant screen above the information desk, gone black.

27

turn the transmitter in my pocket back on. "We're on the plaza!" I shout. "Where are you guys?"

"Cross Reforma! Toward the Starbucks!" Ken's voice in my ear. "We're in the alley behind it."

I grab Sun's arm, pull him into the road. We lurch through the traffic in the huge roundabout, a blur of screams and screeching brakes, and sprint across the dingy garden in the shadow of the huge statue of Christopher Columbus. As I run, I close Mark's knife and slip it into the pocket of my jumpsuit.

And as we race through the road on the other side, Longdai's orange helicopter comes thumping around the side of the building, hurtling toward us, blowing Lijia Nu'erhachi's white cap off my head, drowning out the world.

"This way!" I shout at Sun, veering down the side street behind the Starbucks. The taxi's waiting at the corner with its rear door open. Sun dives in first and I'm right behind him, a jumble of limbs in the back seat, the door still ajar as Ken hits the gas.

"What in the flaming bejesus was all that?" Mark exclaims

once we're upright. He's wearing a sombrero so big that his headrest pins it against the roof of the car when he turns to look at us.

Pain radiates through my torso, and I groan in agony as I try to turn my head and look at my shoulder.

"Huàn ge wèizi," Sun says—*Switch seats with me.*

"NOBODY TALKS." Ken is weaving the cab through Colonia Juárez, the older, denser business district south of La Reforma, at a terrific pace. "NOT A FUCKING WORD FOR TEN MINUTES."

We bounce up a curb, tear across a parking lot, zoom into another alley. The orange helicopter has ascended higher above us now, and in the window of sky framed by the rooftops, I glimpse a larger blue model—Mexican police. Cruiser sirens squall from the surrounding roads, fading, doubling, and rising again as Ken flies out of the alley, across three lanes of oncoming traffic, and onto the tree-lined pedestrian path along the median of Avenida Insurgentes.

Sweat pours down my face, my damp skin hot and cold all at once, my mouth choking dry. I look at Sun, and he gestures with his hands. I slide into the left seat as he climbs over me. He tumbles against the door as Ken veers left to avoid a skateboarder. The cab clips a flower kiosk, a bucketful of pink camellias scattering across the hood.

Sun rights himself and cuffs Mark on the shoulder. When Mark tears his eyes away from the horror movie playing in the windshield, Sun makes a wrapping motion with his hands. Mark reaches into the foot well and retrieves the black rubber med kit. Sun pops the latches, locates a pair of forceps, and starts cutting away my sleeve.

Mark puts an open water bottle into my hand, catches my frantic eyes with his. "Easy, pal," he says. "You'll be okay."

"I said nobody talks!" Ken hisses through clenched teeth. "I need to hear the sirens. And keep your goddamn faces away from the windows!"

Mark sits forward and raises his hands like, *All right already.*

Ken takes a hard right and Sun smashes into me, igniting a fresh explosion of pain in my shoulder. The cab careens off the median. Sun shoots a glare in Ken's direction, then reopens the kit on the seat between us and fingers through its extensive contents. He plucks out a tube the size of a glue stick and holds it in front of me. I have to mop the sweat out of my eyes with the cuff of my sleeve in order to read it: MORPHINE AUTO-INJECTOR.

I nod to him, my breath still pumping shallow and fast. He pops off the red cap, presses the other end into my thigh, and depresses the plunger with his thumb, a pinch like a bee sting.

Then he's back in the kit, selecting another packet. Tearing it open: a spongy white square. He reaches past me, grabs my seat belt, and buckles it around me. Buckles his own. Pulls a tongue depressor out of the kit, slips it between my teeth.

I bite right through that fat popsicle stick when he presses the square sponge against the ridge of my shoulder blade. I'm still spitting balsa fragments out of my mouth when the fat warmth of the morphine hits my heart and flutters my eyelids.

Sun takes the water bottle out of my hand, pours some into my mouth, some over my head and face. He leans forward, his hand still clamped on my shoulder.

"He will go into shock," he says to Ken.

"I don't give a single fuck," Ken barks. "I said don't talk!"

We're fishtailing around Glorieta de los Insurgentes now, filling the air with burnt rubber and fried clutch. He straightens out in time to rocket across the huge traffic circle onto Avenida Chapultepec.

"Drive smooth so I can help him. Or you will pay a price," Sun says in his matter-of-fact manner.

Ken's eyes snap to Sun's face in his rearview for a fraction of a second. Then he leans forward and looks up at the helicopters. The cruiser sirens sound more distant now.

"We'll lose these birds under the Periférico in five minutes," he says. "If you can shut the fuck up."

"Five minutes," Sun confirms.

Ken slams his foot on the accelerator.

Sun sits back and wraps his right hand around his grab handle, his left hand still squeezing the vortex of pain in my shoulder.

Minutes pass in a patchy fog, blackness ringing my field of vision, my eyelids popping open each time Ken swerves from lane to lane. When I next surface from the warm bath of opiate haze, we're on the lower level of the Periférico, the ring road that encircles Mexico City. Sun and Mark are watching the orange and blue helicopters through the blur of load-bearing columns. And then they disappear from view as we sink deeper underground.

Ken merges into the left lane, pulls us into the lee of an eighteen-wheeler. Mark rolls down his window, throws his sombrero out of it, and climbs halfway out of the car with his feet on the seat. I hear him pawing the roof above me, pulling off the decal spray-painted with one set of taxi registration numbers, revealing another. Then he drops back into the car, rolls up his window, and attaches a mesh sunshade to it with a suction cup.

Sun affixes similar shades to the rear windows. I slip back into my drooly reverie. Dad's voice echoes through my head.

"Zhǐyǒu guòqù de huíyì néng ràng wǒmen tòngkǔ. Zhǐyǒu duì wèilái cúnyí shí wǒmen cái huì hàipà."

—Pain only exists in our memories of the past. Fear only exists in our doubt of the future.

Car sounds, sharp words, the reverberations of driving underground, the brightness of the day, the city morphing into hills shrouded in cloud. Mark saying, "Supposed to go unnoticed . . . plastered all over the news . . . rest of our pathetic lives in a hole underground"; Ken saying, "Take it up with Pearce . . . cameras in those birds . . . probably burned me, too."

And I'm laughing a little to myself thinking, *Mole people, even worse than raccoons*, when—OUCH—pain jolts me awake like a hatchet smacking my right shoulder.

I blink my teary eyes open, unhappy noises leaking out of my mouth. Sun shows me an angled pair of tweezers holding a tiny object: an oblong ball like a lead M&M. My right shoulder is bare now, the sleeve of Lijia's jumpsuit and my white T-shirt a mess of bloody fabric on the seat.

"One more ball," he says.

"They shot me," I murmur. "With a shotgun."

"Not well," he says. "Most of the balls missed. Two stopped against your, ah, jiānjiǎgǔ."

"Scapula."

"Try to relax." He sticks another tongue depressor between my teeth, then dives back into my shoulder with his tweezers.

"IT'S NOT THAT BAD," I scream.

Mark casts an alarmed eye back at me.

"Nǐ gànmá zuò zhème duō"—*Why are you doing all this?* I wheeze at Sun. —*You didn't have to be here.*

He studies me for a moment before saying, "Wǒ xiǎng huánqīng wǒmen zhījiān de zhài"—*I want to settle the debt between us.*

—*You think that's possible?*

—*My marriage with Lianying is fake. It's only for the green card.*

He pauses, and my mind goes red hot as I realize what's coming next.

—*But I have feelings for her. I cannot talk about it with her until you and I have reconciled.*

And it occurs to me that this must be the moment he's been waiting for. The moment when the sociopath who murdered my father expects me to say we're cool.

I shake my head.

—*She pities you,* I mutter. —*Nothing more.*

He stares at me without reaction. Then he turns back to the kit, extracts another individually wrapped syringe, and holds it in my face: HEMOSTATIC GRANULES WITH APPLICATOR.

"This is necessary to stop the bleeding," he says. "It will also hurt."

He places his left palm on my back, pushing me toward the door, and inserts the applicator into the first of my two wounds. A galaxy of pink stars spools across my vision, and the stars become a flurry of black snow, and then the flurry becomes a sheet.

When I wake again, Sun is tapping my right hand with his left. He catches my eye and shakes his head very slightly. Then he draws a character with his index finger on the back of Mark's seat. 敬—jìng—*respect*. And then, beneath it, 言—yán—*speech*. Respect speech? What? I close my eyes, shake the druggy fog from my head. It's not two characters, but one: 警—jǐng.

Warn.

I look back to his face, but he's looking out the window now, his hands folded in his lap. I gingerly push myself upright in my seat. Most of my bare shoulder is covered with a patchwork of gauze and tape, the rest of me prickled to gooseflesh by the powerful AC. The dull ache spikes into razors when I try to move my right arm, so I fish around with my left, find the bottle of water in the pocket of the door. Take a sip, check the time: 12:02.

It's been an hour since we left the Baoli, and now we're on some curving dirt road, flanked on either side by a hilly landscape of waist-high shrubs and modest pines.

"Where are we?" I ask.

"State of Mexico," Ken says. "Out of the range of DF cops. We'll lie low here until we can make contact with Keystone."

He takes a right onto another dirt road, this one even narrower. The cab's suspension bounces us around as we climb higher into the hills, deeper into the clouds. A quarter of a mile later, we come to a stop in front of a cattle gate across the road.

Ken cuts the motor, pulls the keys, and hops out.

"Motherfuck," Mark says. "Is this it? Why'd he park so far?"

I look forward between the front seats. The gate looks twenty feet wide. Ken parked us sixty feet away from it.

Mark pulls the handle of his door just enough to pop the latch. I glance at Sun, see him do the same.

Ken's arriving at the gate now, glancing back at us, pulling something from his pocket. And despite the drug haze and the pain, the next five seconds play out in my head as clear as crystal.

"Go go go go go," Mark is saying, and I'm summoning some final reserve of strength to push open my door and run a dozen steps before the pink-and-white Hyundai explodes.

28

The blast launches me airborne.

Gravity slams me back down.

I taste dirt and scream, coil reflexively into a ball. Then I spot an object dropping out of the sky. Roll away an instant before it smashes into the earth beside my head.

A brick of transparent plastic, its cracked surface printed with bold black letters: TAXI.

Ringing in my ears. The crackle of flame. The creak and pop of settling metal. I push the ground away, climb to my knees, and peek through the shrub between me and the car. On the other side of the flaming hull, I see Sun Jianshui on the ground, motionless and prone.

Walking toward him from the gate is Ken, pistol drawn.

I drop flat, hyperventilating fast and shallow. Mark and Sun saw it coming. They saw the holes in Pearce's polemics and Ken's bogus plan. I was never expected to make it out of the Baoli. That was why Sun, instead of faking a seizure, got himself escorted to the security center: so that he could help me escape. That was why Mark lent Sun his knife. And they knew Ken would try to eliminate us, so they stayed alert even after we made it out of the city. Mark anticipated the car bomb when he saw how far Ken had parked from the gate.

Really impressive. Right over my head. But not quite enough to stop the same old story from playing out. The bad guys still win, and who writes history?

Fury floods my veins. I steel myself and crawl back to my knees. Ken's approaching Sun in a crouch, his head on a swivel as he scans both sides of the road. I reach into my pocket for Mark's balisong.

It's not there.

And the last hour flashes through my head. The helicopters, the sirens, the med kit. Sun tweezing shotgun pellets out of my shoulder. Further back. Pouring water over my head. Reaching across me to fasten my seat belt.

"Hey, Ken!" Mark steps into view on the other side of the cattle gate, a couple hundred feet down the road, just out of range of pistol fire. His hands raised in surrender. "Let's talk it over!"

Ken wheels around to aim at him and freezes mid-turn, twisted into an arc, as the balisong handle pops out of his side.

And now I see Sun on his knees, left hand on the ground, right hand extended in the follow-through of his expert throw.

Ken howls, his body contorting. Hops twice to his right as if he could still dodge, his arms held awkwardly at shoulder height, his neck craning down to see what stung him.

And he seems to see the knife and remember the gun in his hands in the same instant, swinging it to aim in Sun's direction.

Almost in time.

Sun's first kick, a crescent right like the crack of a whip, catches Ken's wrist and sends the pistol flying. His second, a roundhouse left, snaps across Ken's face and sends him staggering back. Sun quicksteps to stay with him. Yanks the knife out of Ken's side.

Ken manages to lift his hands a few inches, palms open. He's saying, "I didn't have a—" when Sun slashes the knife across his throat before the word "NO" can make it from my mind to my mouth.

A moment later, I'm standing over Ken's burbling, convulsing body as Sun searches the bushes for the pistol.

Mark limps over, takes one look at the car's shattered windshield, and then abruptly grips his knees and starts puking.

Sun returns from the bushes with the gun in his hand.

"Are you injured?" he asks Mark.

Mark shakes his head, tries to speak, retches again.

"He's not good with broken glass," I mutter.

Sun rests a hand on Mark's back and says, "You did well." Then he kneels next to Ken and starts going through his clothes. "He planned to leave here without the taxi. There must be another vehicle." He pulls a ring of keys from a pants pocket. Then he extracts Ken's wallet and tosses it to me.

It bounces off my chest and falls to the ground as Sun walks toward the gate.

Mark spits a final time into the dirt and then joins me beside the body.

"Holy hell," he says.

"You knew this was going to happen," I say. "You gave Sun your knife."

"Would've told you. Didn't think you could keep it together." He tips his chin toward Sun. "He agreed."

"How'd you know?"

"Like Longdai has payoff videos floating around on their LAN? Horseshit." He shakes his head. "Pearce is after something else."

Ken's eyes have stopped rolling now, and aside from his twitching hands, his body is still.

"You played along anyway."

"I felt we had some advantages. They clearly thought we were morons. Anyway, what choice did I have?" He scowls down at Ken, then turns to Sun, who's walking back from the gate. "Find a ride?"

"Can you drive a motorcycle?"

"You're kidding me." Mark's palms go to his temples.

"No, I am not kidding you."

"What kind of bike?"

"Honda." He closes his eyes for a moment. "CBR600RR."

"There's no way three of us are going anywhere on a crotch rocket like that."

"There is yes way." Sun tips his head at me. "He is light. I am lighter."

Mark studies the ground for a minute. Then he says, "I'll ride to the next town, swap it for a car, and come back to get you guys. Should only take an hour."

Sun shakes his head. "We leave together."

"You think the three of us will make it a mile? After what we just pulled?"

"They will expect us to be leaving the city, not entering it."

Mark's face twists into an incredulous expression. "Let me get this straight. You want to ride threesies on a sport bike *back into Mexico City?*"

Sun nods. "If we want to hide, we need local help. Our local help is with Juliana. Is that incorrect?"

"No fucking way!" Mark says. "I don't care about your hard-on for big sis. We're not going back into the city. That's my only offer. And you can't ride without me."

Sun says, "I can learn," and turns to start walking back toward the gate.

"Wait a minute!"

Mark reaches for Sun's right hand, the one holding the keys, and Sun whips around, striking Mark's forearm downward with his palm. He feints a kick and Mark dodges back, making fists. Sun draws Ken's pistol from his waistband and pulls the slide to chamber a round.

"HEY!" I step between them and raise my good hand like, *Cool it*. "Nobody's shooting anybody! Sun's right: we need local help. We can't run with no cash, no clothes, no provisions."

I give Sun a hard look. After a beat, he lowers the gun. I turn back to Mark.

"If there are roadblocks, we don't know if we're inside or outside. We have to hope that we can make it to Art and Jules without being noticed."

Mark's face stays mad. I see the freshly broken thing within him: the thin hope that he'd emerge from this ordeal unscathed and paid. Now he's calculating his odds on the road on his own. How well was he photographed at the Baoli? If he splits now, will he ever see his share of Pearce's money? He grabs Ken's wallet off the ground, snatches out the bills, and counts them. Flings them back to the ground and screams a four-letter word. Puts his hands back on his knees and stares at his right foot as he taps it to a rhythm that only he can hear.

Then he bends over and gathers up the bills that haven't already blown away on the breeze.

"I get the helmet. And no tickling." He jabs a finger in Sun's face. "You know how to lean?"

The worst part is next, when I have to ditch the jumpsuit and steal Ken's jeans. His shirt is ruined with blood, so I end up wearing Sun's suit jacket over my bare skin. I ride between the two of them, my left hand wrapped around Mark, my right limp at my side, Sun perched behind me on the rear cowl.

The two miles of bumpy dirt road are brutal, the pain in my shoulder jagged and intense. When we hit the paved road again, the relief is exquisite. Adrenaline washes out of my blood, and I slip back into a warm morphine muddle. Mark takes it slow, drafting trucks, keeping toward the center of traffic clumps. It's hard not to feel conspicuous. But most of our fellow drivers seem determined to avoid looking at us anyway.

At the city's edge, we hit a straightaway with a roadblock of federales: camouflage jeeps fronted by officers with tactical helmets and M16s, waving cars to the shoulder. But as Sun predicted, they're only hassling people headed out. Mark guns the bike, and we rocket past the line of traffic.

Then we're back in DF, rolling down backstreets toward the poorer eastern neighborhoods.

The city is eerie, the streets strangely quiet. People seem more glued to their screens than usual. We pass a few storefronts and lobbies with crowds gathered around TVs. I feel Mark and Sun notice it, too, an alertness to the difference in the air. The knowledge that we must have caused it.

But we don't stop. Too risky. We don't find out why DF is on lockdown until we arrive at Art's cousin's restaurant. Pozolería Urbana, on Vicente Guerrero, in Iztapalapa.

29

It seems that every restaurant in Mexico City has a flat-screen TV prominently mounted on the wall facing the door, showing not the Pumas game but a slideshow of the food on the menu. Just in case you're a passerby with a weakness for low-res temptation. Or you horfed your enchiladas so fast that you forgot what they looked like.

Pozolería Urbana is no exception. At the moment—around four in the afternoon, five hours after our incursion into the Baoli—the restaurant is closed, the lights are off, and all of the windows are shuttered against prying eyes and the broiling sun. Jules, Art, Sun, Mark, and I sit dispersed around the dining area, isolated by the grudges that divide us. We're all watching the TV above the service counter, which is mirroring Jules's phone over the Wi-Fi. She's tapping through livestreams from every major news station on the continent.

They're all showing the same thing.

"For centuries, we have tolerated a world order in which the richest countries exploit those who have less. All in the patronizing guise of Enlightenment."

Lai Yixun stands at a white podium, the bright sun casting lens flare off his diamond tie clip. His epic backdrop is the multicolored facade of Terminal One. When I glimpsed the live video of this speech on the Baoli Jumbotron this morning, I assumed he was speaking Mandarin. But apparently English remains the lingua franca between China and Mexico.

"The powerful countries say, 'We grew wealthy by burning fossil fuels, but *you* must not do so because they pollute too much. We achieved hegemony using nuclear weapons, but *you* must not develop them because they are too dangerous.' These powerful countries consider themselves to be 'exceptional.'"

He does air quotes with his fingers, a wry smile on his face.

"Today, China demonstrates a different model of global leadership. Instead of withholding our technologies, we share them with—" Lai pauses mid-sentence as a man in a black suit rushes up to him, wraps his hand around the foam tip of the microphone, and whispers in Lai's ear.

Each time I see it, I think about where I was at that exact moment. Perhaps in the atrium of the Baoli, falling on my face after failing to hurdle the barrier around the turnstiles. Or still down in the corridor, sliding on my belly through a puddle of Pine-Sol.

Lai's face screws up, his aplomb replaced first by disbelief, then rage. He storms away from the podium. Murmurs spread through the crowd as a third man takes his place and says something about technical difficulties, postponement of the ceremony, please cease all recordings—but nobody's listening. The cameramen aren't even filming him anymore.

They've refocused on the maglev train, a sleek rocket now sliding into view behind him. Racing across the desert at 280 miles per hour. Brisk and smooth as mercury.

Not slowing down.

The screams begin before the crash, but it all happens so fast that I don't notice that sympathetic detail until CNN replays the footage in slow motion. First: lots of screaming voices, rendered low and bloaty by the stretching of the sound waves. Next: the silver train folding upon itself like an inchworm as it smashes into the station. The shock wave generated by the impact shatters the glass walls of the terminal in a spectacular diagonal progression. The middle of the train, arching upward, obliterates the grand facade of multicolored panels. And then gravity catches up to the train's tortured joints, and it tips toward the camera, snaps in half, and crashes onto its side, a final row of glass fountains erupting from its windows.

Mark is squeezing his eyes shut, cupping his hands over his ears.

"Must we, Mother?" he moans.

"Shut up," Jules says. "They're about to show a statement from the Chinese Foreign Ministry."

We've been sitting here for two hours now, squabbling like ill-tempered cats, absorbing each new development like a punch to the kidneys. I'm back in my own clothes, which Jules transported here, along with the rest of our stuff, from Hotel el Paraíso. There's an improvised sling around my right arm and an unfinished bowl of tofu pozole on the table in front of me. My appetite made an appearance as the morphine wore off. But I lost it again when Al Jazeera broke the news of the Chinese aircraft carrier disembarking from the naval base in Venezuela, cruising toward the Gulf of Mexico.

Mark's sitting alone at a table in the far corner of the restaurant. He's finished his pozole as well as two thirty-two-ounce bottles of Pacífico, and he's working on a third. Jules and Art share a table on the opposite side, and Sun's sitting cross-legged on the linoleum, leaning against the wall, his palms rested on his knees.

Art's dad, Rafa, is faceup on the kitchen floor, snoring gently. The family resemblance is striking, except that Rafa is several inches shorter, and his long hair is blown out and streaked with bleach. When he lay down half an hour ago, I expressed some surprise that he was capable of knocking off for forty winks in the middle of an international crisis.

Art shrugged his giant shoulders and said, "Siestas reduce stress."

Ken's sport bike is blocking the locked door. His suppressor pistol sits on the table in front of Art, along with Mark's balisong and a long-barreled revolver. When we staggered in two hours ago, coated in layers of dried blood and dust, Art pointed this revolver at our heads while Rafa emptied our pockets. Jules stood behind them, her arms crossed over her chest.

Then Jules sat us down in the dining room, showed us the shocking footage of the train crash, and explained that she'd be calling the shots from now on. I hadn't given her my real crypto account number when I called her from the pool house, but I had done so four nights earlier, when I called her from the hotel. She transferred the entire balance to a crypto wallet of her own on Wednesday after reaching Art on the phone.

He'd quoted her the modest sum of three hundred thousand pesos to provide a hideout for three hired guns on short notice. Instead of agreeing, she gave him my share of the APEX money—at current rates about ten times what he'd asked.

"She said that your recent behavior had been extremely annoying, and that she'd feel better if I had that money instead of you," he told me, smiling smugly and turning his palms up like, *Who am I to argue with that?*

I stared from him to Jules with my jaw hanging open. He placed the tofu pozole in front of me, as well as a cloth napkin and a wooden spoon. Then Jules explained that she'd transferred him Sun's share of the crypto, too, when Longdai released our surveillance photos an hour ago. The stakes had gone up, she explained, now that we were the most wanted fugitives in the country. As for Mark's share, she said she'd decide what to do with it later.

Mark took it poorly. First he bit the side of his thumb so hard I could see it turn white. Then he struck a conversational tone.

"It seems we've gotten blurry on the boundaries here," he said. "You aren't *my* sister, or *my* banker, or *my* hot ticket to citizenship. And frankly, all this nuanced family beefing is causing me a migraine. So how about you hand me back my knife and transfer me my goddamn cyber peanuts, and I bid you a permanent adieu?"

Jules shook her head. "You know where we're hiding. If you take off and get caught, how do I know you won't give up our location?"

"Who said anything about me getting caught? I was in and out of the Baoli in fifteen minutes, wearing a hat and sunglasses! I wasn't down in the tunnel, playing shotgun hot potato like these buffoons."

Instead of answering, Jules pulled out her phone and queued up the surveillance photos on the restaurant's TV.

Intruders A, B, and C. Longdai's smart surveillance algorithms had reconstituted thousands of images from the Baoli's security cameras into mug shots. Intruder A—that's me—in Lijia's jump-suit, straight on, brightly lit, on a plain white background. Sun is Intruder B, looking extra severe in his navy blue suit.

Intruder C is Mark in his tourist garb. The software that amalgamated the images had managed to digitally remove his sunglasses. His eyes in the photo are a void gray instead of green. But the pizza-slice scar on his cheek is plain as day.

Mark stared at the photos for a long minute. Then he shot a death glare at Jules, marched behind the bar, and helped himself to his first Pacífico.

He downed about a third of it as we watched the crash a second time. I saw him cringe as shards of glass rained out of the desert sky.

"It could be a coincidence," he said. "It was the first time they ran the train, right? Or maybe we were sent to make a scene at the Baoli, create a diversion while someone else—"

"Uploaded a virus?" I interrupted him. "One that messed up the operating system of the magnetic track? You think someone else did that?"

He shot me an irritated glance, then quickly looked away. *Pearce is after something else*, he'd said as we stood above Ken's dying body.

I was still digesting the fact that he'd gone along with the plan anyway, and never breathed a word about his suspicions to me.

I glowered from him to Sun. His face was impassive, as usual, and he was pressing the pads of his thumbs into the wiry muscles at the base of his neck. One train crashed, one throat slashed, one country pushed to the brink of invasion, and Sun Jianshui was massaging his pressure points. And as Jules changed the channel and the maglev train reappeared, whole again, racing toward Terminal One again, I saw Ken dropping to his knees in the road, blood gushing from the thick scarlet line across his throat, his face frozen in a mask of shock.

The image has replayed over and over in my head for the past two hours, as the world waits for China's response, as the mayor of Mexico City declared a lockdown until "los fugitivos que perpetraron esta atrocidad puedan ser encontrados"—*the fugitives who perpetrated this atrocity can be found.*

So much for keeping my head down and surviving in the shadows. Nobody in Mexico City will mistake me for qīngtíng diǎnshuǐ—the dragonfly that skims the water's surface.

Now I'm the cannonball that obliterated the pond.

"Look, if you wanna be in charge? You need to make a plan," Mark is saying to Jules. "We can't just sit here until the SWAT team smokes us out. We have a very distinctive combination of complexions, okay? Someone probably IDed us when we rolled up!"

"Iztapalapans don't like talking to cops," Art says. "Anyway, most of the people around here hate the airport."

"Oh, great." Mark kicks over a chair. "So we're safe as long as we never, ever leave our cozy pozole prison."

"Will you please shut the fuck up?" Jules's eyes are fixed on the screen. "We need to hear this."

"Shit," I'm saying at the same time. "Shit!"

The spokesman for the Chinese Foreign Ministry is speaking over a photograph of Lijia Nu'erhachi, looking haggard.

"—a Longdai engineer who was apprehended while attempting to board a flight to Spain. Mr. Lijia confessed to accepting payments from foreign agents in exchange for access to restricted areas of the Baoli Tower. It is now understood that these foreign agents introduced a software virus that caused the crash of the maglev train."

The coverage cuts back to the spokesman, who is reading from a script at a drab podium flanked by massive Chinese flags. As he speaks in Mandarin, CNN pipes in simultaneous interpretation into English. "Mr. Lijia confirmed that he received payments from the three intruders whose attack on the Baoli Tower was captured by surveillance cameras earlier today. We are now releasing the surveillance footage in its entirety. According to Mr. Lijia, these foreign agents were operatives of the United States of America."

After a weighty pause, the spokesman continues, reading from his notes in a monotone that the interpreter matches. "This cowardly attack is a flagrant insult to the people of both Mexico and China. Unfortunately, we can observe that these actions are consistent with decades of arrogant American interference in the affairs of sovereign nations. Our joint investigation is ongoing, and we will leverage all necessary resources to commensurately respond to this nefarious atrocity."

The Foreign Ministry spokesperson squares his papers against the podium and hits the camera with a withering look.

"The People's Republic of China is not intimidated by the aggressions of a clumsy empire," he concludes. "Fire will be fought with fire."

Then the feed goes dead, replaced by CNN's Crisis Coverage

team: three star anchors sitting around a curved desk, pale-faced and stunned.

"¡Diosito lindo!" Arturo exclaims. "This is some shit right here."

"You should get out of here," I say to Jules. "You don't have to be part of this."

"That was true on Tuesday, too, Victor. I didn't have to come down here, did I?"

"The stakes have gone up, like you said. We are walking dead, Jules! None of us will ever escape this. But you can go home right now."

"I know that, okay? But I wouldn't want to miss your theatrical debut." She turns back to the TV screen, which is showing newly released surveillance footage from the Baoli. I'm walking down the stairs from the mezzanine, wearing Lijia's blue jumpsuit, haloed by a yellow circle labeled INTRUDER A.

"Jules, this isn't a joke! You need to go while you can," I say. "I never should've involved you in the first place."

Now she turns away from the screen to scowl at me. "Wow, Victor, that is so patronizing! You're excused from deciding anything for me!"

She stands up now, crosses the room, and sits down at my table to berate me some more. "You know something, Victor? You spend a lot of time stewing in the past, but you're not the only one with regrets! I could've gone with you to that house in Pasadena. I could've said, 'Hey, maybe let's call the cops instead of shooting each other in the leg.' But instead I threw you my car keys and said I wanted out. Well, now I want in. You and Sun are the only family I've got. I'm not going to run away like you always do. I'm not going to abandon you just because you have less common sense than a lemming."

I open my mouth, but for a moment, nothing comes out. Then I say, "You married the guy who killed our father, and *I'm the one lacking common sense?*"

Jules sets her jaw and presses her lips together hard. Her nostrils flare as she takes a deep breath, and I see her choosing her words.

"I chose to forgive Sun, and now I have a friend I can always count on. What can you say for yourself about the choices you've made? Look where they've gotten you!"

I'm fumbling for another retort when Mark cuts in.

"I hate to interrupt Hanukkah," he says, "but this may be important."

We turn to the TV, which is now showing a split-screen interview. In one panel, there's the same poised journalist who so recently spoke with Lai Yixun in a conference room at the Baoli Tower.

In the other panel is Niles Pearce.

30

This brazen accusation from the Chinese Foreign Ministry is an insult to the American people," Pearce is saying. "Frankly, Ally, I'm astounded."

I'm on my feet now, stepping closer to the screen. Niles looks a lot like his younger brother, but his blond hair is longer, and his eyes are blue, not gray. The chyron at the bottom of the frame reads: SENATOR NILES PEARCE III (R-MO).

"The United States government has not authorized any operations in Mexico City related to Longdai and their extravagant airport. As chairman of the Senate Intelligence Committee, I would know!"

"Senator, the Chinese Foreign Ministry has released surveillance footage of three men staging a dramatic attack on the Baoli Tower. A Longdai engineer has confessed to taking bribes from American operatives. If the United States isn't behind today's attack, who is?"

Niles Pearce clasps his hands in front of his chest. "This train crash only took place a few hours ago. Before jumping to conclusions, let's take a look at what we know and what we don't know. A visual spectacle—with zero casualties, let's not forget. Then, almost immediately, a confession from one of Longdai's own engineers. And the footage of these 'intruders,' the so-called 'American operatives'—" Now it's his turn to do air quotes. "Do those men look like SEAL Team Six to you?"

The journalist blinks rapidly. "I'm not sure I follow, Senator."

"Ally, this train crash has all the hallmarks of a false flag attack. We know that Lai Yixun is a student of history. The Mukden Incident: a pretext for the Japanese invasion of Manchuria. The Gleiwitz Incident: that's how Hitler took Poland! Now, consider the net result of this train crash. A Chinese carrier steaming toward the Cantarell oil field. If you're a Chinese expansionist, I'd say this outcome looks a lot like Christmas."

Niles Pearce shrugs his shoulders and opens his hands on either side of his face. He has the same boyish smile as his brother, the same slight drawl that has him pronouncing the *h* in his "whats." He seems to be enjoying the opportunity to perform on camera.

The journalist doesn't share his upbeat tone. "That's quite a statement, Senator. Is it fair to say that you categorically deny American involvement in the maglev crash?"

Pearce nods solemnly. "I assure you, the United States government had no role in this incident."

"One last question, Senator. What can you tell us about the reports of increased activity at naval bases in Louisiana and Texas? Is the United States preparing a military response to the Chinese carrier group headed to the Gulf of Mexico?"

"That's a question for the president, Ally. But I will say this: the United States has always stood up for the sovereignty of our fellow democracies."

"Unbe-fucking-lievable." Mark springs to his feet, starts pacing around, his hands flying up to his head. "These frat boys are trying to start a war."

Jules hits mute on the stream and fixes Mark with a puzzled stare. "What do you mean, 'these frat boys'?"

"The guy who hired us to plant the bug was his brother," I say. "Whitney Pearce. He's a security contractor."

Mark rests his elbows on the bar and presses the heels of his hands into his eye sockets. "Who the hell names their kids Niles and Whitney, anyway?"

"You're saying Niles Pearce knows what you did? And he just lied about it on national TV?"

"Oh, Niles knows all right. Unless their family is as dysfunctional as yours," Mark says. "First Whitney sends us on a suicide mission to sabotage the Chinese. Now Niles spreads the theory that China is running a false flag. Each side thinks the other crossed the line first."

"So he didn't lie," I say. My skin goes cold, and the truth tightens around my skull like a vise. "He said the government wasn't involved, and they're not."

"The president is a dove. He would never green-light an operation like this," Mark says. "The Pearces are hawks. Neocons. They're freelancing."

"Niles Pearce ran for president, too." Jules stands up now, her hands falling limply to her sides. "He got thrashed in the primaries."

Art's face screws up into a grimace of disgust. "Are you saying that country-club cornball and his brother planned this whole shit show to provoke your president?"

Mark nods. "Hundred to one, the president has no clue what's going on. From his view, this is a Chinese power grab," he says. "He'll retaliate by trying to kick them out of Mexico. That's what Pearce wants. Everything he said to us was a lie! Buying painite, exposing corruption, planting spyware—it was all a ruse to trick both sides into a fight."

I shake my head in disbelief. "They care that much about the Monroe Doctrine?"

"It's not the Monroe Doctrine. It's the money." For the first time since I met him, Mark looks truly appalled, and he speaks with no trace of humor in his voice. "They're drumming up business."

Jules looks at him with a quizzical expression. "Elaborate."

"If there's a war in Mexico, the United States will need contractors like APEX to stabilize the country. Secure convoys, tactical advisers, green zones. Hundreds of millions in taxpayer dollars. The fun's over in Iraq and Afghanistan." He turns to her with this bewildered look on his face. "Whitney Pearce wants a new playground."

"Well!" Art hops up and strides toward the kitchen. "I think I'll have one of those Pacíficos. Anyone else?"

"Yo también," I say.

"Make it three." Jules turns back to Mark. "So we go to the US embassy. Tell your version of the story."

He shakes his head. "End up in prison."

Her eyebrows go up. "Not worth it? To stop a war?"

"Don't you get it? Nobody will believe us. It's his word against ours." He starts pacing the room again, his voice filling up with spite. "That's Pearce's play: the *false* false flag. If he says it's Longdai who hired us, how could we prove him wrong? We're plausibly deniable. That's why he chose us."

"He's right," I say. "We can't prove any connection between us and APEX. We have no evidence."

"Maybe we can make an evidence," Sun says.

We turn as one to look at him. He's in the far corner of the room, crouched by my backpack. He's got Song Fei's notebook and hair clip in his hands.

"What are you saying?" Jules asks.

"Ally is short for Allison. Allison Weiss. The lady on the TV."

Jules and I exchange perplexed looks. Art pauses in the middle of popping the caps off three beers and says, "Uhhh."

"You mean the news anchor?" Jules says. "What about her?"

Sun is looking at me. "Allison Weiss," he repeats. "Àilìsēn wàisī."

I spring to my feet and dart over to Sun, who hands over the notebook, already open to the list of dates and names. Atlanta, November 12: 艾莉森-外丝—àilìsēn wàisī.

"Arizona is not on the list," Sun says. "Song Fei did not see the Grand Canyon."

"I'm experiencing feelings of confusion," Mark says.

Sun paces to the center of the room. "I wonder why Song Fei went to visit American journalists and politicians. To tell them something about Longdai? I don't think so." He shakes his head. "I think she never defected from Longdai. This was a lie she told to Whitney Pearce, but she was working for Longdai all along. Whitney Pearce was breaking the ban on painite that his own country created. So it's very dishonest. This is what Lai Yixun complained most about United States: hypocrisy. He sent Song Fei to make a trap for Whitney Pearce."

"That's some ace guesswork, pal," Mark says.

"I am not doing guesswork," Sun insists evenly. "'Hēishǒu làn-quán, tiān gāo huángdì yuán.' *The black hand abuses its power. The sky is high, and the emperor is far away.* Whitney Pearce is black hand and your president is emperor. The poem is a coded message, correct? Why would she make a coded message in Chinese characters?"

"To send back to Longdai," I say, catching on. "She must have known that APEX was watching her, so she sent her intel in code. A photo of a poem with some misplaced radicals—"

"—she could sneak it past a wiretap," Jules finishes my thought.

"But you said Lai sent Song Fei to trap Pearce," I say to Sun. "What was the trap?"

Sun holds up the hair clip. "Remember what happened before we met Pearce the first time."

I picture Miller and Pabst picking up Song Fei in their party limo. "They strip-searched us."

Mark bonks himself in the forehead with the heel of his hand.

"The hair clip is a recording device. She wore a wire on Pearce!"

"So you see. Song Fei was not a defector. She was a spy." Sun smiles slightly, pleased with himself for recognizing a scheme worthy of his own machinations.

"So what? Even if all your guesses are correct, and even if we could access the recording, that wouldn't get us anywhere," Mark says. "It's right there in the notebook: Song Fei flew to Atlanta. Allison Weiss *already heard* that tape. Audio? C'mon. You can fake that. People don't trust anything these days."

"How about video?" Sun asks Mark. "Whitney Pearce is breaking the boycott by buying painite. So we make a geotagged video showing the box of painite in his office. We could use the bodycam with GPS that is in your luggage."

Mark frowns at his duffel bag, sitting unzipped at Sun's feet. "Of course you searched my luggage."

My throat closes up. My stomach does a flip. "You're suggesting that we go back to the mansion?" I manage to croak.

Sun does his little shrug. "There was a large tree hanging over the pool house. I saw the code to the back door."

"We'd need access to the neighbor's to get up that tree," Mark says. "And that's just entry. Those branches wouldn't hold a rope. We'd need another way out. And let's not forget the platoon of steroidal apes who live there. Why are we even discussing this? You're batshit crazy! We should be talking about how to disappear."

Jules shakes her head. "Nuh-uh, pal. Nobody's disappearing." She points at the screen, where the train is crashing in slow motion once again. "You guys did that. You can't run away from it. This is bigger than our lives."

Mark scoffs. "I'm pretty sure Whitney Pearce did that, not me. We got conned, okay? We were supposed to be installing some harmless spyware."

"You knew all along that you weren't."

"I was doing a job! One that I had precious little opportunity to decline, I might add. False flags, train crashes, aircraft carriers—this is a big pond, and girl? We are small fry." He drains the last of his Pacífico and then marches toward the kitchen, turning his head back over his shoulder to say, "If you need someone to blame, go lecture those spooky blond frauds. Don't put this at my feet."

"Okay, that's *such* bullshit." Jules darts forward and blocks his path, snaps at him with such vitriol that his chin retreats toward his Adam's apple. "You're all 'poor little me,' 'just doing my job'—like you're a straight, white, able-bodied male with no responsibility for your actions! Well, guess what? You're not small fry! You're a shark in denial."

She stands there in his way, red-faced and radioactive, and the air between them crackles with tension until Mark raises his hands. He backpedals a few steps, plucks one of the untouched beers off the bar in front of Art, and holds it against his neck.

"Is it hot in here? Or is it just flamingly judgmental?" he asks the ceiling. Then he turns back to Jules, speaks in a tone of weary resignation. "You're a sharp tack. I suggest you fight a ten-year war for oil sometime. Might take the edge off some of those convictions."

Mark's excuse for everything: *I've seen the dark side, I know how the world works. Trust nobody. Believe in nothing. And never let your guard down—or your best friend will stick a knife in you.*

Thanks to this attitude, Mark saw Ken's betrayal coming and saved my life. But now we're top three on the country's most-wanted list. Perpetrators of "nefarious atrocity." If we're ever going to see daylight again, we're going to have to try a different approach.

"We couldn't do it without you," I say. "So what if she paid you your share?"

"What the hell are you even talking about? Filming ourselves as we burglarize a mansion full of mercenaries? That's insane! There's no way we can get in there. Let alone get out."

Mark glares at me incredulously, but I hear the wonder beneath his words. He knows I have an idea. I tip my head toward the screen.

CNN is broadcasting another protest on La Reforma, the biggest one yet. The attack on the maglev has galvanized the protesters. More signs, more naked cowboys, more white trucks filled with gunmen. The crowd swells like a stormy sea in front of the Baoli. There's a new barbed-wire fence around the building, and on the other side of it, Longdai guards in black jumpsuits mingle with Mexican riot police in urban camo, stoically enduring the hail of insults and litter flung their way by the crowd.

I turn to Sun. "When you were in the security center, could you tell who was in charge?"

He tips his head to the side for a moment, and his slight smile reappears. "I think it was last guard who came through the door. The woman you shot in the hand."

I look back to the screen. In the traffic circle on the other side of the plaza, the one Longdai's helicopter chased us through mere hours ago, a group of masked men in gray-checked flannels are throwing cables over the statue of Christopher Columbus, tying them to white trucks, mounting a Lilliputian assault on the massive bronze monument to the Italian explorer.

#NOCHINOPUERTO

NUESTRO PAÍS, NUESTRA TIERRA

MÉXICO PARA LOS MEXICANOS

"We can't do it on our own," I say. "But maybe we can ask for help."

31

The more we talk about the plan, the more it feels logical and right. We'll start by asking for NGAP's assistance: a way to get into the APEX mansion and a place to hide afterward if we succeed. If NGAP agrees, we ask for more help from Longdai: a way to get out of the compound and the password to Song Fei's hair clip. If Longdai agrees, we break into the mansion later tonight and record a video that proves that Pearce has been violating the painite boycott. Combine that video with the recording of Pearce asking Song Fei to plant spyware at the Baoli, and we can show that APEX is the true instigator of this international crisis. Then everybody calms the fuck down, and Whitney Pearce gets banished to Neptune.

"Are y'all sure we shouldn't jump off a very tall building instead?" Mark says. "It'd be no less dangerous, and we'd get to experience the miracle of flight."

"It's in NGAP's self-interest to help us," Jules points out. "And Longdai's, too."

"Yeah, well," Mark says. "I have this niggling doubt that they won't see it so clearly as you do."

"It's risky, but Mark, what's the alternative?" I say. "Go underground for the rest of our lives in a country where everyone knows we started a war?"

"You think we'll make out any better if this plan works?" he protests. "You think the Mexican authorities will say, 'Hey, these scum-sucking saboteurs were operating under a couple of false assumptions when they obliterated our shiny new toy, so we'll let them off with a slap on the wrist instead of forty frickin' years in the electric chair'?"

"I don't know what will happen to us," I admit. "We have to hope that whoever decides our fate will see that we tried to undo some of the damage we caused."

Mark stands up from the table and throws up his hands. "Whatever you say, Liberace!" he exclaims, walking backward toward the kitchen and the fridge full of beers. "We'll go out with a bang!"

Jules scowls as he turns his back, but Sun smiles.

"Tā hěn Měiguó," he says—*He's very America.*

"You sure you can count on him?" Art asks me. "Seems like he might come all the way off his hinges before we even get to the fun part."

"He'll play his role," I say. "He knows it's our best shot. He's just salty because it's not a very good one."

"No," Sun agrees. "It is not."

A grim silence settles over us. We all see the reality of our situation. We're about to step onto a minefield with blindfolds on, and once we start moving, we won't be able to stop. I look at each of them in turn, grateful to at least have some company on this perilous path.

Then I check Dad's Casio. It's almost six p.m. now. And we have a lot to do.

"So what's the best way to make contact with NGAP?" I ask Art.

"Mmm." He studies the calluses on his palms as he thinks

about it. "There's a place near here we can poke around. The Santa Muerte shrine. Wouldn't wanna roll up there too deep, though."

"I'll go with you," I say. "The others can wait here and rest."

"Would three be 'too deep'?" Jules asks.

Art says, "Probably not."

"Then I'll go, too."

I say, "I don't think that's a good idea."

"Um, I love you, Victor, but your bedside manner has a high fatality rate. This is persuasion, not hockey. I'll help with the talking," she says in a tone that brooks no rebuttal. "C'mon, we need to figure out Pearce's neighbor's address first."

While Jules and Sun use her phone to search Google Earth for the APEX mansion, I log onto Huayiwang on Mark's laptop and peruse the Politics forum, searching for arguments that might sway NGAP to assist us in exposing Pearce. All we have to do is convince them that a big fight is coming—and that they should help us try to stop it.

The online pundits have made a flurry of new posts in the last hours, forecasting how the maglev crash could spark a global military conflict, gaming out various iterations of the first Sino-American War. Hypersonic missile barrages on Okinawa and Guam, pitched sea battles in the Taiwan Strait, dogfights over the Spratly Islands. Could China disable our GPS networks with cyberattacks? Could the United States pinch off oil shipments at the Malacca Strait?

Meanwhile, dire news continues to arrive in a steady flow. The Mexican interior minister holds a press conference to announce full cooperation with the Chinese investigation, which will include a Special Reaction Team from the People's Liberation Army. The US Air Force is flying surveillance drones over the Cantarell oil field. And someone leaks a blurry video of what looks like a battalion of Chinese soldiers, dressed in the black jumpsuits of Longdai security, boarding Y-20 Kunpeng transports at the PLA base in Hong Kong.

Then the chief of staff of the Mexican army speaks to reporters, contradicting the interior minister, stating that no Chinese troops will set foot on Mexican soil.

So the Mexican government is already dividing along battle lines. My skull starts buzzing like there's a nest of wasps inside it. I shut the laptop, head to the bathroom, and splash cold water on my face. When I emerge, Art eyeballs my right shoulder, where my black T-shirt is wet with seepage from the shotgun wound.

"There should be a first aid kit in here somewhere." He ducks through the doorway into the kitchen, returns with an enameled tin box. Then he helps me out of my shirt as Sun starts cutting bandages and tape into the right shapes.

"Put your hand like this," Sun says, maneuvering my arm so the skin of my shoulder pulls taut.

Art cocks an eyebrow at him. "Not your first twirl around the dance floor," he remarks.

Sun pulls open his collar, shows Art a scar that makes him wince.

"Their dad removed a bullet from me on a mah-jongg table when I was fifteen."

"You need stitches," Art says to me. He holds a bandage in place as Sun applies tape.

"I'm free tomorrow if you are," I say.

He does his low, gentle chuckle. Then he says, "If you can charm these narcotraficantes, they'll have you covered."

Before we leave, he hands the weapons and the motorcycle key to his dad.

"No dejes que se vayan," he says to Rafa, tipping his head toward Mark, who's working on another Pacífico, and Sun, who's back on the floor, studying the ceiling.

Mark rolls his eyes. "Like we have anywhere to go. I feel as popular as Osama bin Laden on September twelfth. Except instead of some cave in Tora Bora, I'm in a bathroom stall at Delmonico's."

Jules eyes him with a dour expression. "If we're going to do this, you might want to sober up."

He nods somberly. "Your feedback has been forwarded to the relevant departments."

Then he picks up the clicker and starts surfing channels.

We follow Art through the kitchen, out the back door, and into the alley where his truck is parked. I lie down in the back to stay out of sight as Art pilots us across Iztapalapa. With my head behind the passenger seat, I can see Jules watching the city pass by her window, a deep furrow in her brow.

"I respect what you said back there," I say. "I'm sorry for suggesting that you weren't deciding for yourself."

She looks at me around the side of her seat.

"Thanks for hearing me."

"I just wanted to say that we can try this without you. You can still walk away. Your picture isn't plastered all over the news."

"You don't value my help very much, do you?"

I grimace as the truck bounces over a pothole. "It's not that. I just don't want you to get hurt because of me."

She chuckles bitterly and shakes her head at me. "You still don't get it, Victor. I've *been* hurt because of you." She turns back to the window, and the afternoon sun catches her profile, lighting up the amber of her eyes, a shade paler than mine. "Do you remember when Mom was in hospice? She told us that we had to look after each other. I told her not to worry, Dad will take care of us. But she made us promise anyway. You do remember that, right?"

Warm emotion rushes to my eyes, and I say, "I remember."

"I thought it was her pain meds talking," she says, anguish written on her face. "Anyway, I was fourteen. All I wanted was my own space. Dad was so overbearing, and you were, like, his little clone-slave. Giving him nightly reports on how many push-ups you could do, constantly reciting his medieval proverbs. So I kinda forgot what Mom said. Maybe I forgot on purpose. Then all that shit happened last year. Mom knew, right? She knew that Dad's past wasn't all the way behind him. She asked me to look after you, and I didn't."

"It's not your fault, Jules," I say. "You told me not to go to Beijing, and I went anyway."

"I know it's not my fault. I'm explaining to you why this is what I want. I'll stick my neck out for you, even though you're an imbecile."

She smiles, and I manage half a smile in return.

"I get how you felt after Dad died. I was alone, too," she continues. "I had to look after myself because nobody else would. Then Sun showed up with Dad's money. He could've kept it, but he wanted to make amends, even after all the awful things Dad made him do. He's a selfless person."

When she mentions Sun, the scene of Ken's death floods back to me like ice water in my intestines.

"He killed a guy today, Jules. Cut his throat just like he cut Dad's." I shake my head. "He'll do anything to get what he wants. He'll always be that way."

She closes her eyes and sits with this information for a minute, pain still creasing her forehead. But when she opens her eyes again, they're filled with kindness. "I didn't ask him to come with me to Mexico. He wanted to help you," she says. "When I was asking you to turn yourself in? We knew that the cops would start looking for him after hearing your story. He said he would disappear again if it meant that you could be free. So don't be so sure about what he'll always be like."

"You can't trust what he says," I say. "He always has an ulterior motive. He told me that he has feelings for you. He actually wants my blessing."

"I know how he feels. We live together. I'm helping him, and I'm the first person he's ever known who's not some sketchy underworld operator. But he's not pushy about it. Just pensive," she says. "Like someone else I know."

Art coasts to a stop and puts the truck in park. "Y'all need a minute?"

Jules shakes her head. "Let's do this. And thank you. You're taking risks by helping us."

"It's not a big thing. You scratch my back, et cetera."

"No, really. Thank you."

He studies her for a moment. "You kids keep it lively, gotta give you that. But also, I'd like to see you clean up this mess before the tanks roll in."

He gives each of us an intent look. Then he says, "Let me do the talking here. These people are all right, but it's best not to, you know, overdo it on the eye contact."

We're parked in front of a row of abandoned houses, their crumbling walls covered in vivid tags, the empty street littered with debris. I see a crowd ahead of us at the next intersection. Men and women of all ages, a lot of clothing very baggy or very tight.

"We can find NGAP here?" I ask.

"We can make inquiries here." Art opens his door and eases himself out of the truck.

As we approach the intersection, I see that the crowd is actually a procession that's moving along the center of the next street. The sidewalks are lined with dozens of framed portraits, each one a little altar on a baby blanket or a place mat, adorned with plastic flowers, candles, candy, and a lit joint or cigarette smoldering in a shot glass. Beside each of them, a figurine of a girl skeleton, wearing a robe or a frilly gown, holding a cross or a scythe or a globe. Covering her ears. Covering her eyes. Standing on a pile of skulls.

"That's Santa Muerte?" Jules asks.

Art nods and says, "La Flaca."

The Thin Girl. The Saint of Death. A folk goddess, he explains, banned by the church. But the people here—pickpockets, sex workers, coyotes, sicarios—they're Catholics who are just as dedicated to Santa Muerte as they are to Jesus. Maybe because they feel weird asking Jesus to protect their sister from Border Patrol. Or to watch over their brother for six years in San Quentin.

"She looks after people who live in the shadows," Art says. "People who face death."

The people in the slow-moving line brood in stoic silence. From up ahead comes the sound of voices raised in chant: "¡Por arriba! ¡Por abajo!"

—*Above us, below us.*

Art hands a ten-peso coin to a little girl with braided pink hair. The girl passes the coin to a woman trailing behind her, then gives Art a handful of candies in return. We proceed from altar to altar, adding our pieces of candy to the offerings. The sun is low in the western sky now, the longest Sunday of the year coiling into history, and I'm imagining men in flak jackets surrounding the pozolería. American warships chugging toward the Taiwan Strait.

"We need to do this to make contact with NGAP?" I ask.

Art squints at me and says, "Yeah, let's go with that."

When we reach the front of the procession, I see the shrine itself: a storefront packed with candles, white roses, and other offerings. Towering over them, a black-robed skeleton with rhinestone eyes and a Mona Lisa smile.

The pilgrims filter in one at a time to make their pleas. A shirtless man in jeans crawls parallel to the line, pausing every few feet to touch his head to the asphalt. A companion makes his path by moving flattened cardboard boxes back to front, back to front. The crowd on the other side of the shrine takes up the chant again.

"¡Se ve, se siente! ¡La Santa está presente!"

—*She is seen, she is felt. The Saint is present.*

"Wait here," Art instructs us, and then walks over to the chanting crowd, starts talking to a guy in a gray-checked flannel.

I look from portrait to portrait on the street altars: a man mugging tough in mirrored shades; a teenage girl in pigtails, smiling big. Brothers and sisters, mothers and fathers, gone but not forgotten. A guy sitting on the curb, eating chicken and rice off a paper plate, catches me reading his huge T-shirt, which is silk-screened with an image of English words spray-painted on a brick wall.

The words say: WHAT BREAKS YOUR HEART?

"¡Ya llegaron los chinitos!"—*The Chinese are already here!* he hollers, flashing a grin that's short a few incisors. "¿Quieres comer, campeón?"—*Want to eat, champ?*

He elbows the guy next to him, who scoops chicken and rice from a pot on the sidewalk onto two more paper plates.

I haven't got much of an appetite, but this doesn't seem like the moment to refuse anybody's hospitality. So I take the proffered plate and say thank you.

He gestures for us to sit on the curb next to him. I'm bracing myself for some kind of razzing, but the guy throws an arm over my shoulders, taking care to avoid the sling. He nods at me intently, and then tips his chin toward the shrine. "La Santísima," he says—*The Most Holy.*

Then he looks at my plate.

I fork a bite of rice into my mouth. It tastes like soup cubes.

"¿Está rico, no?"

I nod. "Está muy rico."

The guy claps me on the back and turns back to his companions. Jules and I watch the crawling man and the other pilgrims at the front of the line as we eat. The closer they get to the shrine, the more raw and solemn they become. But when they emerge, they join the lively group on the other side, sipping giant beers, passing joints, taking group photos in front of the best graffiti.

"¡La niña está presente! ¡La niña te protege! ¡Gracias te damos, Santísima Muerte!"

—*The girl is present. The girl protects you. We give you thanks, Most Holy Saint of Death.*

The mellowing sun floats west, glinting off broken windows, casting a golden glow on cinder block walls. The girl with the pink braids hops past us on one foot, holding her mother's hand for balance. And suddenly, the last fragments of my armor fall away and Mom and Dad's deaths rush back to me, filling the void they left in my chest cavity, soaking me with a sorrow as cool and blue and deep as the afternoon sky above el Distrito Federal.

I close my eyes and sit for a long minute in that bottomless sadness. When I open them again, Art's walking back to us, accompanied by an adolescent boy about half his height, a wisp of a mustache on his upper lip, his hair stiff with gel.

"¿Son ellos?" he asks Art.

Art nods. "This is Pablito. He'll take you where you need to go."

Pablito tips his chin back to look down his nose at us.

"You're not coming?" I ask Art.

"I gotta drop by the rope store," he says. "Anyway, it's better if not too many people see what you're about to see."

"Jeez." Jules bugs her eyes.

"You'll be fine," he says. "Probably."

"Remember, we need at least a hundred meters," I say.

"I hadn't forgotten," he rumbles, and then he lopes off in the direction we came.

32

Pablito leads us away from the shrine. As we turn the next corner, a white pickup comes bouncing down the potholed street on squeaky shocks. The driver pulls the hand brake and hauls on the wheel, spinning the truck around as it screeches to a stop in front of us.

Pablito vaults into the bed and looks back at us expectantly.

Jules climbs in first, then turns around to pull me up. We're barely seated when the truck roars into motion, sending us grabbing for the sides. With each bump, my shoulder sings with fresh pain, and I feel wetness spreading through my T-shirt once again.

"¿Vamos lejos?" I gasp at Pablito—*Are we going far?*

He shakes his head, his face devoid of expression.

The air cools. Twilight descends. After about ten minutes, we arrive at a complex the size of a football stadium. The driver pilots us into a vast parking lot, alive with the coming and going and parking and honking of hundreds of cars, vans, and trucks. People pushing carts weave among the vehicles, whistling at each other like basketball coaches as they avoid collisions by inches in the waning light.

"¿Qué es este lugar?"

Pablito looks at me derisively. "La Central de Abasto," he says—*The Center of Supply.*

And as we pull closer to the hangar-like bays at the center of the parking lot, I see that they contain a wholesale market of epic proportion. We pass a dozen stalls stocked with great pyramids of carrots, a city of papayas, a labyrinth of limes. Boom boxes pumping mariachi and dubstep form overlapping halos of cacophony. Klieg lights punch stinging white holes in the dusk. A calico cat prowls the ridge of a watermelon mountain.

I check my watch. It's almost nine now. "¿No cierran?"

Pablito shakes his head. "Twenty-four seven," he says, the scornful smile dancing across his eyes again.

We round the corner to the far side of the market, where semi-trucks back up to the bays in waves, unloading crates and pallets by the thousands. Our driver hits the gas, zooming toward a row of identical tractor-trailers at the edge of the parking lot, then coasting to a stop in front of them.

Pablito nimbly leaps out of the truck and beckons for us to follow. After we climb out, the truck screeches away. He leads us along the row of white tractor-trailers, stops behind one, knocks a rhythm on the back door, and flings it open.

All I can see within is darkness. Jules and I exchange a look, and then she climbs into the back of the truck, and I follow. Pablito hops onto the step, grabs the door handle, and brings it down between himself and us with a slam.

Darkness. The earthy, peppery odor of—what, radishes? Then, without warning, a spotlight snaps on within the depths of the truck.

My hands fly up reflexively to shield my eyes.

"¿Quiénes son?" A man's voice, loud and demanding, reverberates against the steel walls.

"¿Ya sabe, no? Soy Intruder A." I remove my hat.

"¿Y ella?"

"Mi hermana."

"¿Por qué está aquí?"—*Why is she here?*

"Quiere ayudarme"—*She wants to help me.*

Silence for a moment. Then the truck starts moving with a jerk that throws Jules and me against the closed door behind us.

"¿Adónde vamos?"—*Where are we going?* I ask.

The voice ignores my question.

—*She doesn't understand Spanish?*

—*Not much.*

—*And how will she help you?* A second voice, this one higher, a woman's, and equally authoritative.

I turn to Jules and translate the question, both of us still shielding our eyes with our forearms.

"Tell them that you're an idiot who's going to get himself killed if he keeps listening to the wrong people."

I interpret her words into Spanish. A couple of chuckles.

—*Maybe you already got yourself killed.*

The first voice. I'm not really sure how to respond, so I take a page from Sun's book and shrug my shoulders.

—*Why do you seek us?* the second voice asks.

—*We share a common goal.*

—*Why do you seek us?* Again, louder, harsher.

No small talk, I guess. All right. I figure I have one chance to make my pitch, and if I screw it up, like they said, I'm already dead. No big deal.

—*We need a place to hide. Somewhere outside the city.*

—*And a doctor,* the second voice points out.

—*Yes, that, too.*

—*So.*

—*It was Whitney Pearce who sent us into the Baoli. APEX. You know who that is?*

A moment of hushed conference between the voices.

—*We know Whitney Pearce.*

I explain that we were mere pawns, that Pearce lied to us about our objective. I give them our theory of his motives: to provoke a conflict between China and the United States, opening up more demand for his mercenary services. I cap it off with my conjecture of how this conflict will play out, trying to sound more confident than I feel.

—*The Chinese are overextended,* I say. —*They'll take the opportunity of open hostilities to recapture Taiwan. The Americans will dislodge them from Latin America. The Mexican military will side with their old friends from the north. No World War this time. Just a skirmish. Two giants testing each other's defenses.*

I pause for emphasis before concluding: —*And Mexico will suffer the most.*

"O quizás Taiwan," replies the second voice, a hint of mockery in her tone. "Pero todavía no nos has dicho que nos puedes ofrecer"—*You still haven't said what you are offering us.*

—*I can expose Pearce's scheme. The United States will have to back down.*

—*You have proof?*

—*I can get it. Tonight.*

The voices confer again.

—*Then we're left with, what? Billions in debt and a Chinese air force base in Baja? Maybe we prefer the gringos.*

I hesitate. Look at Jules. She gives me a nod. I take a deep breath.

—*We may be able to sort out your Longdai problems, too.*

—*How will you "sort out" our Longdai problems?*

I tell them.

Silence descends for a moment. Then the spotlight shakes as the truck reverberates with laughter.

A third voice, gravelly and deep, speaks for the first time.

"¡Órale! Estás mas loco que un cabra"—*You're crazier than a goat.*

"Completamente absurdo." The woman's voice.

I shrug my shoulders.

—*We accept that we may fail. Anyway, helping us will not cost you much.*

—*Just a place to hide*, the first voice intones. —*A way to get there. And a doctor.*

"And a computer," Jules adds, recognizing our demands repeated back to us. "With good editing software. I prefer Premiere, but Final Cut would be fine."

I translate, earning a few more chuckles, and the first voice says, "Buen software, claro que sí."

—*You only have to provide these things if we make it out of the APEX compound tonight. If we fail, you've risked nothing.*

The voices confer again.

—*Nothing more? This is all you ask?*

—*There's one more thing.*

A sigh. —*Of course.*

—*Do you know who lives at 11104 Boulevard de los Virreyes?*

33

They let us out in a different corner of the epic parking lot, with a new white pickup waiting to collect us. Or maybe it's the same white pickup, just without Pablito in the back. Can't tell. Can't see much. Even with Jules's help, I barely make it into the bed.

As the pickup starts moving, she slaps me in the face.

"Hey. Bubba. Hey," she says. "Stay here."

"I'm awake."

"Plan doesn't work if you're in a coma."

"Had some morphine around noon," I say. "There's, uh. Fatigue factor."

She hugs her knees to her chest.

"I should've listened to you. Turned myself in," I say. "Prison would've been better than getting shot and causing a war."

Her lips press together in a line. "What would Dad say? 'Fù shuǐ nán shōu.'"

—Spilt water is hard to gather.

"You hated Dad."

"Sure, it's that simple, dumbass. I hate you, too."

"I could go to prison now. Stop off at the hospital," I say.

She nods brightly. "Hand off the baton, I'll take it from here."

We both know I won't. "I'm Intruder A, not you." I try to tap her nose with my finger, but miss. "And Mark would bail."

"Dude needs you. But he'll never admit it."

The pickup slows to a crawl, inching through a procession of a dozen handcarts stacked with crates of avocados.

"He doesn't need me." I tip my head back onto the side of the truck. "He just needs someone."

I hear Jules shrug. "Like everyone else," she says, and slaps me a couple more times. "No sleeping."

"I only need. Tofu. Pozole," I say.

By the time the pickup delivers us to the restaurant, my cheeks are raw from being slapped. I'm just conscious enough to be impressed by Jules's strength as she hauls me through the kitchen.

"Those kickboxing classes. Must be. The bomb." I raise my eyebrows as high as they go, but my eyelids stay shut.

Chairs scrape across the floor. Harried voices. More hands, laying me on a table.

"—fair amount of blood," Art is saying.

"—more of that broth," Mark is saying.

"—a stimulant," Sun is saying.

I manage to peel an eyelid open, see Sun giving Art a pointed look. Art purses his lips and rocks his head back and forth. Then he steps away and calls out, "¡Oye, Pá!" I hear a brief argument in Spanish, the kind of talk you'd like to never have with your father. And then he's back, holding a tiny spoon of white powder in my face.

"Snort it, kid," he says.

I muster enough breath to make a skeptical noise.

Sun says, "You must raise your heart rate."

He covers one of my nostrils with his thumb and tips my head forward, and all of a sudden, my eyes are wide open again, and I'm sitting up on the table.

"Gak!" I observe.

"Easy," Art says.

Jules's eyebrows knit together. "I think we're in new territory."

Mark shakes his head. "There was that one time? At that dive in Beacon Hill?"

I'm blinking rapidly, scraping my upper lip over my front teeth. "That was baking soda."

"Potato, potato." He eyes the little vial in Art's hand. "You know, my shoulder's kind of bothering me, too."

Art screws the tiny spoon back into the vial, tosses it back to Rafa, and says, "You might need the ER."

I shake my head, the drugs lighting up my mind with vim. "I'm fine."

"Pressure is crucial," says Sun. He's holding a roll of surgical tape from the first aid kit.

I picture my twin entry wounds beneath the wet bandages. Crimson blood oozing through the crystallized hemostatic powder.

"Okay," I say, and then do some yelping as Jules holds up my elbow and Sun runs the tape under my arm and over my shoulder several times.

"Wow! All right! The gate to the neighbor's house will be un-locked tonight, and the owners will be out until one a.m. NGAP will have a driver waiting for us at the Hipódromo. We do the thing."

Mark's eyes go big. "Those maniacs said yes?"

I nod. "They're not too keen on the idea of APEX turning Mexico City into Baghdad."

"So what's the signal?"

"You'll hear us."

"Man. *Man.*" He rubs his eyes. "Shit just got real."

"Shèbèi dōu zhǔnbèi hǎo le ma?"—*You've got everything ready?* Jules asks Sun.

He turns his head to indicate Mark's backpack and mine, repacked with the weapons we've accumulated on our journey, as well as some additional gadgets from Mark's duffel.

She goes to him and gives him a hug: not a sister's hug, or a lover's hug, but a roommate's hug. A really good roommate.

"Bǎozhòng"—*Take care of yourself,* she says, and he nods again. I see the spring coiling in his body, the readiness to act. And in that moment, I know he'll play his part to perfection.

"Thank you," I say. "For keeping me alive."

He looks at me with his usual blank intensity. The corners of his mouth move upward about a millimeter.

I look away before emotion takes over, not quite ready to forgive my father's killer while coming up on party drugs.

"Jules," I say. "What do you say? Would you send Mark his share?"

"Oh, yeah. Fine." She pulls out her phone.

Mark goes stiff like he just remembered leaving the oven on. "I never set up an account. I could do it now. Five minutes. Aw, fuck it." He's standing there with his backpack on, his hands gripping the shoulder straps. His stance unsteady. His face pale as bone.

"If you don't make it there"—he frowns at his shoes—"no amount of money's going to save my ass. But hey." He starts toward the back door. "I call shotgun. Oh. Too soon?"

Art shakes his head. "You and Sun should take that motorcycle. That way, you'll at least have a ride if Victor and Jules get, uh. Held up," he says. "I'll drop them at the Baoli."

34

Art puts the truck in park and kills the engine on the far side of the huge, dark roundabout. The protesters have left the plaza now. The traffic on La Reforma is sparse. The Mexican police are gone from the other side of the fence, but the Longdai security guards in black jumpsuits remain.

I check Dad's Casio. "Ten forty-four," I say.

"Hey," Jules says. "The summer solstice is at ten forty-six."

And so we sit for a moment as the hidden sun reaches the northernmost point of its celestial journey for the twenty-fifth time in my life, finding me in a vegan chef's truck, watching four naked men in cowboy hats pick up trash around a smashed bronze of Columbus.

"Heck of a day," Art says.

"Thank you for everything," I say. "You should ditch the truck. I'd feel awful if anything happened to you because of the help you gave us."

Art gives me a sardonic look. "Kid, like your sister said, we're all making our own calls here. You didn't force me to take any risks

I didn't feel like taking," he rumbles. "Trust me, I've done worse for less. If you think you're living fast, you should've seen me at your age."

He extracts his soft pack of Pall Malls from his breast pocket, taps one out, and stares at it for a moment before tucking it behind his ear. "Thanks to you little punks, ol' Rafa gets his ninth life. And I'll have enough left over to open the finest plant-based cantina that Salamanca's ever seen. So. You're welcome."

I shake his right hand with my left, and Jules gives him a hug. Then we hop out, Jules slinging the rope over her shoulder. We walk across the roundabout toward the fence. When we reach the plaza, I glance back.

The truck is still there, but all I can see through the windshield is the glow of an ember.

"Bu yào kào jìn!" shouts one of the guards—*Do not approach!*

We slow our steps and raise our three functional arms in the air. As we get closer, I recognize a few of the guards from this morning's scuffle. The skinny guy I bashed in the chest with the mop. The older, stocky one who shot me, the one Sun kicked in the head. He's got a stripe of white tape across his nose. The buff one who asked me, —*Mr. Lijia, is something wrong?*

"Wǎnshàng hǎo," I say. "Shì wǒ, Rùqīnzhě A."

—*Good evening. It's me, Intruder A.*

And as Jules and I step up to the fence, the light from the atrium's windows falls onto our faces. The guards who didn't meet me this morning are peering forward. The ones who did are flinching back. Nobody seems quite sure what to do.

We lie down on the ground.

"Wǒmen shì lái tóuxiáng de," Jules sings to the paving stones— *We're here to surrender.*

A hushed discussion takes place, and then I hear one of the concrete post stands scraping across the ground. Footsteps approach us. Hands frisk my ankles, waist, pockets, finding nothing.

And I'm thinking, *See the bandages, have some mercy, and please don't grab my right arm*, when the guard doing the frisking grabs my left arm and yanks me to my feet.

I look into his face—the older guard with the stripe of tape across his nose—and silently thank him. Then another guard wrenches my right wrist forward to cuff it to my left, and I squeal like a piglet.

"Ānjìng"—*Quiet!*

Nose Tape pushes me through the gate. He mutters something to his smartwatch and tips his head to the side, listening to a voice in his ear. Then he issues a few instructions to the remaining guards before leading us into the building. On the other side of the revolving doors, the vast atrium is a spooky variation of itself from earlier today, when it was filled with the merry bustle of money being made. Now the presiding mood in the Baoli is hushed like, *Someone did a boo-boo.*

And my skin tingles as I remember that I did that boo-boo, and only I can undo it. I feel like skipping. Is it the blood loss, or maybe the drugs? When I turn my head to look at Jules, I see that she, too, has a lively expression on her face, despite the lack of entry wounds on her body and cocaine in her sinuses.

She was right: it feels better to face the music. I'm finally turning myself in. Yes, in another country. For another crime. But for the first time in sixteen months, I'm owning it. Me, Victor Li. Intruder A.

Nose Tape pulls a remote from his pocket and points it at the turnstile, which slides open. He walks through without breaking stride. The escalator on the other side is stationary now, and he descends the steps at a jog. The underground corridor is once again lit bright as a tanning bed. There's labeled masking tape all over the ground, the vestiges of ballistic analysis.

And then we arrive at the door to the security center, and Nose Tape swipes his badge again. The gravity of the situation returns to me. I remember what's at stake: my life, for one. Jules's, too, and many others. *Quizás.*

The door unlatches with a digital plink.

The interior appears as Sun described it: lots of cool white light, keyboards, monitors, and wheely chairs. Hum of electronics, odors of warm circuit and screen cleaner. And a barred cell right there in the far corner of the room. Space is limited underground, I guess. Still, putting your prisoners within sight of your security operations seems like a bad idea.

Unless you can make sure that they never see the light of day again.

The trio of security center denizens stand up as Nose Tape leads us across the room to the cell. He swings the barred door open, stands aside, and turns to fix us with a baleful look.

"Ladies first," I mutter, and Jules affects a curtsy as she steps in and sits down on the short steel bench. I sit down next to her. The door slams shut. A latch slides into place.

"Shēnshàng yǒu dōngxī ma?"—*Anything on their persons?*

The last security guard to emerge from the security center—the one who Sun said was in charge—is talking to Nose Tape now. There's a purple bruise on her chin where Sun hit her with the jug of cleaning fluid, and her right hand is wrapped in white gauze from wrist to palm.

—*She had this.* Nose Tape holds out the rope.

—*I have these, too,* Jules says, pulling two rings off her fingers and holding them out to the guard in her cuffed hands.

One emerald, one sapphire.

The woman in the black jumpsuit peers at the rings in Jules's hands, takes them from her, holds them up to the light. Then she turns around and orders everybody out of the security center. She turns to Nose Tape.

—*You, too,* she says.

He shoots her a wounded look before shuffling to the exit.

She produces another remote from a jumpsuit pocket and aims it, one at a time, at the three security cameras in the room. One by one, the little red lights on the cameras go dark.

She rolls a chair over from a computer console and sits down in front of our cell. Folds her arms across her chest. Studies us for a long minute.

Then she unfolds her arms, sits forward with her elbows on her knees, and holds the rings in her palm between us.

—*Where did you get these?* she asks.

—*Your suitcase,* I say.

35

It takes me about ten minutes to get through the first part of the story, from Hull Secure Facilities to Los Tres Piratas. Jules chimes in now and then, helping out when my vocabulary fails me. The first time she does this—when she supplies the word for fugitive, "táowǎngzhě"—I give her an incredulous look like, *When did you learn that?* Apparently, living with Sun Jianshui has improved her Chinese just as much as his English.

"Jiù yìshí dào tāmen shì bǐjiào zhùmíng de, Měiguó jūnshì, uh, zěnmeshuō," I'm saying—*We realized that they were a relatively notorious American, uh, how would you say it*—

"Hétóngshāng," Jules interjects.

"Hétóngshāng?"

"Contractor."

I shrug my shoulders and repeat, "Hétóngshāng."

Song Fei holds up a finger like, *Just a minute.* She pulls a phone from her pocket, stands up, and paces to the other side of the room.

"How do you think it's going?" I ask Jules.

"Good, I think. It's her, that's one. And she's listening."

"That's two."

She comes back a minute later and says, "Jìxù shuō"—*Keep talking.*

Another ten minutes, and we're caught up to the present moment and the plan we made. Her eyebrows shoot up when we tell her the terms we agreed to with NGAP, including the concessions they want from Longdai in exchange for their help tonight.

—*I know it's a lot to ask. We just want to set things right. We had no idea what Pearce intended*, I'm saying. —*If I'd known the kind of damage we were causing—*

She puts her hand up to silence me again. Fills her cheeks with air and lets it out slowly.

Then she says, —*How did you recognize me?*

—*We knew from Pearce that you were Longdai security, and then we realized that you lied to him about having defected*, I say. —*It made sense that you would come back to Mexico after being deported from the United States. And that you would be here, running the security center. When I shot at the barrel of your gun this morning, I injured your right hand. On the forestock. Which means your left hand was on the trigger. I knew from the handwriting in the notebook that you were left-handed.*

She holds her bandaged right hand in front of her face and smiles incredulously.

—*Circumstantial evidence. What if you were wrong?*

—*It would've been a lot harder to explain to someone else*, I admit.

—*Anyway*, Jules says, —*this was our best idea.*

Song drums the fingers of her left hand on her knee. —*Well*, she's saying, when the door slams open and Lai Yixun barrels in.

Song hops to her feet, meets him between us and the door. He cranes his neck to look at us, his hands clenched into fists. She puts a hand on his shoulder and redirects him to the other side of the room. Speaks to him in low tones as he makes impatient facial expressions, hands on his hips.

"Hoo boy," Jules says.

"Rough day at the office," I say.

"Let me talk," she says. "Keep your head down. Because it's your face that he's been hating all day."

They come walking over now. Lai stops in front of the cell and drills me with a contemptuous glare.

Jules stands up.

—*I am Li Lianying. His sister.* She strikes a conciliatory tone. —*We're very sorry about your train.*

Lai looks from Jules to Song and back.

—*Is this really happening?* he says.

—*We want to expose the people who are behind this,* Jules says.

—*So you confess! Publicly!* He spits the words in my direction. —*Tell the world that APEX hired you to do what you did.*

Jules shakes her head. —*You know that won't work. We can't prove anything without your help.*

He scoffs. —*You want my help.*

—*We can help each other. If we can prove that APEX instigated the conflict, then you'll be vindicated, and the United States will be humiliated. The president will stand down. He doesn't want war. Pearce is forcing his hand.*

Lai stares incredulously at her for a moment, then runs both palms downward over his face. —*Tell me clearly, so I understand, how you could prove that Whitney Pearce is behind this.*

—*Well*—Jules counts on her fingers—*one, first-person accounts from the intruders about what happened.*

—*Confessions.*

—*Confessions, sure. Two, the audio recording that Song Fei made of Pearce asking her to infiltrate the Baoli and buying painite from her.*

He turns to Song Fei and says, —*I thought you lost that recording.*

She looks at Jules.

—*It's in the hair clip, right?* Jules asks.

Song nods curtly. —*I was afraid to back it up. I was under constant surveillance. If I were caught in the United States, I would be treated as a spy.*

—*Even though you were just trying to warn them about APEX,* Jules says to her.

Song Fei casts her eyes downward. —*The Americans I met were not receptive.*

—*Because when Americans look at you, they don't see a person,* Lai sneers. —*Only a foreign threat.*

—*Well,* Jules says, —*not every American thinks that way.*

"I spent two years at your top university." Lai switches into his deliberate English. "Every week, somebody asked me, 'Yixun, what's the Chinese perspective on this issue?' If they even bothered to learn my name. One professor called me John for a whole semester. Another called me Chucky."

"Okay, that sucks," Jules admits amiably. "I've had alienating experiences, too. But some people were nice to you, right?"

Lai scowls and switches back to Mandarin.

"Tí wài huà," he says. —*We're off topic. You have the recording, plus your confessions. That's not enough to prove anything.*

—*The third part is visual evidence,* Jules says. —*We go back to the APEX compound in Las Lomas tonight, break into Pearce's office, and record a geotagged video showing how much painite he's collected.*

—*Their counter-narcotics operation in Las Lomas is conspicuous,* Song Fei points out. —*A video showing painite there, combined with my audio recording of Pearce, could be persuasive.*

—*You approve of this plan?* He stares at her goggle-eyed.

—*I think the evidence may be adequate to expose APEX.* She speaks carefully. —*It would be very difficult to obtain.*

—*Intruders B and C can do it,* I mutter to Lai's knees, trying to sound as deferential as possible. —*But they need a way out of that compound.*

Lai gives me a look like I'm dog shit on his shoe.

—*And you expect us to provide that.*

—*Just sixty minutes with your helicopter.*

—*Your audacity is astounding.*

I tip my head back and forth. —*Forty-five would probably do.*

Lai turns to Song. —*You're the security expert. What is your assessment?*

She paces a few steps away, studies the floor, paces back.

—*I believe they are competent. After all, they bypassed our protocols this morning,* she says ruefully.

Lai scrunches up his face and furiously scratches the back of his neck. —*One hour in the helicopter. We hand you off to your cartel friends. You disappear to a secret location. Then when will you release your video?*

—*I can edit it pretty quickly. It'd be best to have a first-person account from Song Fei, too.* Jules thinks on her feet. —*We don't have time to do that now, but we could send the car back for her. The same drop-off spot at the Hipódromo. Tomorrow at noon. No tracking. No communications devices.*

Lai looks to his subordinate again.

Song Fei squares her shoulders. —*I am not afraid.*

—*But you have to announce partial forgiveness of the airport loan first,* Jules says, —*and a training program.*

—*Debt forgiveness is not on the table!*

—*These are NGAP's conditions to play along. They'll drop the protests and support the airport,* Jules continues patiently. —*You only have to forgive thirty percent of the debt. And train Mexican people to use your technology and work alongside your staff at the airport. Half the workforce has to be local. And not just the bottom half. Every level.*

—*You think I can make that kind of decision on my own?* he exclaims.

—*If you announce it publicly, Beijing wouldn't dare contradict you,* I say. —*It would be too messy.*

—You're asking me to make a unilateral decision that would enrage my superiors!

I jump to my feet.

"We're asking you to live up to your words!" I shout in English, knowing he understands me perfectly. "You're always claiming that China will be a different kind of world leader, but that's a lie! You're not different—you just want power, market access, puppet governments. How do you sleep at night?"

"I sleep very well!" he roars back at me. "How you Americans love to lecture. You forget who wrote the rules! You criticize our friendship with Myanmar, and what about your alliance with the Saudis? You say we must not build bases near your borders, and you station thirty thousand troops in Seoul. Fifty thousand on Okinawa! How stupid do you think we are?"

Our faces are inches away from each other on opposite sides of the bars. Lai's pulse pounds furiously in his temple, and I feel my own in my ears. But my eyes fall away first. I can't defend my country to him. I know how poor an example the United States has set.

It's Jules who answers him. She switches back to his native language to do it. She speaks softly, her cuffed hands wrapped around the bars. *—You're right. Everything you said is true. I don't think you're stupid. But the Mexican people aren't stupid, either. They're already marching in the streets.* She takes a step back from the bars and shrugs. *—If you do this, you'll show them that China can be more than merely the latest empire in town. And at the same time, you'll be exposing American hypocrisy at the highest level.*

—And if you refuse, Pearce's false flag story will stick, I point out. *—China will look like the aggressor. And you'll probably lose the airport anyway.*

He looks from me to Jules and back, his jaw clenched, his nostrils flared. Then he slams his palms against the bars, grabs the nearest office chair by its back, and flings it across the room.

It smashes into a row of monitors, sends them crashing to the floor.

"Fuck you both! You're already dead!" He jabs a finger back toward us. "Nobody tells me what to do!"

He storms out of the room, slams the door hard enough to shake the bars of our cell.

The security center falls silent. I slump onto the bench. Song Fei sits on the floor, rests her head against the wall, and closes her eyes. We spend a few minutes like that, digesting.

Then Song Fei's phone buzzes. She reads a message. She turns to look at us.

There's the slightest of smiles on her face.

36

Song Fei stands on the landing skids and gives the pilot explicit orders over the intercom.

"Bié guǎn qítā de zhǐlìng. Jiù zhè xiē. Míngbai ma?"—*Do not obey any instructions other than what I've just told you. Got it?*

"Míngbai"—*Got it.*

"Rènhé yìwài zhuàngkuàng, zhíjiē liánxì wǒ"—*If anything unexpected occurs, contact me right away.*

"Míngbai." He keeps a straight face, maintains his professional demeanor. But he seems less than totally comfortable with the situation.

She gives him a thumbs-up, pats the side of the helicopter, and takes off her headset.

"Nàme wǒmen míngtiān jiàn, ba," I shout—*So we'll see you tomorrow?*

She puts the headset back on and says, —*What did you say?*

—*We'll see you tomorrow?*

Her eyes go down and to the right. —*You made a good argument.*

I think Lai Yixun likes the concept of saving the airport and embar-
rassing the Americans. But if he announces the debt forgiveness without
the approval of the party leaders, they could give him a relatively severe
punishment.

—*What are you saying?* I shout.

—*If I don't make it, make your video without me!* she shouts back.
—*You can save a lot of lives.*

—*But NGAP will kill us if he doesn't meet their conditions!*

—*Then I hope he does!*

And before I can respond, she takes the headset off again, sets
it next to the binoculars on the seat across from me, and slams the
door shut.

—*Ready?* the pilot says.

Jules and I exchange a look. Then she gives him a thumbs-up.

"No going back now," she says. "We have to do what we can."

I nod, queasy to my core, as the helicopter rises into the night
sky and Song Fei shrinks beneath us, the white dot of her face
framed by her black hair and jumpsuit. She stands there, looking
up at us, at the edge of the big yellow circle painted on the helipad,
perched atop the Baoli Tower like a graduation cap.

"Are you okay?" Jules asks.

"My shoulder hurts like an alligator bit me," I say. "But I don't
feel sleepy anymore."

I guess there's a faint smile on my face because Jules says, "Even
if she shows, she's not going to make out with you."

"I hadn't talked to a girl in a year," I say.

"Woman," she corrects.

"Love will keep us alive!"

She rolls her eyes and says, "I loathe the Eagles."

I check Dad's Casio: forty minutes past midnight. Preparing the
helicopter ate up a lot of our time. Mark must be wound tighter than
a rat trap by now. The window that NGAP promised us at the house
behind the APEX compound will close in less than half an hour.

Fortunately, helicopters don't sit at traffic lights. It only takes us three minutes to fly from La Reforma to Las Lomas. And then I'm staring down at the mansion, the dark lawn, and the pool house. The same place I woke up eighteen hours ago. But now it feels like a different city, a different life.

The pilot's voice pipes into my headset.

"Dì yī ge dòngzuò?"—*First maneuver?*

"Děng yí xià"—*Wait one second.* When I pull the door open, the roar of the rotors grows even louder. I grab the binoculars from the seat across from me. The pool house is dark. Good. There are lights on in the mansion, but none on the second floor. Even better.

"Hǎo a. Dì yī ge dòngzuò," I say—*First maneuver.*

The pilot drops us toward the earth. Close, closer. He levels off about two hundred meters above the south side of the mansion. The main entrance. Across from the pool house. Close enough that we're loud on the ground.

So Mark and Sun can hear us. And so anyone walking around the grounds will be looking at us, trying to figure out what we're doing here, while behind them Mark and Sun clamber up the cypress tree that overhangs the pool house.

I set a timer on Dad's Casio for sixteen minutes. Stare down at the roof of the pool house. *Come on. Come on. Come on. There.*

A flashlight blinks up at us. Five pulses. Short long short long short. The starting signal.

I hit start on my watch and heave an exhale.

"Dì èr ge dòngzuò"—*Second maneuver,* I say to the pilot, and the helicopter climbs back into the sky.

I fall back into my seat and share a grim smile with Jules. Nothing to do now but wait. For the first three minutes, Mark and Sun are lying flat by the top of the stairs, waiting to see if Pabst and Miller heard them drop onto the roof.

If they did, and they came up to investigate, they might be fighting right now. That's Sun's responsibility. Nothing I'd worry about. He's already studied their hands, their eyes, their gaits. And with Jerry's night vision goggles on his face, he has another advantage. If things get hairy, he'll use Mark's knife or Ken's suppressed pistol. Nothing lethal, we agreed. Perhaps a slash across the Achilles tendon. A bullet in the calf. Just like how I shot him at that house in Pasadena.

I check my watch.

13:16 to go.

Pabst and Miller could already be bound and gagged. Or they didn't hear a thing. They're still in the pool house. Perhaps they moved back to the mansion this afternoon. Sun and Mark tiptoe down the stairs along the outside of the building. The windows are dark. The coast is clear.

They sit tight for another two minutes, crouched at the corner of the house, to avoid getting ahead of schedule. We can't see them, and they can't talk to us. If they move on the mansion too soon, they could stir up trouble before we get down there to haul them out.

So we wait a few more excruciating heartbeats.

And the next time I look, the Casio says 9:42. They should be moving across the lawn now, crawling on their bellies so they're not silhouetted against the light from the pool. Sun first, using those night vision goggles to watch where they're going. Mark behind him, the bodycam strapped to his chest, capturing great footage of dark grass dragging along the lens. No real danger here. Even if someone's out for a midnight stroll, he won't be expecting them. A couple of quick kicks, a jab in the throat, and a palm strike to the elbow crease. The fifth point of the lung meridian, where qi pools.

That's how Sun explained it to me after I saw him knock someone unconscious for the first time. Back then, in my dorm room at San Dimas State, it seemed like the coolest thing I'd ever seen. Now I'm hoping that I never have to see it again.

7:32.

They should be at the back door now. Sun's pulling off the night vision goggles. Punching in the code—and praying, praying, praying that it hasn't been changed since last night. Opening the door a millimeter, listening for footsteps on the other side. Someone's there. A quick skirmish—and hopefully a quiet one. Or no one's there. Wait another minute.

5:00.

Now the tricky part begins. They're slipping up the stairs to the second floor. Is the hallway empty? Probably. But what about Pearce's door—is there a strip of glowing light beneath it? Or is it dark? Is it locked?

If it's locked, time to get creative. Mark's only experienced in picking padlocks. Maybe he can handle a deadbolt. Or maybe they're using the hammer and screwdriver from the tool kit in the Pozolería, taking the door off its hinges—quickly, quietly! If they have to kick it in, they kick it in. Still, locked is better than unlocked.

Because if it's unlocked, that means Pearce is in there. Mark hangs back. Sun tiptoes up to the door. Knocks twice. Does his best impersonation of Miller's Brooklyn accent. What did we decide? *Keystone! Need ya downstairs!* Make it sound urgent but confusing. A prank? A crisis? An important phone call? What's up? Pearce sticks his head out. Sun's already gone. Down the other staircase at the far end of the hallway. Calling him again. Or fighting someone he encountered. But he's armed and resourceful. Hopefully he can handle it.

3:00.

Sweat pours down my face. My heart's going like a jackhammer. Jules's eyes tick back and forth between my watch and the window like the pendulum of Pearce's grandfather clock.

"Zhǔnbèi dì sān ge dòngzuò!"—*Prepare third maneuver!* I shout into my headset.

"Shòudào!"—*Copy!*

Mark has to be in the room by now. He's picking the padlock

on Pearce's African blackwood box. Sun's guarding the door. Or fighting on the stairs. Leading Pearce and whoever else on a chase through the mansion. Mark's opening the box. Making sure his bodycam gets a good shot of the contents before he shoves them into his pocket. Not rubies. Not costume jewelry. Painite.

Or he can't pick the lock. They've been discovered. Sun's barricading the far stairwell with furniture, firing shots over people's heads. Mark smashes the box to bits with the hammer. Or he shoves it into his backpack. Not ideal. Not good at all. When we get it open later, what will viewers say? *Deepfake. Camera tricks. I know how they did that. It doesn't prove anything.*

Still, better than nothing. And regardless, Dad's Casio says 1:00 now. Time to go.

"Kāishǐ xiàluò!"

We drop through the air toward the mansion again, this time faster. Low enough for the rope to reach the ground. And now we're on the other side of the compound: the north side, by the pool house.

As we descend, I lean out the door. Jules grips the back of my belt with her left hand and a grab handle on the ceiling with her right. One end of the rope is fastened to a bulkhead inside the helicopter. The other end is tied around the handle of a teakettle that we borrowed from the security center, giving the rope some tossable weight. We also tied four loops in the rope, six feet from the end.

If everything goes right, Mark and Sun will be hanging from those loops for three or four minutes until we can land at the drop-off point: the Hipódromo de las Américas. A racecourse, two miles to the north, where NGAP promised to station a vehicle to smuggle us out of the city.

"Gāodù jiǔshíwǔ mǐ"—*Altitude ninety-five meters!* the pilot announces.

—*Twenty meters to the south!* I tell him.

—Copy!

—Ten to the west!

—Copy!

I clear my mind, exhale my breath, and underhand the kettle onto the lawn.

It lands where I want it: in the grass, near the side of the pool, across from the pool house. Where there's some light for Mark and Sun to see it. But as far from Pabst, Miller, and Pearce as possible.

—Ascend on my mark!

—Copy!

The timer on my watch hits zero and starts beeping, barely audible over the noise of the rotors. Nothing happens. The mansion remains dark. *Beep. Beep. Beep.* I click it off and sit forward in my seat, leaning out the open door. Jules hovering at my shoulder.

Nothing. More nothing. But lights begin blinking on in the neighboring houses. A helicopter flying very low, not going anywhere. Conspicuous. And then a light snaps on in the pool house.

"C'mon, c'mon, c'mon," Jules is chanting.

The back door to the mansion swings open and Sun sprints out, Mark right behind him. They disappear into the dark of the lawn. I turn and see Pabst and Miller in front of the pool house, looking up at us, trying to figure out what the hell Longdai's helicopter is doing above them. They don't see Mark and Sun, who remain cloaked by darkness as they approach the pool.

And more lights blink on in the first floor of the mansion.

I squint down at the lawn, seeking their shapes moving through the dark—there they are! Then the back door of the mansion flies open again and a blond head rushes out. Pearce, with a scoped rifle in his hands. And in front of the pool house, Pabst pointing, his mouth open, his words drowned out by the thump of the rotors. Miller out of sight. No—coming back out the door with a pistol in each hand. He tosses one to Pabst and lifts the other in front of him in both hands, aiming into the shadows on the other side of the pool.

Muzzle flashes in the dark: Sun fires first. Art's revolver—louder, more of a deterrent, better for this stage, we decided. Warning shots only, we agreed.

But Miller and Pabst both crumple to the ground.

Jules shrieks into her headset. Her hands fly to her mouth. Most of my fingers are already clamped between my teeth. I pull them out so I can yell at the pilot as Mark and Sun reach the rope and grab hold of the loops.

"Shàngshēng! Shàngshēng!"—*Ascend! Ascend!*

And as we begin to climb, I see Pearce in the light of the colonnade, taking aim across the dark lawn. Drawing a bead on Mark and Sun as they swing skyward. The crack of the big-bore rifle rends the air.

I see Mark's back spring into an arc. And I scream—*NO!*

Sun fires a shot at Pearce, then drops the revolver and wraps his right arm around Mark's torso. I see Mark's hands loosen on the loop above his head. And for a moment, Sun manages to hold Mark's limp form aloft.

Then Sun's arm swings free, and Mark's body drops, drops, drops, and splashes into the pool.

As the helicopter turns north, Sun sways on the rope beneath us, still backlit by the glowing pool, still hanging on to a loop with his left hand, an object clasped in his right.

Straps fluttering in the turbulence.

The bodycam.

37

The vulture glides lower, spirals tighter, grows from a mere dot in the sky to a black-winged behemoth that blots out the sun. It alights on a fence post on the far side of the arroyo. I keep still. Avoid eye contact. The vulture does the same.

For the first time in hours, my attention slips into the now. I stop reliving last night, cease my contemplations of what might happen this afternoon. Breathing as shallowly as possible, I watch the vulture side-eye the skeleton at the bottom of the arroyo. Some kind of dead little desert pig, the digitate shadows of its rib cage lengthening as the sun slides past noon.

Go ahead, I'm thinking. *Scavenge away. Surely there's some flesh left on those bones. Go ahead, you goldbricking sky scrounger. Don't mind me.*

The vulture complies. It steps off the fence post, glides into the arroyo, and hops toward the skeleton. A smile threatens the corners of my parched mouth. A little action around here, finally, after hours of nothing but stark sun and dire thoughts.

But the vulture hops right past the sun-bleached bones. Up the near side of the arroyo. Toward my outstretched legs.

Not yet, bird! I spring upright, sending it squawking back into the air. I snatch a rock from the ground and hurl it skyward. *Try again tomorrow!*

Then I become aware of fresh silence at my back, where voices have been constant until now. I turn around and see Sun and Pablito watching me from the patch of shade beside the adobe ranch house. They look away before my eyes meet theirs.

"Now you try," Sun says to the boy.

Pablito nods and drops into a stance. Sun swings a right hook at his head. The boy catches the outside of Sun's fist with the back of his hand, spins it into a wrist lock, pulls Sun twisting to the ground at his knees. He releases Sun's wrist and smiles shyly. Sun pops back to his feet.

"Good," he says. "Again."

Pablito bites his lip and drops back into his stance.

"No lo arruines demasiado, Pablito!"—*Don't fuck him up too badly!* hollers one of the guards from the roof. He guffaws at his own taunt and takes a swig of his Tecate. One of the others taps him on the arm with the butt of a pool cue and says, —*Your shot, bro.*

The roof is much nicer than the interior of the house. They've got a shade structure built from palm fronds, a Bluetooth speaker blasting narcocorridos, and a barrel filled with Tecates and ice. It might be mistaken for a pretty chill scene if it weren't for the fifty-caliber machine gun mounted in a pile of sandbags at the southwest corner.

Southwest—that's the direction of the unpaved lane that leads to the front of the ranch house. On the other sides, only arid hills and the occasional clump of spiny, stubborn conifers. Nada más. Dusty nothing for miles in every direction.

The only way up to the roof is a ladder that we've been forbidden to touch. Still, I have the feeling that if Mark were here, he wouldn't be sitting on the shade side of the house, playing footsie with the vultures. He wouldn't be methodically teaching a twelve-year-old how to dislocate elbows. He'd be up on that roof, winning at pool. Drying his fingertips on the cuffs of his crew socks before every shot.

If Mark were here.

Memories flit unbidden before my mind's eye. Mark staggering up to Calder's Eagle, telling me he hates my guts. Rubbing his palms together as we sat on Bin Twenty-One, eating cinnamon rolls that tasted better because we couldn't see them. *There's a big score in here somewhere*, he said. *I know it.* I feel his wet sock on my neck after he stopped me from strangling Jerry Hull, and I see him holding Song Fei's painite up to the pale dawn sky, and his words echo in my head: *I could tuck this little Valentine into my pocket, call us even, and walk away.*

Instead, he'd chosen to trust me again, and it'd cost him his life. What if he hadn't? Where would he be? I picture him running his arcade, swapping out the taps, repairing the Pac-Man. Classic rock till eleven, Motown till close. But that never would've happened. I don't know where Mark Knox would be, but I know he'd be alone, looking out for number one, nurturing a new dream.

A score that will change everything.

I walk through the open door into the stifling heat of the ranch house, through the sparse living room, past the splintering table where Jules remains hard at work. In the kitchen, I splash tepid brown water from the sink onto my neck. A solid line of carpenter ants marches across the counter to the jumbo bag of barbecue pork rinds—the only sustenance that the guards have offered us. I eat a few without tasting, sip water from a gallon jug.

"How's the shoulder?" Jules calls from the other room.

I blow ants off a handful of rinds and bring them to her.

"It's fine," I lie. When we arrived at three in the morning, the doctor was waiting. He sewed me up more quickly than seemed considerate. Then he leapt into his Volvo and sped into the desert without so much as a *Two Advil and plenty of rest*. My shoulder is still throbbing in time with my pulse, and I can't reach my ear.

She takes the pork rinds from me and pops one into her mouth. "Thanks. I'm about done. Will you tell me what you think?"

I pull up a chair. Jules hits play and sits back. The video starts with the surveillance tapes from the Baoli. The next part, we filmed here: Sun and I confessing our crimes, explaining how Pearce set us up to sabotage the maglev. She follows that with some background on APEX, mostly screen grabs from Wikipedia, combined with her own voice-over.

After that comes the audio recording from Song Fei's hair clip. She gave me the password on the roof of the Baoli, right before we boarded the helicopter.

"ygxxm168," she said.

I patted my pockets for a pen.

"Yǒnggǎn xiǎo xióngmāo," she blurted out, her face flushing red.

—*Brave little panda. Sixteen August is my birthday.*

Brave panda indeed. The recording showed that she'd expertly deceived Pearce: lamenting her role in Longdai's bribery schemes, hinting at her admiration for the United States, keeping it short so he could fill the space. Pearce took the bait. He waxed righteous against corruption before getting to the point: if she'd do him the kindness of dropping off some spyware at the Baoli, he'd purchase both of her four-carat stones.

The recording goes longer than that, but Jules clipped it after the incriminating offer. The final segment is our smoking gun: the link between Pearce, Song Fei's tape, and our confessions. Time-stamped, geotagged footage from last night showing the box full of painite in Pearce's office.

And the footage is good. The second floor of the mansion had been empty. Mark made short work of the locks on the door and the blackwood box. He poured a dozen painites into his palm. He tilted them to catch the light. Our plan worked well, right until the end.

The whole video is twelve minutes long. Jules started working on it as soon as we arrived this morning. Her bloodshot eyes are shadowed purple, and she's clawed her pixie cut into an impressive bird's nest.

"You did a great job."

"Think it's enough?"

I purse my lips. "Since the helicopter in Las Lomas made the news last night, it's hard to dismiss."

"The recording from Song Fei is the only confusing part," Jules says. "Like, 'Wait, who's this voice?' It'd be better to have that taped confession from her, too."

I check Dad's Casio: ten minutes to two p.m. The numbers on the display are so faint that I can barely read them. The batteries are finally dying.

"If she's coming, she'll be here soon."

Last night, it took us about two hours to get here in the back of yet another white truck, this one with a topper on the bed. I felt woefully exposed, having expected NGAP to spirit us past the roadblocks rolled up in carpets or floating in the belly of a milk tanker. Instead, we sat there in the truck bed with our forearms on our knees. The federales waved us to the side of the highway. Pablito pressed his finger to his lips, and they looked directly through us as if we were ghosts.

I wished Lai Yixun had been there to see it. It was a nice reminder that Mexico would remain out of his reach, no matter how many bribes he paid.

This morning, the truck left the ranch house around ten to meet Song Fei at the Hipódromo. There could be traffic. There could be war. A lot of things could happen.

"Have you checked the news?" I ask.

"Uh-huh. The Chinese carrier group reached the Cantarell oil field. It looks like they're setting up a blockade. The whole Mexican navy is floating a mile away."

"Anything else?"

"Well, every base in the Pacific is a flurry of activity."

"Every base big enough to matter."

"And Longdai announced a press conference at four. At the airport site," she says. "It could be the debt forgiveness. The training program."

"It could, or it could not."

"True," she says. "We need to be prepared."

We talk it over for a few more minutes. Check the file size of the video, the upload speed of our satellite hotspot. We have no idea when our guards will tire of waiting for Lai Yixun to meet NGAP's conditions. In the end, we decide to upload the video before the press conference. Then we'll schedule an email for a couple of hours later to distribute the link to several news channels at once. Whether Lai comes through or not, Jules says, we'll tell our side of the story.

"That's how it's gonna be, then," I say.

She nods grimly.

I blink slow like, *Okay.*

"It's the right play, Victor," Jules says. "This is what it's all about."

"Cleaning up after my terrible mistakes?"

She shakes her head. "We're lighting up the shadows. People will ask questions they didn't ask before."

"You don't know that's true."

"And you don't know it's false," Jules says. "I'll get it all set up. But first, I need some air."

When she steps outside, I take her seat and run a dozen searches on the laptop. "Mark Knox parents." "Mark Knox baseball." "Mark Knox army engineer." "Knox family Montana." "Tina Knox." "Tina Knox Montana." "Tina Tyler Knox Montana." Nothing. Nowhere. Either no results or too many. Twenty minutes later, I'm no closer to finding someone I could send Mark's money to, someone who would want to know what happened to him. Someone who could share the weight of grief hanging around my neck like an anaconda.

When Jules comes back, I'm watching raw footage from the bodycam, poring over the final minutes. The helicopter rotors drown out all sounds except the crack of Pearce's rifle. The camera swings wildly on the strap in Sun's hand. I pause on a frame that captures the pool, study the blurry shape that's floating there. Drag the slider a frame forward. And another. Did he move?

Jules rests a hand on my good shoulder.

"Go back to the beginning," she says.

I click stop. I click play. It was quiet then, and dark. Mark's crouched at the base of the cypress tree. He's aiming the bodycam at his face, and the wide-angle lens renders his nostrils enormous.

"Testing, testing," he whispers. "Intruder C here, but you can call me Al. That psychopath over there is Intruder B—hey, wave! We'll do this better later, but here's the score: these jarheads set us up, so we're gonna steal their candy and film it all for your infotainment. Don't forget to Like and Subscribe!"

The video cuts and resumes on the roof of the pool house. Sun aiming his flashlight into the sky. Short long short long short. And somewhere up there, in a helicopter, a countdown begins.

Jules pushes the lid of the laptop shut. She wraps her arms around my head while I cry like a lost child.

"It's not your fault."

"I know."

"He was a good dude."

"He was a jackass."

"Okay, but he was *your* jackass."

I cry awhile, and then my sore face falls calm. Silence replaces my sobs, finding us like this: steeped in peril and pain, bound by blood and truth. The silence expands, swallowing Sun's voice, then Pablito's. It engulfs the knock of the pool balls and the music from the roof. For a moment, the silence is almost whole, allowing only heartbeat and breath.

The moment stretches, the heartbeats slow. Our breaths fall shallow and our ears grow keen. For silence is never a void, always an absence, a prelude, a pause.

And then, the sound of a motor in the distance, and wheels on an uneven road.

ACKNOWLEDGMENTS

The structure and soul of this novel owe a great deal to the creativity of Ari Nieh, my coconspirator in storytelling, games, and imagination throughout childhood. You talked through many early versions of the story with me, and you gave me the ideas for the puzzles that lie at the heart of the plot. I needed you on this one, so thank you, Ari!

My supremely steady agent, Bonnie Nadell, provided crucial edits and advice. I feel immensely fortunate to count myself among her writers. Heartfelt thanks are also due to her colleagues Austen Rachlis and Lauren Christiansen.

Sara Birmingham, ace editor: I am grateful beyond words for the care and keen eye you brought to this project. Working with you has been an absolute dream. Miriam Parker, Sonya Cheuse, Martin Wilson, TJ Calhoun, Meghan Deans, and everyone else at Ecco continue to be positively wonderful to me in every interaction. Thanks very much to Allison Saltzman for designing a sizzlin' jacket cover and to Mary Beth Constant for providing precise and thorough copy edits with good humor. And here's a huge loving shout-out to Zack Wagman: you got this whole thing rolling because you believed in Victor Li and me.

To create the world of *Take No Names*, I drew on several excellent studies of history, politics, and place, including Shannon K. O'Neil's *Two Nations Indivisible: Mexico, the United States, and the Road Ahead*, Jo Tuckman's *Mexico: Democracy Interrupted*, Carmen Boullosa and Mike Wallace's *A Narco History*, Alma Guillermoprieto's *Looking for History*, Sean McFate's *The Modern Mercenary*,

P. W. Singer's *Corporate Warriors*, Patrick Radden Keefe's *The Snakehead*, Bonnie Tsui's *American Chinatown*, and David Lida's *First Stop in the New World*.

David Lida was also a welcoming friend and guide during my time in Mexico City, as was Isabel Rice, who went so far as to crash my visit to the Santa Muerte shrine in Tepito to make sure I didn't get myself in trouble. My talented fellow students in the Taller de Novela at Casa Tomada and our brilliant instructor Daniel Saldaña Paris taught me much about the concerns of contemporary Mexican writers and provided invaluable feedback on an early draft. Alejandro Arballo and Juan Pablo Beltrán Mainero helped me review the Spanish language and mexicanismos in this novel, and Ruby Lai did the same for the Chinese. The three of them are to credit for the authentic and accurate use of these languages in this text; all errors are my own.

Aleah Houze, Rachel Barrett, and Rigas Hadzilacos contributed to the revision process with insightful notes, as did Nicole Mones, my mentor in authorhood. I'm grateful to Brad Basham for his eye, his time, his car, and his couch, and to Steven Patenaude for the good deals on headshots and hot tips. During a period of unrelenting distraction and continual disaster, I would not have been able to complete a novel without the encouragement of steadfast friends who hyped me up whenever my resolve wavered: in particular, Breanna Chia, Michael Patenaude, and Olga Desyatnik. My family—Susie, Ari, Camellia, Uzi, Geordie, Helen, Linda, Rob, Carol, and Sidney—is my foundation, and alone, I am nothing. This book is a story, I hope, of how little we can achieve and feel on our own, acting out of fear and self-interest, compared to when we lower our defenses, set aside our petty resentments, and open our hearts; many people have helped me learn this vital truth through their love and compassion, but none so much as you, Tess.